W9-BLR-060

In 2076,
what will we be celebrating?

America's future begins today—and all around us
we see the ideas and techniques sprouting up that
will shape how we live when the next big birthday
party happens. Where will the technology of organ
transplants take us? The environmental protection
movement? The leisure-time explosion? Sex change
on demand? The arms race? The exponential expansion of knowledge? Zero population growth?
The data processing revolution? Instant global
communications? Acrosol propellants in the upper
atmosphere? The women's movement? Biofeed-
back? Ectogenesis? Situation ethics?

For tantalizing answers to these and dozens of
other concerns about our next hundred years, just
pick up this provoking entertainment and start
reading these adventures by the country's most
nimble students of the future.

PETER S. ALTERMAN   KARL HANSEN
CAROL EMSHWILLER   JO ANN HARPER
ROBERT CRAIS   MARGE PIERCY
WILLIAM JON WATKINS   JAMES
STEVENS   HARLAN ELLISON   SONYA
DORMAN   VONDA N. McINTRYE   PETER
DILLINGHAM   ROBERT E. VARDEMAN
and JEFF SLATEN   JAMES SALLIS and
DAVID LUNDE   PATRICK HENRY
PRENTICE

Books by EDWARD BRYANT

PHOENIX WITHOUT ASHES (1975)
AMONG THE DEAD (1973)
CINNABAR (1976)

2076:
THE AMERICAN TRICENTENNIAL

Edited by Edward Bryant
Associate Editor, Jo Ann Harper

PYRAMID BOOKS 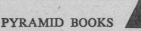 NEW YORK

2076: THE AMERICAN TRICENTENNIAL
A PYRAMID BOOK

Pyramid edition published April 1977

Library of Congress Catalog Card Number: 77-74713

Printed in the United States of America

Pyramid Books are published by Pyramid Publications (Harcourt Brace
Jovanovich, Inc.). Its trademarks, consisting of the word "Pyramid"
and the portrayal of a pyramid, are registered in the United States
Patent Office.

Pyramid Publications (Harcourt Brace Jovanovich, Inc.).
757 Third Avenue, New York, N.Y. 10017

ACKNOWLEDGMENTS

To Jean Holmes Harper
and Lorin Wendell Harper

To Anne Van Kleeck Bryant
and Edward Winslow Bryant

The United States themselves are essentially the greatest poem . . . Here at last is something in the doings of man that corresponds with the broadcast doings of the day and night.

—Walt Whitman
Leaves of Grass

Knavery seems to be so much the striking feature of America's inhabitants that it may not in the end be an evil that they will become aliens to this kingdom.

—George III: 1782.

CONTENTS

FOREWORD: COMING ATTRACTIONS

Any writer would have to be a fool to pretend to know *exactly* how the future will unwind. The contributors to this anthology are no exception to that rule, though perhaps they are more astute prognosticators than most. The shotgun effect operates in both speculative fiction and the relatively new science of futurology: if you generate a sufficient number of scenarios, *some* are bound to come true.

Obviously every extrapolation in *2076: The American Tricentennial* cannot come true. There is, I hope, a balance to the book. There are lighter visions and dark; both Utopian and dystopian portrayals of the future. When I first solicited submissions for this book, I requested manuscripts which would avoid the clichés ("No nuclear war and/or pollution survivors prowling the ruins of Philadelphia on July 4, 2076; no thought-police kicking down the doors of the last American rebels"). I wanted stories or poems that would explore the possible textures of life in third-century America, or at least in whatever socio-political entity might have replaced it. What I was looking for were possibilities. I think my writers have come through nicely.

My hope for this book is that it will provide some entertainment, food for thought, and nourishment for debate. If you receive all three, then you will be considerably more enriched than if you had partaken of most of the other Bicentennial-linked artifacts of the red, white, and blue "Buy-centennial" year. That brings up a point I want to address. This anthology project was not undertaken as lightly as most topical creations, though admittedly it would have been much more difficult to bring about in any other year than 1976:

One afternoon I got a telephone call from one of the contributors to this book, who said, "Hey, I'm doing a story about the Tricentennial. Do you know a market that'd want something like that?"

"No, but there will be," I said; and I should like to thank Norman Goldfind of Pyramid Books for implementing that inspiration. Now, one year and half a million words of manuscript reading later, you hold the result.

—Edward Bryant
Denver
June 1976

INTRODUCTION: FLASHFORWARD TO 2076

Peter S. Alterman

> I hold that man is in the right who is most closely in league with the future.
>
> —Henrik Ibsen

> The future isn't what it used to be.
>
> —Arthur C. Clarke

Brooklyn native Peter Alterman took degrees in English literature at the State University of New York at Stony Brook, Adelphi University, and the University of Denver, where he earned his Ph.D. studying the relationship between science fiction and the modern novel. Though teaching English part-time in the University of Colorado system, he also works as a data management administrator for the U.S. Office of Education. He has had extensive training in physics and communications electronics. In his spare time he writes fiction and nonfiction. Thus it seemed to me that Peter Alterman was a logical choice to write a broad-spectrum, futurologically oriented overview serving as introduction to this volume of fiction and poetry about America's third century.

INTRODUCTION: FLASHFORWARD TO 2076

It used to be that only science fiction was concerned with the world of the future. Now, however, every segment of society is busily engaged in extrapolating, planning, and building America's third century. Science fiction is hard pressed to keep up with newspapers. Space exploration, rockets, laser beams, death rays, things we're used to thinking of as science fiction, are now real. The future is rapidly becoming the present, and the present is more science fiction than we realize. Take bioengineering, for example. It's in the midst of an awesome revolution and we aren't even aware of it. I don't have to remind you of Viking's landing on Mars July 20, 1976, of the Venus, Mercury, and Jupiter flybys, and, of course, the landings on the Moon. We are, in fact, in the midst of a new migration into the solar system. We don't realize that the future has crept up on us —we're still reading fiction about its eventual arrival. Acceleration is a problem for science fiction as well as for society in general.

This introduction, I guess, is an apology, because it's almost impossible to predict what is going to happen in 100 years. What was predicted for 2100 in 1955 is already taking place. Advances in solid state electronics have already made it possible to have wristwatch access to a computer. We have the technology now to do away with a telephone system operating through wires. We are very close to having broadcast power. Fusion energy is just down the road: that means a cheap, unlimited, non-polluting source of energy. As we begin to implement the advanced technology which our culture gives us, we find that everything we've predicted is already old hat. Science fiction must run very hard to stay in place. The time lag between science fiction and science fact is getting smaller and smaller.

Science fiction has historically concerned itself with the

effects of future technology on people. Isaac Asimov once said that it's the job of science fiction to extrapolate the human effects of technological advancement. Engineers can predict the internal combustion engine, but it takes a science fiction writer to predict the traffic jam. Or, as Gardner Dozois says, it's one thing for us to predict the automobile, and it's another thing to predict the sexual habits of the teenager at a drive-in movie.

However, new disciplines have sprung up within the last decade which have usurped this perspective. Futurology, the systematic study of the future, has recently come into vogue. Business uses it to predict technological breakthroughs. The military, of course, is highly sophisticated in the use of prediction for technological, strategic, and scientific purposes. All of us use futurological prediction on a regular basis. Environmental impact statements, for example, predict what's going to happen to our culture and our environment in 10 years, 20 years, 50 years. The SST issue is basically a futurological one. What it *will* do to the ozone layer, and what the ozone layer damage *will* do to life on Earth. That doesn't sound like science fiction, yet it is.

Let's consider the arrows we have to watch, the path we are now following. An overall view of current trends leads us, I think, to four important areas. The first one is the communications breakthrough. We now have computers that can practically be programmed in basic English. No more FORTRAN, no more COBOL. With this capability, every one of us, especially our children, will be able to use computers as naturally as we turn the pages of a book, or turn on a TV set.

Communications satellites make instantaneous contact with any part of this Earth possible. Arthur C. Clarke was responsible for developing that particular concept. In the U.S. and India communications satellites beam all kinds of information into remote areas, proving that it is economically feasible to educate large groups of people this way. The summer and winter Olympics and special events like the landings on the Moon are carried live to practically the whole planet. Communications satellites are continually going up and every one that goes up is cheaper to launch, cheaper to run. The cheaper they are, the more frequently they will be used.

Communications advances have given us new electronic

devices we can wear on our belts for communication or calculation. Had I the money or the inclination, I could have a hand-sized walkie-talkie on my belt with which I could talk to anybody in a four-state region. That's now.

The communications breakthrough is twofold: it puts us in contact with more people more easily, and it brings us instantaneous access to more information than ever before. It's not necessary to know a lot of facts—it's necessary to know how to "access" a lot of facts. And that's getting easier and cheaper to do.

A second trend is the development of alternate sources of energy. Fusion power is right around the corner. Solar power, practical and inexpensive, is not only around the corner—it's sneaking up on our roofs: significant headway in expense and efficiency is being made. Wind power, too, is being utilized more efficiently.

A third breakthrough is in biomedicine. It started, in the popular mind, with Christiaan Barnard's heart transplants. But we've had transplants and artificial organs for years now; we're just getting better at designing and applying them. Recipients are staying alive and functioning better.

We can create artificial life, or the preliminaries to artificial life—test-tube life. With computers, we are at the point of learning how to create artificial intelligence. We have the technology for genetic manipulation, a major area of ethical concern among biomedical researchers. Even though he can't smile without hurting himself, the bionic man *is* around the corner, albeit without an atomic device in each elbow.

The fourth area of major concern is the depletion of our resources. I say that's a current trend, but it's been going on since the first man or woman found that you could take clay, fire it, and make a vessel that wouldn't leak. But we are getting to the point now where our resources are rarer and more expensive to get to. That means we're constantly on the lookout for more and different sources of metals, of energy, of water. We are beginning to realize that the only major new sources are out in space. The Moon is a treasure trove. Isaac Asimov, in the early fifties, wrote a story about Martian colonists who went to Saturn and brought back a worldlet of ice. The point, of course, is that in order to maintain a necessary level of resources, and thereby technology, we are going to have to go out into space.

The Earth Resources Development satellites have been

designed to find new sources of metals, foods, etc., on Earth. One purpose of Skylab was to discover new resources. Even finding them on Earth involves going out into space. And although the concept of nationalism is outmoded and destructive, it is the force that will push us out there.

The United States cannot exist as it has without moving to another area of resource development, of expansion, of industrial potential. It's getting more and more expensive to get tin from Bolivia, but we can get tin elsewhere. The U.S. doesn't have a death wish. Neither does the Soviet Union. Neither does Bolivia. We will move out into space. Once we're there, we won't last long as little individual states. But we won't get there unless we force ourselves, and nationalism, I feel, is the propellant.

All this continued advancement, and it is advancement, requires a growing technological foundation. Much as I don't like to give points away to my engineer friends, we cannot do without advanced technology. And we cannot do without a large and effective scientific establishment engaged in basic research, because, in the long run, technology does *not* make our lives more complex. It makes them simpler. It is easier to keep a house in 1976 than it was in 1876. The rules are different, and what we gripe about is learning new rules. But they make life easier. We can know more, more quickly, than ever before. And I think that should give us pause, because our view of the future should be a very optimistic one. Full, proper control of our environment and our society is leading us to a better life. It is our obligation to learn how to live—to learn the new rules.

There are many potential disasters which could befall us. If we don't solve the energy problems, which is to say if we do not take advantage of fusion power, solar power, wind power, and geothermal power, the future could very easily be Og and Zog crawling out of their cave below Los Angeles and beating each other to death for breakfast.

If we don't solve the pollution problems and the waste problems which face us, the future could be Og and Zog crawling out of their cave below Los Angeles and walking across the sea to Catalina Island, where they beat a rabbit to death for breakfast.

If there is a new ice age (and that's one thing that's being predicted) it'll be Og and Zog crawling out of their cave south of Los Angeles and beating a polar bear to death for breakfast.

Or if California actually does fall into the sea in 1984, Og and Zog will crawl out of their cave and swim to the surface south of Los Angeles, and kill a tuna for breakfast.

If we have no solution for the resource problems, if we don't go into space, if we don't find new sources, Og and Zog will crawl out of their cave south of Los Angeles and eat sand for breakfast.

While the problems which face us are always greater than the possibilities for solving them, we are, somehow, still here. Again, this puts me in the position of being a bright-eyed optimist, and I'm not. There are certain crises we must weather. We must control our urge to blow ourselves up in a nuclear holocaust. We must find solutions for overpopulation, for the potential famines which threaten the world. We must find solutions for the depletion of our resources and for the pollution problems. I believe that, one way or the other, we will, because we must.

There are, however, certain inertial forces in our culture which impede rapid change—religion and law, for example. What happens if we build basic intelligence into a chimpanzee so it can be a house servant, as Arthur C. Clarke has suggested, or if we create turtle people or snake people, as Cordwainer Smith projects? What if you catch the chimp diddling your daughter in the broom closet? You take out your shotgun and boom—there go 100 years of bioengineering. Is that murder? We're already having trouble defining the legal boundaries of birth and death. What legal and ethical questions would be raised by intelligent chimps? Or dolphins? If we unplug life-sustaining devices from terminally ill patients, is that murder? What law does, essentially, is to maintain continuity from the past through the future. We may disagree with it, we may need to change it. But that continuity remains. And it slows us down. The legal profession will have to be accounted for in any advances we wish to make.

Religious, moral, and ethical values like the primacy of life now come under attack. Many of the problems we're having stem from conflicts betwen new social realities and old moral ideals. The abortion question is one example. Euthanasia is another. If the primacy of life is something we believe in, what do we do about the severe overpopulation of the earth? Brunner's *Stand on Zanzibar* is one attempt to inquire into this particular issue. Obviously, there has to be some accommodation. We have to discover new values. Our old values are a drag on absolute technological advancement.

Let's talk about the biological revolution. A revolution is taking place in sex, physiology, gerontology, disease control, psychology. We're pushing back the onset of old age. Someone who is 50 is no longer old in our society. People are old, not when their hair turns gray, not when they start to wrinkle, but when they hit around 70. And that's a purely arbitrary age. We will have to deal with the problem of old age simply because there are going to be too many people over 70, over 80, over 90, more people hitting 100 and doing something once they're there.

What is the nature of a society of active, vital 85-year-olds who have been retired for 20 years and have absolutely no reason to expect that they're going to drop dead next week? Are we going to have the situation Walker Percy describes in *Love in the Ruins,* where all the older folk from Ohio buy Airstream trailers, drive down to Florida and meet each other and talk about their Airstream trailers, then drive to Arizona and meet each other and talk about their Airstream trailers?

It is now possible for a male to become a functional female, and a female to become a functional male. Transsexuals are sterile so far, but that doesn't necessarily mean they always will be. It's getting easier to be whichever gender you choose. What happens if any male can go into a hospital or clinic, as Samuel R. Delany describes in *Triton,* and come out a genetic and biological female 17 minutes later (or vice versa)? What is that going to do to our society? The concepts of male and female, masculine and feminine, are going to have to change even more, and with them, family and child-rearing.

The major diseases are being conquered one by one. It's getting rarer for someone to die at the age of 40 from natural causes. The more we learn about diseases and our bodies' defense mechanisms, the more we will learn about controlling and altering our bodies.

What happens to us when we can add a third arm? It's a reasonable extrapolation of transplant technology. Instead of putting on new jewelry, we can put on new limbs. Instead of wearing clothes we can wear diamonds set into our bodies, assuming, of course, that we can afford diamonds.

Our concepts of fashion are going to change. Delany has characters with lions' manes and with cosmetic dragons coming out of their shoulders. Our concepts of self-recognition are going to change. It's going to become easier to be unique and to identify ourselves as individuals.

Body banks are another possible result of transplant technology. As spare parts become more necessary for increasingly older people, where are we going to get them? Well, we can grow them, and I'm sure we will, or we can carve them out of people who are newly deceased. Larry Niven has written some very interesting stories about what kind of society we would have should we expand the latter practice. If you need a part, what better place to get it than from a convicted criminal, one who is useless to society, one who speeds or jaywalks? Or in the worst of cases, one who does not believe as we do?

Cloning technology is already well under way. We can clone many lower orders of creatures; we soon will be able to clone ourselves. Science fiction stories and novels abound on this theme. One obvious thing we can do with cloning is to create an army of identical units. That ought to terrify you. What kind of a society will a clone society be? Ursula Le Guin gives us a vision of clone culture in "Nine Lives." What happens if you have 8 other selves to live with all your life? If some of you are male and some of you are female and you have sexual relations with one of your clone brothers or sisters, how do you define it? Normal sexual relations? Incest? Self-abuse? Oh, the problems we're going to run into.

Conception without sperm can be made to occur by stimulating an egg cell. The offspring is genetically identical to the mother, so you don't get males. What happens when you don't need fathers to have babies? What will it do to families? To the gene pool?

Ectogenesis will bring with it many social problems. Ed Bryant has a wonderful science fiction idea, borrowed from Shulamith Firestone, concerning ectogenesis: what happens if a movie starlet should become pregnant by design and choose to have her child externally brought to term? She can *rent* a mother. Bryant's question is, what happens when our society has created a large group of socially mistreated foster mothers? It's bound to happen without controls.

And, of course, there are cyborgs. How much of a woman can you replace before she ceases to be a woman and becomes a highly independent machine? What would happen to the world of professional sport if a cyborg were to play for the Denver Broncos? He could be tackled by a whole team and never go down.

Another issue in the biological revolution is eugenics, the planned improvement of the human race. We are rapidly gaining the ability to control genetic makeup. No more glasses, no more hay fever, no more flat feet. That's all wonderful, right? Who's going to decide what we should breed for? Many Hitlerian scenarios come to mind.

All these issues will confront us in our lifetimes. We will probably live a lot longer than we expect, so we'll see a lot more than we'd ever expect. Certainly our children will have to cope with these problems. And these concerns are not to be taken lightly. They are problems of greater magnitude than those we face today, precisely because we have no standards by which to decide what constitutes a human being, what constitutes life, or what constitutes sentience.

We don't only define ourselves physiologically, but psychologically and sociologically as well. Our age is the first in which a person defines himself by what he does rather than by where he was born. What does work do for us? It provides some sort of social organization and ego support. It provides us with a natural area of expertise in which to excel, but it should not be the justification for existence. We should learn that we don't need to work to "be someone." You can be someone through hobbies. You can be someone in family relationships, social relationships, intellectual or athletic activities. In other words, your role doesn't have to be defined by the job you do. And your "job" need not be "work" in the traditional sense.

We need avocations, we need other "work." To be a great stamp collector, to be a great radio amateur, to be a great amateur publisher of magazines, some area in which to excel, some area in which to employ oneself. Not for financial gain, but for recognition and social contact. This has to happen.

We retire earlier and we live longer and more usefully. We are doing more volunteer work and creating new hobbies. The hobby industry proliferated shortly after World War II. Before that, you'd work until you dropped, and they'd cart you away. We all know men and women who dread retirement because all they've done is work all their lives. They don't know what to do. And if it's bad now, imagine how bad it's going to be within 100 years, when no one will have to work. We must learn another meaning for "work." If we don't, we're in for wars of boredom. We're seeing the beginnings of this problem now. Why is it that historically unemployed people are the most unsettled part of our population? It's very simple: boredom. They have nothing to get up for in the morning, nothing to look forward to. With nothing to do, people become frustrated, and their frustration breeds violence. Minor injustices become magnified because they are the only significant events in an otherwise dull life. The best way the human race has ever devised for siphoning off excess energy is to put 10,000 people out on a field and have them run at each other with sticks and clubs. Are we going to turn into a military state simply to resolve the question of what to do? Certainly we have better solutions.

Our culture is always being accused of collapsing into decadence, and I guess it is. But decadence is merely the educated response to boredom. Instead of beating someone over the head with a club, you write pornographic poetry. That's also an aggressive act, if not a physical one.

The American system of government and political vision is ideally suited to a leisure culture: it demands our regular, active participation. We have a right and a duty to be tavern politicians, and we will have more and more time for that role. Politics is one of the most valuable ways we could spend our time. America is probably going to last a lot longer than any of us expect it to, because its politics are so ideally suited for decadence.

Liberal arts education is also appropriate to a leisure society. Even though literacy is no longer necessary in this society and is already a rare commodity, it has values we are going to need. Reading is a much more engaging and strenuous process than watching television. And if what we're looking for is things to do, passivity is what we should walk away from. If we want to entertain ourselves, we should do it actively.

Literacy *will* come back, not just the ability to read headlines and write one's own name, but the ability to read critically, deeply, and with understanding. The arts and humanities will become more and more important, not only for entertainment, but for enrichment. They teach us critical reasoning. They figuratively lengthen our life span by enabling us to experience past, present, and future. And they engage our minds and hearts for long periods of time on fundamental human issues. A liberal education serves us in the way we experience the world, in the way we perceive details, in the way we organize our lives and find satisfaction. It may not assist us in solving everyday engineering and accounting problems, but it is invaluable for helping us fit engineering and accounting into our lives in a meaningful way. It will help us understand the rules of the new worlds we will be living in.

The exponential growth of knowledge and specialization will demand continuous education. The only solution for C. P. Snow's two cultures question is further education. And if you have 60 years with "nothing to do," education is perfect. You can never know even a fraction of all there is to know; you can never master everything. You're always running toward a receding horizon, and being enriched by the race.

Literacy, critical reasoning, and the growth of knowledge and specialization will be enhanced by data processing. Access to information and manipulation of data will be made easier. If you can carry your library on your wrist and communicate with it, imagine how much you can know and do: you can ask specific questions and receive specific answers, helping you synthesize pieces of information more effectively than you can now. Having a library with you at all times will help you apply new and old knowledge to the everyday world, thus making you and that world less everyday. Education will profit from this final extension of the "university without walls." Finally, your leisure time will be richer because you will have vast storehouses of entertainment with you at all times.

As one simple byproduct of the data processing revolution, within the next fifteen years, an increasing percentage of our schoolchildren will learn computer access in elementary school. It's happening now. We teach them how to read in order to know; we're going to teach them how to use computers for the same purpose.

An obvious outcome of all these changes in ourselves and our lives is a global culture. In the United States now, we are tied together less by accident of birth than by our preferences in food. This country is becoming more and more unicultural. We have a uniform idea of what the good life is, because we all see it on the same commercials. Television has leveled us. We all have similar standards, because we're all being trained to have them. The media soup around us is constantly providing standards of dress, behavior, and even language for 215 million people. And as America goes, so goes the world.

Take language, for instance. English is now the most widely used scientific, technical, and literary language in the world. Airline pilots speak in English everywhere. Although the Chinese dialects are still the most spoken languages, followed by Urdu, Hindi, and the other languages on the Indian subcontinent, the language that is most used in the twentieth century for communication between cultures is English. Does that mean that everyone on the Earth is going to be speaking English? Yes. Communications satellites bring English everywhere, and that's the clue. Our greatest export is communications, and the rest of the world is a captive audience, learning our ways of necessity.

Does that mean that we're all going to become one people, all eat, dress, and live the same? No. The old differences are breaking away, true. Despite the last gasp of cultural separatism going on now in this country, a steady degradation of old uniquenesses continues. The old differences are even fading in Europe. To be Italian more and more means that you come from a particular part of Europe, not that you have a unique cultural heritage or way of life. That's a problem. We *are* getting more and more homogenized.

One of our traits as humans, however, is that we're constantly creating little groups. We have a need to find our niche in a social order, and the social order must be small enough for us to maintain our own identities. If we cannot live in the twenty-first century with our present social groups, and all indications are that we won't, then we will create new social groups to serve our needs. The nature of the family and child-rearing may change, but the family and child-rearing will stay a part of our lives. We need stability, we need to accept our roots. As primates, we are social organizers. We will remain social organizers on the larger scale and on the smaller scale.

A global culture is obviously too unwieldy for the individual, so we will create our own new little niches. Within a homogeneous world culture, we will create new distinctions. And, as always, these distinctions will serve to identify us with a larger group and at the same time call attention to our uniquenesses.

In the new world, much will be uniform, standard, and controlled. For those who need the possibility of chaos and disorder, there is a need for frontiers, psychological as well as physical. There are two new frontiers opening for us, vast enough to accept all our growth and our rowdiness: the sea and space.

The sea will go the way of America—first the province of adventurers and pioneers, then the farmland of hundreds of thousands of citizens. Space pioneering will do the same, and will give us a solar civilization with economic and military outposts on Mars, the Moon, eventually on Venus and some of the outer satellites of Jupiter and Saturn. This pioneering is already well under way.

We will have a global culture which will continually be redefined. And we have the potential for a society of greater freedom and greater access to knowledge, with less privacy, perhaps, than ever before. In order to control the freedoms we are going to have in 2076—freedom over our bodies, our families, our environment—we are going to need strong ethical bases for making decisions. Old values are rapidly eroding in our own time. I believe that the ethical basis for our decisions is going to rest upon some sort of computer-connected apparatus which we will consider reasonably infallible, just, and humane. We will accept some sort of parent figure, a centralized ethical, political, and legal authority.

It has been suggested that we will return to the New England Town Meeting for our political authority. I think not. Many issues will be too complex and technical for people to feel confident about making decisions on them. We're going to need expertise, and if we use our leisure wisely, we will each be an expert in some small area. But we will look to data processing to help us digest information and make wide-ranging technical decisions.

We can very easily fall into a dictatorship. The more choices we have, the easier it is to ask someone else to make decisions for us. It takes education, courage, foresight, and the ability to withstand anxiety to make independent decisions. It's too easy to take on a dictator. We must not.

I don't believe that we will allow ourselves to die. With luck, perseverance, knowledge, and intelligence, we will look back after 300 years still a young, growing culture.

—Peter S. Alterman, Ph.D.
University of Colorado at Denver

A RED, WHITE, AND BLUE FOURTH OF JULY
Karl Hansen

It seemed an intriguing idea to both open and close this book with stories set precisely during America's Tricentennial celebration. The following story is not the most Utopian vision that our great-grandchildren could hope to see. Speculative fiction is sometimes taken to task by readers and critics alike for its frequently pessimistic orientation. There is a simple reply: no matter how dim the forecast, at least a dystopian story projects that there *will* be a future; and perhaps the warning will have a salutary effect. In the tradition of *1984* or *Brave New World*, "A Red, White, and Blue Fourth of July" forces our attention to the means we might employ to save ourselves from a horrific future. But how should we define the goal? And how high a price would we be willing to pay for salvation?

Karl Hansen was born in Salt Lake City (his maternal great-great-grandmother trundled a pushcart across the plains with Brigham Young early in the nineteenth century). A 1976 graduate of the University of Colorado Medical School, Dr. Hansen plans to specialize in emergency medicine. In the best SF manner, he once was a Future Scientists of America regional winner for a project called "Memory Transference in Planarian Cannibals."

A RED, WHITE, AND BLUE FOURTH OF JULY

Sometimes a face seemed almost familiar, like a childhood friend now lost to fragments of memory. Recognition wavered tantalizingly near, the way glimpses of an almost forgotten dream will linger for a time during the half-wakefulness of morning. Eyes teased him from the silence of shadow. Faces mocked him with the serenity of death. Yet he knew their deaths could not have been easy. Quick, yes, but not easy. Every neuron must have exploded with pain as the cellular water crystallized within. For an instant, they must have felt as much agony as an organism was capable of perceiving. Pain should have pulled their faces into terrible grimaces.

Then why did each wear a smiling mask? He had asked himself that same question too many times, when he thought of Rence, and remembered her face—free of hate, finally. In the instant of death had she found peace? Had she known, and is that why she meant to have him follow? Or was it to taunt him one final time? There were no answers from her rigid lips.

Kurtz rode in quiet along the edge of the shadow of the wall. Air danced along the polished skin of the cab; the scream of its parting was muffled to a murmur. Permaplastic wheels spun noiselessly on the shining stainless-steel track.

Sunlight splayed across the city; only a narrow margin of shadow still lay next to the wall. The shadow's edge crept toward the wall as the sun rose. Faces floated like pale balloons within the shadow, their bodies concealed by the darkness. As the shadow diminished before the sun climbing to zenith, tatters of garments would be seen hanging from the bodies and they would appear as clothed statues; dry, frozen flesh now white as ancient marble underneath the shreds of cloth. And as brittle: arms and legs would be seen scattered along the base of the wall, sheared cleanly from the torsos. In the light, some of the faces would lack noses, or ears. Forgotten dolls, he thought, imperfect statuary now discarded and forgotten. But not entirely forgotten. And with the same smile carved into each stone face and the same sapphire eyes.

The monorail track paralleled the wall, curving with it around the city. From below, the wall was substantial, standing almost three thousand meters high, the top edge indistinct as the wall melded into the hazy air. Not at all like it appeared from his apartment window. Fifty stories of elevation and twenty-five kilometers of distance transformed the wall to a wavering black ribbon set on edge, the top surface distorted by the madly swirling currents of heated air sent streaming upward by the fringe disturbance of the mass-field. From his apartment, the wall seemed ethereal somehow, perhaps fragile, almost a magical structure erected from the summer daydreams of a timid child. But beneath the wall, the feeling was different. The faces could be seen beneath the wall.

Kurtz looked away from the wall, away from the faces waiting there. He pushed a memory away, refusing to let himself think of her. Besides, he had more important things to consider. Today was the Fourth of July, the day of the Tricentennial. Today was the day of the Contest, and it was almost half finished.

But his gaze kept returning to the wall, searching for a face lost among the dry images, just as his thoughts were wont to return to another time in his life, seeking meaning that had somehow become misplaced.

The surface of the wall was impenetrable, completely opaque, a blackness absorbing all radiation that fell on it —paralyzed force, deep and dark as the pupils of a dead man's eyes. Kurtz felt the coldness of the wall sympathetically, a coldness that sucked energy from the sun and wind to perpetuate that energy into force that held air molecules tightly within the matrix of a field, stabilizing a force grid, forming the reticular membrane of the mass-field comprising the wall. He knew that if he reached out and touched the wall, his hand would be seared with cold, frozen solid instantly as the wall absorbed the heat from his flesh— solid enough for the tissue to shatter into sharp-edged crystals.

He closed his eyes, suddenly afraid of seeing his own

face leering among the smiling death-masks at the edge of the wall, eyes shining blue.

He was tired from the overnight trip from New York. It was past mid-morning before he had finally arrived in Denver and transferred to the local rail system. He could never sleep in the underground trains, always feeling tense and nervous from childhood claustrophobia. Sometimes he wished there was still air travel, that airplanes weren't so wasteful of petroleum fuel. Fusion power had made available abundant electrical energy, but petroleum was scarce —too scarce to be used for fuel; it was needed for plastics, fabrics, medicines, and the thousands of other products that were synthesized from it. Electrical motors and batteries were still too heavy to be used in aircraft. And synthetic fuel was too costly. So now they had to content themselves with surface transportation.

As a child Kurtz had made one of the last jet flights and remembered the journey with the simple awe of childhood. The open land below had been too novel to frighten him then. The billowing white clouds beside them had been too beautiful. But even from high in the air he could see the long rents of the open pits, with huge mining machines busily working the leading edge, and the sheen of stagnant water pooled at the bottom of the pits. With evening, the faint splotches of the blue dead zones appeared, glowing in the darkness. Where the land was dark, food could still be produced. Only time could reclaim the dead zones; only the natural decay of radio-isotopes and the normal degradation of chemical wastes would eventually return the land to productivity. And then only if further contamination could be prevented. So inside each dead zone was the light of a walled megacity.

Tiredness spread over him; he began to doze. He could not remember the last time he had taken a vacation. There was always so much that needed to be done, and there was really no place to go—all the megacities were the same. He knew he was working too hard and had been for years. Twenty years ago he had been placed in charge of children's programming for a local cerevision station. That was when he had first begun working long days, seven days a week. Renee could never understand how important he considered his job then. If children could be molded early in life, they would adapt much better as adults. Maybe some of the madness could be prevented. He had driven himself to do a good job. He knew it was unfair to Renee. But why couldn't she have understood? Why did her loneliness have to turn to bitterness and scorn? He thought the baby would help. But it hadn't. Now twenty years later he still worked too hard. But someone had to. Everyone could not give up.

The city was quiet; the streets that flashed by on the right were empty of people and the buildings seemed still and serene. Not at all like the Fourth of July should be: no parades, no laughing throngs of people, no picnics in the park with baseball games and watermelon and little boys stinging their fingers with firecrackers. Of course the Fourth hadn't been like that for a long time, so long ago that he knew his memories could not be real, and were instead delusions constructed from the fragments of life glimpsed through the cerevision. Sometimes he wondered which of his memories were real; some of the fragments were his own, if only he could sort them from the others, the ones that had been generated in his mind by the cerevision.

He knew why the city was so quiet; he knew what the people would be doing. Because today was the Fourth of July, the day of the Rebirth-76 Contest. Everyone had a cerevision. And all would be in use today.

He leaned forward and switched on the cerevision unit in the console of the cab. The spherical translator crystal glowed. He closed his eyes, allowing the images emanating from the cerevision to build in his mind. No two people experienced the cerevision exactly the same; there was constant feedback between the unit and the mind, allowing continuous perceptual modification. All morning he had followed the progress of the contest, but for some reason had been unable to steadily view it, feeling the need to sometimes have his mind free of cerevision images.

Rebirth-76 had been conceived to commemorate the American Tricentennial. For a year, there had been nightly recreations of history, tracing the birth of the nation and its subsequent development for the past three hundred years. Through the cerevision, it seemed as if one were a participant in the actual event, because a person's own experience and memories were used by the feedback circuit to build a vivid and personal background dimension to the general structural pattern provided by the cerevision. Over a year, the entire American experience had been conveyed:

Each citizen had been a colonist, a patriot (and a Tory), a pioneer, an Indian fighter (and an Indian), a mountain man and a buffalo hunter, a gold-hungry prospector, a riverboat gambler, a gunfighter, a dance-hall girl, a rebel and a Yankee, a cattleman and a sheepman, a rustler, a lumberjack, a farmer, a factory worker, a miner, and an astronaut stepping on the moon. All the wars had been fought again, the railroads and dams built once more; the forests cut, the land cleared and planted, iron and coal stripped from the ground. And cities grew, spreading out, spewing forth their wastes, until the walls had to be built to contain the pollution, and there were a hundred great megacities, each a hundred kilometers in diameter, and each with ten million inhabitants. One billion Americans. Each city had presented its own history and development during the course of the series. There was an air of intense desperation to the cities' presentations, and a sense of sadness, because the nation no longer had the resources to keep its cities from undergoing an inexorable decline that had first begun more than a hundred years earlier. The walls had only delayed the process for a time. Now the critical time had come.

By pooling the resources of all hundred megacities, one city a year could be saved; they could afford to save just one. It would require a century to save all the megacities. So it was decided to let the cities compete for salvation, using the Rebirth-76 series on the cerevision. Ten megacities were selected on the basis of their presentations to have declined the most in the past one hundred years, and therefore to most deserve being resurrected. Each was allowed an additional hour of cerevision time on the Fourth of July. From these presentations the people would select the winner.

Only one would win and the others would continue to suffer for at least another year, but the chance of salvation would provide an uplift everyone needed. Besides, through the cerevision, everyone could experience the reward of the winner.

For the past year, Kurtz had been the director of Denver's presentation effort, and had just now returned from delivering the final cerevision presentation to Contest Headquarters in New York. For the past year, Kurtz had lived with the reality that despite the cerevision, only one megacity would actually win.

The Public Rapid Transit cab sped quietly next to the wall. Heat, reflecting from the buildings beside the track, rippled from the bright, stainless-steel rail in shimmering waves. Above the margin of the wall, the edge of the sky was blue—the demarcation between the pure air of the countryside and the foul, hazy air of the city. Fatigue pressed from behind his eyes. A glimpse of a remembered image disturbed him. When he was tired, he could not control the memories that always nagged at his consciousness. He closed his eyes, not even trying.

A LAKE—SUMMER—AT TWILIGHT

Trees line the shore of the lake. The sunset ebbs from its surface as the gentle summer wind sends ripples across the water. Track along the lake shore. There is a grass-covered hill behind the edge of trees. People sit in small groups on the hillside, sprawled on blankets spread out on the grass.

An old man and a young boy sit side by side upon a faded flannel blanket. In the background, blurred by loss of depth-of-field, a softball game is being played. A dull thud of bat on ball is heard, and then the cheers of the offensive team urging the base runners to advance. The boy has been crying; his eyes are still red with tears.

OLD MAN

They sure don't know how to celebrate the Fourth, these days. No sir, not like we used to, not at all. Oh, we had picnics, just like now, but there were automobile races, and swimming and boating. Sometimes we would drive to the mountains. But we always came back before dark, so we could be sure and see the fireworks. [He looks at the boy's face, hoping to see a smile brighten it.] The firemen shot them over the lake on the night of the Fourth of July. The rockets would explode in the air; at first, just a brilliant burst of white light and a giant puff of gray smoke. Everyone covered their ears as the concussion waves beat down on us. Then, as it got darker, they started shooting the good stuff. There were streamers and fountains and corn-poppers. Everyone oohed and ahed. But before you knew it, the fireworks were over, and all that was left were cinders sizzling on the lake. Yessir, a real red, white, and blue Fourth of July.

The boy looks up to the old man and then beyond him.
The wall can be seen, rising to blend into the sky. The sky
is gray overhead.

                         BOY
      They never had a chance, Grandpa, did they? [His
      eyes are alive, darkly.]

                       OLD MAN
      Your parents? No, they never did. But it's better not
      to think too much about them now. [Wistfully] It's
      a shame there aren't fireworks displays anymore; that
      would help you to forget. [Reminiscing] That was al-
      ways the best part of the Fourth for me.

                         BOY
      Never a chance at all. And they knew it all the time.

                                    CUT TO:

A CONCRETE VENTILATOR HOUSING—NIGHT—
IN THE COUNTRY
A louvered panel is pushed outward from the inside of the
ventilator housing. The screak of metal bending and scraping against cement is heard. A gap forms between the panel
and the wall. A leg protrudes from the gap, then another
leg, then a torso, until a figure of a man stands next to the
housing. More people crawl from the ventilator, both men
and women, and mill about, waiting for everyone to get
out. Behind them is the faint glow of the dead zone sur-
rounding the city, and even further away the dark wall and
the city itself. Ahead lies the dark land still free of contamination. Finally, the last one climbs from the ventilator
duct, and they all begin walking toward the dark, slowly
and cautiously at first, then skipping and dancing, and their
whispers turn to laughter, as they realize they are free.

A FIELD OF SPRING WHEAT, BORDERED
BY WOODS
They cross the field. In the wood, unnoticed, starlight
gleams on metal. The night air is pleasantly cool, the sky
clear. Some couples hold hands, touching for the first time
in years. They stop at the edge of the wood, resting on grass
still soft with spring dew. Some begin to make love, openly,

calmly, slowly, knowing the darkness will last until morning.

Quiet movement begins in the trees. A twig snaps under pressure. Then the assembled machines dart from the wood and are upon the people, slashing with arms designed to prune orchards or weed fields, crushing flesh between tool-steel pincers, shearing bodies in half with sharp plowshares. The night is quiet, disturbed only by the soft sound of bodies breaking, the silent movement of machine joints; no cry is voiced by any of the people.

The machines leave, returning to their other duties. There is much work to catch up with before morning. The starlight breaks into prismatic colors from the surface of glass optics.

CUT TO:

THE BOY AND THE OLD MAN
It is dark now. The boy begins to cry silently.

OLD MAN
Go ahead and cry. You'll feel better afterwards. I know how much you miss them. When you're older maybe you'll understand.

BOY
Why did they leave, knowing all the time? Why couldn't I have gone?

Kurtz awoke abruptly as the cab eased into a passenger loading platform. For a moment, he thought he was home, but the buildings were wrong and the wall was still next to the track. He realized the cab was stopping to pick up another passenger. He had hoped to have a direct route home, and was annoyed by the prospect of sharing the cab.

There was only one person standing on the platform, so perhaps he would not be delayed long.

The cab stopped and the door slid smoothly open.

Kurtz could see the woman clearly through the open door. The wall-wind swirled about her, blowing brown hair out long in front to hide her face, billowing her pants to open the slits along the sides, revealing glimpses of the dark-tanned skin of her legs. She hesitated, as if deciding whether to board the cab. Then, as the door was closing, she slipped inside and sat opposite Kurtz. A hot gust of the wall-wind followed her into the cabin.

The woman pulled strands of hair from across her face, then began combing it with her fingers. Kurtz could see her face clearly. For a moment a sense of *déjà vu* came to him, a fleeting ache for the loss he had never forgotten; there was something about her face, some quality that reminded him of someone else, two others, a mother and daughter. She was about twenty-five; as old as his daughter would have been, as young as his wife had been. But there was something else the same. Something about the eyes. It seemed important that he should remember.

The cab accelerated away from the loading platform. Kurtz looked away from the woman, away from her eyes, and the memories they evoked, staring once more at the bland surface of the wall.

He knew little of the open countryside that lay behind the wall, beyond the dead zone. Sometimes he wondered what it was like to live outside the wall. He imagined himself one of the strange rural people, one of the few outcasts who had chosen to remain outside the walled cities when there was still a choice, to run the mechanized farms that produced food for the city people. The land was too important to allow it to be further destroyed by the wastes of the cities, or for any more land to be taken out of production due to urban sprawl—food production was marginal at best, just barely meeting the cities' requirements in a good year. So the cities had been walled to contain both urban pollution and further growth. Almost all the population had lived in the sprawling urban centers, anyway. Now, the countryside was nearly deserted, with vast distances between the few rural habitations; broad fields of green crops lay on both sides of old, crumbling highways, with dull, graceless machines tending the fields, the sun glinting from their polished bodies as they worked the land.

Like all city dwellers, Kurtz was terrified of the wasteland outside. He shivered, thinking of the machines out there. As a child, he had seen on the cerevision that the machine bodies were hollow inside; the machines were hollow men, devoid of feeling, empty of soul, and the only way they could get a soul was to catch a naughty child and steal his. Then the machine could take the child's place, and live his life, while the poor, soulless child was doomed to take the place of the machine, toiling endlessly in the hot fields. Cerevision experiences were almost as vivid as real ones; even now, when he thought of the machines, he felt a little twinge of dread. And he also had a personal reason to hate the machines, a real memory from his childhood: the image of his parents' bodies.

Kurtz had never met anyone from the outside, but he was sure they would be very strange indeed, to live with machines.

"Do you mind?" the woman asked, reaching toward the cerevision switch. Her voice was flat, lacking inflection.

Kurtz shook his head. "No, of course not."

She activated the cerevision and sat back in her seat, closing her eyes. He noticed crow's feet beginning at their corners.

He closed his eyes, settling his mind for the cerevision. The cab went through a shaft of sunlight lying across the track, and the sudden brightness in the cabin startled him awake. He saw her body outlined through the fabric of her shirt by the light streaming through the windscreen, then they passed once more into shadow. He drifted again into the sad, gray life of the cerevision, remembering the interminable hours he had spent wired into a master console, sorting out the fragments of experience that had been recorded by the other ceregraphers, trying to find a common theme among them, to build a unified presentation. He added images from his own mind, stealing from his experience, as well as from his imagination, until his memories mingled and finally became lost among those induced in his mind. But he had found what he looked for in the memories of others within his own subconscious, within the substance of his dreams. Now he again shared the experience of many others, gestalted by someone else in another city, but the images were really the same, the lives no different at all, the dream identical to one he could never forget, the face always Renee's.

DENVER SKYLINE—DAWN

The buildings of the city slowly lighten. At first they are indistinct and shadowy. As the ambient light increases, they are seen coated with grime; their windows are streaked and dirty. A face appears in a window, and watches the sidewalk. Once she would have been very pretty, very young, but now her eyes are dull, washed-out brown. A long time ago the eyes cried. The hair is long about her face. A baby is heard babbling in the room. The face leaves the window. A folded piece of paper has been taped to the glass.

Kurtz felt his attention abruptly withdrawn from the cerevision. For just a moment, he was lifted from his seat by the deceleration of the cab panic-braking, hearing dimly the screech of perma-plastic grinding on metal. He instinctively threw his arms forward, vaguely aware of the woman sitting across from him. The cab lurched, throwing Kurtz across the cab to sprawl on the seat next to the woman. At the same time, he heard the thud of a dull impact, as if the cab had struck something. He knew that was not possible; there were sensors built into both cab and track that would automatically slow and stop it if anything of hazardous size was on the track. But it certainly felt as if they had struck something.

The PRT cab began to slow, no longer braking now, instead coasting without power. The fading images from the cerevision flickered once and were gone. The hum of environmental control machinery was absent. The whine of the wheels and the sound of wind whistling against the skin of the cab slowly subsided as it lost speed.

Kurtz got up from beside the woman, brushing against her as he did, touching the skin of her leg with his hand through a slit of fabric. Somewhere another memory stirred. He looked at her. She did not seem to notice his disconcertion, nor did her face show the consternation he felt; her eyes followed his movement mechanically, her features appeared calm. He returned to his seat.

The forward windscreen had two long cracks radiating from bottom to top, with fine veining along both cracks. Kurtz turned to look out the rear window of the cab: at first he noticed nothing unusual; the track curved next to the wall, sunlight gleaming in patches from its ever-polished surface; the wall stood beside the track, shadow blending into its vague surface; the wall-wind scattered fragments of debris across the track, and swirled dust-devils among the dead statues leaning together in the shadows, tugging at the tatters of clothing still clinging to them. All he could see unusual was a long smudge smeared out on a section of rail, almost unnoticed in the distance.

"See the control cable," the woman said.

Kurtz glanced at her quickly, then again looked out the

rear window. A steel cable stretched over the track from one of the generator struts of the wall to a pole on the other side. The struts were placed every kilometer along the circumference of the wall; the mass-field was generated between the struts. From each strut a control cable passed to the central hub housing the computer maintaining fine modulation of the wall. Kurtz nodded.

"They climb out along the cable and hang from it, waiting for a cab to come along. They have to time the drop carefully. It's become very fashionable."

"You mean . . ." He stopped speaking, overwhelmed by an image that came unwanted to his mind, of someone dangling from a cable, waiting, waiting to hear the crescendo whine of a cab on the rail below: someone he recognized. He turned quickly from the window. The woman's face was unchanged, the eyes the same, forgetting sadness.

"You didn't know? Quite fashionable." She shrugged. "Something precise about it, a certain elegance within the few seconds between the active process of letting go of the cable and the passive culmination of the act. Very psychodynamic."

"Yes," he said. "I see, I mean, I didn't know." The image was still there: the grip slipping, fingers growing weak, the wall-wind tugging incessantly, the rail gleaming far below. He saw Renee in the air, dropping toward the oncoming cab, smiling enigmatically. She knew.

"Why are we slowing down?"

She shrugged again. "A malfunction from the impact, I suppose. A shame, we seem to have lost all power. The Contest was just becoming interesting."

"I guess we wait for a repair crew," he said. "There must be emergency crews on standby call." Even though this was a holiday, he thought. The automatic sensors would alert the maintenance people that a cab was stalled. "All we can do is wait." He paused. "My name is Kurtz, John Kurtz."

The woman looked up. "Lisa," she said. "Lisa . . ." And she stopped speaking, smiling briefly.

Again he saw the sadness in her eyes, and almost remembered.

Inside, it was strangely quiet when the cab finally coasted to a stop. Even the wall-wind was muted by the sealed cab. Kurtz reclined in his seat. Lisa had turned sideways, looking toward the ramshackle buildings that stood beside the track, watching below them. There was nothing to do but wait. Before long help would come. He closed his eyes and tried to relax. But the image was still there, now changing, as he knew it would.

A PRT LOADING PLATFORM—MORNING RUSH-HOUR
The bustle of commuters going to work: PRT cabs zip into the loading platform, doors slide open, passengers crowd into cabs, pushing and shoving for space. The air is hazy with fumes: most of the commuters wear respiratory masks. Their faces take on a certain anonymity—only the eyes are their own, and the eyes are identical: red-streaked and tearful from irritation.

CUT TO:

THE STAIRS TO THE PLATFORM
A young woman pushes her way through the crowd on the stairs. She carries a baby in her arms.

CUT TO:

THE WALL OF A BUILDING
A man's face is seen behind a window on one of the upper floors. He is anxiously searching the sidewalk below. In one hand, he holds a folded piece of note paper. He sees the woman and baby just as they reach the platform.

CUT TO:

THE PLATFORM
The man reaches the loading platform just as the woman and child enter a cab. She turns and sees him before the door closes and the cab leaves. The man forces his way through the crowd and squeezes into the next cab. On the platform behind him, a commuter stumbles, overcome by fumes. The others ignore him, intent on being first in line for the next cab. He lies still on the sidewalk, arms out-flung. Tall towers reach into the tumid air, receiving the supplication of the dead man's hand. The door closes. The cab slips forward.

CUT TO:

THE WALL BORDER

The man walks slowly between the wall and the monorail, knowing he is too late. He finds her on the bank of a dry stream-bed, the water cut off by the wall. She stands a little apart from the other stone figures that line the wall. One arm is held out in front, fingers clenched; the other is outstretched, palm flat on the surface of the wall, as if she had tried to stop herself too late, as she was already falling backwards to lean against the wall. Frost has condensed on her eyelashes, building them into fragile white lace. Her eyes are ice-blue beneath the filigree of silver wire. Sunlight catches in her eyes, and down the line, the eyes of each statue glitter against the null surface of the wall, the light playing from crystallized lenses, frozen aqueous humor. Then he realizes the hand was frozen in a final attempt to grasp something, and pull it close. From behind, he hears the baby cry.

With the air-conditioning equipment shut down, the cabin began to get uncomfortably warm. Kurtz loosened his clothing and wiped the accumulated sweat from his forehead. Lisa was still watching the streets below expectantly. The repair crew should be here soon, he thought comfortingly. But how long had it been already? He was not sure; he might have dozed longer than he had thought. He looked ahead and could see no other cabs on the track, repair or otherwise, nor were there any visible behind them.

The line of sunlight marking the shadow of the wall steadily crept closer to the monorail as the sun rose higher above the top of the wall. When the direct sunlight hit the cab, it would heat up fast, turning into an efficient solar oven without the heat being directed to the heat pumps that normally cooled the interior.

Kurtz suddenly missed the cerevision and the Contest, feeling even more isolated.

The rail was still devoid of movement, still shimmering with heat. The tenement buildings beside the elevated monorail continued to appear deserted and the crumbling streets empty and silent. Lisa persisted in watching the buildings, her eyes darting back and forth, chewing absently on a fingernail.

"What do you see down there?" he asked.

She turned away from the window. Her face was shining

with sweat. "Nothing, nothing yet. Maybe later . . ." And she turned back, watching, expecting.

"When are they going to come?" he asked himself, knowing the heat within the cabin would only get worse the longer they had to wait.

Kurtz sat staring out of the broad windscreen of the cab, watching the hot sunlight drawing ever closer, hoping to see a repair cab coming. But the track remained empty. He must do something soon. Already the heat within the cabin was unbearable. Yet Lisa sat calmly, not complaining, showing no concern.

They would have to get out of the cabin soon. The air was painful to breathe, the seat was burning his skin. He examined the windows; they could not be opened. The entry door was locked and could only be unlocked at a boarding platform. However, there was an emergency hatch that could be opened manually. He crawled behind the rear seat, found the bolts securing the hatch, and undogged them. By pushing with both hands and bracing his back against the seat, he managed to break the wind seal and the hatch cover swung out freely, allowing sunlight to stream into the cabin. Kurtz crawled out of the cab; the wall-wind blew in his face, drying the sweat from his skin. He sat on the hot roof of the cab, legs dangling through the hatch opening, letting the wind cool his skin.

"Move over, give me some room," she said from inside the cabin. He reached down and grasped her hand, helping her climb out.

She sat beside him. The wind lifted her hair behind her, smoothed her shirt against her body.

Below the monorail, the slums of Commerce City sprawled, spreading to the south. To the west were the ruins of an old petroleum refinery, now only rusted pipes and chambers piled in a jumbled mess. The area was a bad section of Denver. Kurtz had qualms about being afoot there. Especially with a woman with him. They might not bother him if he was alone, Kurtz thought. Maybe he should leave her.

"Any ideas?" he asked Lisa.

"We can wait," she said, and laughed: "Or we can walk." Looking into his face: "Or we can do as we each choose."

"Are you from around here?" he asked carefully.

"Close to here. I know the streets, and some of the people. I used to know more."

Maybe she could be a help. "Let's see about getting off the track," he said.

He slid down the smooth skin of the cab, landing lightly on the steel track of the monorail. Lisa came after him. They walked along the rail, searching for an access ladder leading to the ground.

The wall stood solidly to one side. Kurtz tried not to look down, imagining the eyes of the statue faces were watching him, following his movement along the rail. But he could not help furtively glancing toward the border of the wall. The faces seemed sinister in the half-light: nightmare faces, with eyes he distinctly remembered meeting once in dreams—empty, dead eyes, reflecting crystalline blue. The wall-wind carried illusory voices to him in enigmatic snatches; dark whisperings teased him, taunted him, remaining inscrutable, ambiguous of the meaning he sought. He heard Renee's voice amid the murmurs of the wind; she asked after their daughter. He could not tell her, his voice gone. She asked again, then laughed. She knew. She knew why. But she would never tell him, tormenting him to the last. He looked away, knowing there was no life remaining in the dry, frozen figures, that the voices were only in his mind, but shuddering anyway. He began to walk faster, feeling terribly exposed on the rail, wishing desperately he wasn't so much in the open, in plain view of the wall, then began to run, his feet pounding hard on the rail.

"Hey, slow down," Lisa called to him from fifty meters behind. "What's the hurry?"

Kurtz slowed his pace and stopped, waiting for her to catch up, feeling foolish for letting panic overcome him. He leaned on the concrete parapet to allow his racing heart to slow and to enable him to catch his breath. He looked down, toward the buildings. Directly below was the surface of an old freeway. The PRT monorail was built on struts rising from the median of the freeway, which was no longer in use since personal vehicles had been banned. Now the pavement was crumbling with age. The tenements were crowded right to the edge of the restraining wall of the freeway.

Kurtz was breathing normally when Lisa reached him. He carefully avoided looking toward the wall, afraid of what his imagination could create there. It was better to stare down, keeping his eyes fixed on the old roadway, thinking of nothing at all. She stood close beside him.

"Look," she said, and pointed.

There was an old woman walking on the freeway, carrying a satchel on one arm and a small bunch of flowers in her other hand.

"You know her?"

She nodded.

"Where is she going?" he asked.

"To visit her son." She laughed: "To bring him flowers and talk to him for a bit. Jason never answers, just stands there against the wall with the same smile. But she doesn't mind at all. Sometimes she brings him clothes, and dresses him. She carries insulating gloves in the bag, so she can touch him. But mostly she talks to him, telling him about the neighborhood, who's married, who's divorced, all the gossip. She always tells him about the girl he used to see, how well she's getting along." She turned away. "And the flowers she brings stay bright and fresh as the boy stays young."

They stood together, the wall-wind strong in their faces, watching the old woman trudge along the freeway, each remembering something past.

He heard them coming long before he saw them or knew what they were. From among the tenements he heard a distant roar, echoing against the buildings. The old woman started walking faster. Lisa gripped the edge of the parapet tightly.

Kurtz tried to locate the source of the sound, but it was too poorly localized, reflecting from the buildings. Finally he saw thin gray smoke rolling up into the air at the edge of the freeway.

"What the hell?" he wondered out loud.

"They find easy prey today," she said, simply.

The smoke came closer. The rumble of noise became louder.

Then he saw them. As they darted up an access ramp to the freeway, he saw first the shine of the sharp, metal-toothed grills of the cars, with tall exhaust pipes jutting straight up, spewing smoke into the air. The din of the engines waxed against his ears, already ringing in cordant tinnitus. The noise must be deafening on the surface of the freeway, he thought, to be so loud this far away.

He had heard of the renegade motorists that prowled the

deserted freeways in illegal internal combustion vehicles. They hid the cars in secret garages, making replacement parts in their own machine shops, concocting their own fuels out of alcohol and fulminant additives, and ventured out in packs, roaming the streets.

The old woman was running down the freeway, as close to the restraining wall as possible. The cars approached her, veering close as they passed. Black rubber tires kicked gravel against her legs. She was not struck by any of the cars, although their wind spun her about as they roared past.

She stood rooted in place, shaking with fear. The cars sped down the freeway, then slowed to a rubber-burning stop.

"Now they turn," Lisa said. "They come back for another run. Soon she will glimpse their faces through dust-streaked windshields: bright eyes, hard-muscled lines, thin white lips, a jagged edge of broken teeth."

The old woman began running again, still clutching her belongings.

"Do you know them?" he asked, not looking away. The scene below seemed to be occurring in extended time, in a remarkably leisurely fashion.

"I suppose; they sometimes come to the place I work." She closed her eyes briefly. "Sometimes they find no prey on the streets."

The cars streamed past the old woman in single file, each one trying to pass as close as possible without actually hitting her. Their exhaust smoke obscured her briefly.

There was an exit ramp ahead of her. The cars were already past the exit, turning around once more. If she could reach the exit before the cars turned, she would have a chance of escape. There was no hope on the freeway; they would keep zipping past until someone made a misjudgment and came too close.

The old woman stumbled toward the exit.

The cars turned around and accelerated toward her.

She was close to the exit. So close. But her old legs were not quick enough. The cars were approaching.

They once more swerved toward her, racing in a line. The staccato beat of their engines reverberated from the concrete surfaces of the freeway. Flame occasionally shot from the end of the exhaust pipes with the clap of a backfire. They bore down on her. Kurtz knew she would not reach the exit this time.

As the cars passed, the old woman was again partially hidden by gray exhaust smoke, but Kurtz knew he saw the little movement as she leaned into one of the cars. When the air cleared, she lay still on the pavement. The cars sped down the freeway and were now out of sight. Kurtz kept thinking she had only stumbled, that he had been mistaken in what he had seen, and that she would get up. But she remained motionless, flowers scattered about.

"She gave up," he said. "She stopped trying."

Lisa put her hand on his. He turned. He remembered where he had last seen the look that was in her eyes as the sound of internal combustion engines faded. That same lost look he once saw in his daughter's eyes.

A NIGHTCLUB

A woman's face, a girl's almost, but her youth somewhat neglected: her eyes are noticeable—intensity shines from deep inside through her eyes. The tip of her tongue runs along the edge of fine, white teeth, sometimes moistening her lips. The background behind her head is blurred with diffuse light; curls of white smoke rise languorously toward the ceiling.

The woman is standing at the edge of a circular gaming table. There are other players standing with her; they are crowded around the table, almost shoulder to shoulder. Colorful chips are stacked to various heights in front of each player.

The other players' faces are superficially varied: some seem gay, mouths laughing; others are sad, almost crying; some are bellicose, faces frozen into wax life-masks; and some are defiant with wild paranoia. But actually all are the same; the same intensity lies buried in their eyes.

In the center of the table a black steel cylinder rotates about its transverse axis, spinning with blurred speed; its image is melded into a wavering disk. The cylinder is bored and chambered for a 12-gauge shotshell. As long as the cylinder rotates, a microswitch is held open, but as soon as it stops for longer than one second, the switch closes, a solenoid snaps shut, and the shell fires.

The hands of each player rest on a control knob that modulates the magnetic field in which the cylinder spins. As the players twist their knobs, the spin changes according to the summed effect of the magnetic variance. After the cylinder stops, the other players divide the wager of the player before whom it stopped, proportionate to their wager.

Fingers grip the knobs tightly; beads of sweat glisten on polished wood. The players' eyes are fixed with hypnotic fascination on the spinning cylinder; they seem almost unaware of the other players beside them.

The woman bites her lower lip, then laughs wildly.

The players' hands manipulate the knobs; the rotation of the cylinder varies markedly, slowing and speeding alternately.

The woman laughs again.

The faces of the players flash past, frozen in still motion momentarily, then blurring across to the next face. The speed of rotation slows in discrete jerks. As each face appears in isolation, the exhilaration of terror gleams in the eyes. The rotation slows. The faces linger for a longer duration. The woman's face appears, then stays as the motion of the cylinder stops. Her eyes widen, ringed with white sclera. Then she laughs.

A puff of smoke blasts out of the mouth of the cylinder. The woman falls, clutching her abdomen. Blood wells out between her fingers.

A few pellets strike the wall behind the woman, digging loose small chips of marble that fall to the floor.

The woman writhes in agony on the floor. Her lips are pressed together tightly, almost puckered into a kiss. The lips fill the field. They move in whispers, trembling, then cease. Her eyes stay open. The light glares brightly from the pinpoint pupils.

The sound of plastic chips skittering across the table top persists.

Kurtz stood on the balcony of his apartment. The western half of the city was shrouded in the lengthening shadow of the wall. Just minutes before, the last of the presentations for the Rebirth-76 Contest had ended. There would be a few more minutes before the winner was announced; the celebration would be shared by the entire nation, via the cerevision. All day a computer had measured an empathic index, monitoring the effect of the cerevision presentations in the minds of those who experienced them. The city whose presentation had achieved the highest index would win. Kurtz waited nervously. More than a year of his life had gone into Denver's presentation.

The memory of the images from the Contest waned in his mind, replaced by others; the afternoon was a mingled impression of real and cerevision-distorted scenes:

He and Lisa climbing down an access ladder to the freeway, statues glimpsed standing next to the wall, blue stone eyes mocking, following them as they cross the broken pavement, sanguinely expecting to see the cars return, disappointed.

Sitting together in the electric taxi, saying nothing, empty and quiet as the streets, her hand on his, long fingernails digging deep into his skin when the sound of engines echoed faintly, both knowing she would go with him.

Not noticing the food at lunch, sharing a drink.

Making love suddenly.

Later, gently touching the fine white lines on her back, with his fingertips tracing the scars over her shoulders, between and across her breasts, a spider-web of hurt. Asking: "The drivers?"

"Not always." Hesitantly showing him the red splinter hemorrhages under her nails (kissing her fingers), and parallel needle tracks tracing the skin inside her thighs, extending to encircle each buttock.

Tasting her salty tears when she finally cries (kissing her eyes).

Sometimes talking, sometimes touching, sometimes both lost entirely to the cerevision, but always returning.

He left the balcony and walked back to the apartment. The room was dark, illuminated by fading sunlight and the faint glow of the cerevision crystal; her eyes were hidden in shadow. He lay beside her, pulling her close, feeling her skin warm against his.

She turned, kissing his ear. "Slowly, this time," she whispered. "Make it last."

Cerevision images filtered into his mind; the celebration was beginning. Soon they would know if they had won.

He left his body moving toward love with Lisa, his thoughts pulled into the dim reality of the cerevision.

A COFFIN

The dead eyes of a corpse stare vacantly, sunk into old, wrinkled flesh. The dead eyes slowly become living, but the difference is negligible; eyelids occasionally blink away the film that dims the eyes. Spittle flows from the corner of a sagging mouth. The face seems familiar, but evades recognition.

A WALL OF A TOWER

The face peers from a window. The window is joined by row after row of other windows. The same face is behind each window; the eyelids blink in unison, the spittle drools synchronously. The entire wall of a building is composed of windows and the same pale face hangs like a ghost behind each, with eyes opaque.

The eyes brighten, opacity dissolves; something catches their attention.

The window overlooks the wall. Beyond the wall is a dry ridge. Far away, silhouetted by the sky, is a tall cactus. Something sits upon the cactus. The cactus grows larger. A hawk is seen sitting on it, claws gripping tightly into the tough flesh of the plant. The hawk grows larger; yellow eyes glitter brightly. (Kurtz realizes the pattern is not one of his, and knows then that he and Lisa and Denver have not won; a pattern of its own design would be used in the celebration for a city.)

The eyes of the hawk melt, and suddenly everything is brighter, sharper. Kurtz leaps into the air, gaining altitude with slow beats of his wings. He climbs to hover over the thermal currents of the wall, hanging lazily in the air. He sounds his hunting cry before the multifaceted face of a building. The eyes behind the windows follow his movement. Then the glass crystallizes, turning mirror bright. The eyes see themselves reflecting the blue of a flawed sapphire; cracks in the stone coalesce into a bright pupil. A drop of drool falls from the center of their chins.

IN THE AIR ABOVE THE CITIES

Kurtz climbs higher; the air becomes colder, the sky deeper blue. Stars appear in the darkening sky, unwavering in intensity. He hovers over the twilight line extending across the land. Megacities are seen far below, each a bright circle of light surrounded by the faint blue glow of its dead zone. He waits, swooping in slow circles. Darkness covers the land. He is patient, watching the cities carefully. Light dims. His head cocks; his gaze intensifies. He must be sure. He sees the flicker again. Caution is abandoned; he has found the one he seeks. He dives from the sky, cold wind flowing across his feathers, claws extended wide. In anticipation, his nostrils fill with the sweet stench of carrion.

THE TOWER

Kurtz looks out the window, momentarily surprised by the sudden change in point of view. He sees the partial reflection of his dead face from the glass, then notices the faint ion trail of a missile dropping into the atmosphere from orbit, gleaming like a silver wire. For a moment, the sky is dark again. Then a pinpoint of brightness appears over the city, growing slowly, billowing outward. Multicolored fire plays across the surface of an expanding sphere. He again waits patiently. The globe of heat grows larger. The lips of his face smile. The firestorm approaches. A touch of warmth on his face, and he flows inward, drawn to the inferno at the center of the fireball. Heat bathes his body, cleansing him.

A MOUNTAIN OVERLOOKING A CITY

Superheated plasma spills upward over the edge of the wall harmlessly, and the wall contains the rest, growing stronger as more energy is absorbed, protecting the countryside from damage. Kurtz tingles as flame washes over his feathers, and with outstretched wings rides the fire currents upward. He breaks out of the maelstrom into the cool night air over the mountain. He settles on his cactus perch, folding his wings. His wife and daughter stand beside him. Behind them, his parents' broken bodies lie together, and beyond stand a horde of stone images, with upraised arms. Renee leans near. The firelight is caught and held in fissures of shattered ice in her eyes. Her lips touch his with cold.

Lisa lay back. Her hair pulled across his face, crackling with static from the air.

"I was with Jason again." Her voice carried in it the wall-wind.

"I know," he said, remembering his own images.

"He was so young. Sometimes I forget how young we were, how much we hurt. He gave me these flowers." She looked at her empty hand.

His fingers sought to smooth the fine ridges of eschar from her skin.

She held her clenched hand out, rotated it back and

forth, then brought it close to her face. "Will the colors last, the fragrance remain so fresh?"

"For a year, anyway." A sore was bleeding on her back. He touched his finger to the sticky surface.

"A shame . . ." she said, then stopped, listening.

"I wonder." Knowing they could live another year. "You'll stay?" he asked.

"Maybe." Distracted. "Can you hear them?" Listening harder.

Kurtz held the image of fire in his mind, savoring the warmth before it faded.

Blue ice retreated to the edge of his eyes.

ESCAPE IS NO ACCIDENT

Carol Emshwiller

Carol Emshwiller stories are special, as evidenced by both this story and her collection *Joy In Our Cause*. A writer of diverse talents, she recently wrote the voice-over narrations (recording one of them herself) for *Family Focus* and *Pilobus and Joan*, two PBS television specials created by her husband, filmmaker Ed Emshwiller.

An idle but informational footnote: With the 1972 launching of the *Pioneer 10* spacecraft, humankind has made its first serious attempt at communicating with extra-terrestrial civilizations. The first human artifact to exit the Solar System, *Pioneer 10* carries aboard it a gold-anodized aluminum plate with an etched message consisting of such information as an astronomical "map" pinpointing Earth's whereabouts, a schematic representation of the spacecraft itself, and the human figures of a man and a woman. Both humans are portrayed nude. Interestingly, only the male has clearly defined genitalia. It's a small point, but might not the hypothetical finders of the plaque find themselves confused and curious?

ESCAPE IS NO ACCIDENT

I hear myself making a sound like an animal.

I come to slowly.
Dizzy.
Having fallen out of the sky.
Crashed here at two o'clock Eastern Standard time.
No hope of rescue.
But I'm already hoping.

Certainly I must have landed in or near New York, because my first view was of, yes, blue eyes and beard. I didn't recognize him. Lying back in his arms, I was wondering who he was.

He warmed me the best way he could, with his own body stretched out next to mine and all the while making soft word-sounds I couldn't understand.

He guessed who I was.

I never did.

Later on he carried me inside and dressed my wounds. I was a mass of cuts and bruises and childlike at the time.

He always says *he* didn't do it and I never said he did.

I know it's my fault. I came in much too fast. I always do and I think I had a dizzy spell even before. I had passed all the tests devised for it so far but I knew I wasn't up to my usual standards and maybe I shouldn't have tried, but I wanted, just this once, to cross the celestial equator by myself and send back messages of grandeur, hope and good luck, though it isn't every morning you face yourself, plucking out gray hairs and sweating, knowing your reflexes are shot which is maybe another reason why I missed the night side and landed, two o'clock, on the opposite continent right in my own back yard. So *he* says.

"Me, husband." Pointing to himself. "Uh, uh."

"What am I doing crash-landed here in my own back yard?" I ask, but he doesn't understand me any more than I can understand him.

"You, wife. Yeah."

Under the circumstances I feel vaguely as if I had fallen off a ladder while painting the upstairs window sills, but that can't be.

"Me from sky," I say, pointing up. "We got messages. We got the picture with one of each sex, man and woman, and a sun. We understood all that. That's why I'm here."

"Yeah, I get it. Sex an' that."

How many days did I lie there in his bed, semiconscious, feverish and frightened, waking up screaming sometimes, not knowing who I was, and my husband, his hairy arms around me, comforting me? How many days drifting up from sickness and back, his hand on my breast?

"What day is this? What time? What place? I hardly recognize it."

"Me, husband. Uh . . . listen, we call this here pan. This pot holder, spoon, mop an' stuff."

I think he expects something of me now that I'm fully recovered, but I feel I need a long rest and I had hoped, wherever I might be, to have a fairly creative career, and, actually, every time I fell asleep I was hoping to wake up someplace else entirely.

"Hey you . . ."

"I object," I tell him. "I'd much rather have some sort of teaching position. I'm a member of the Association for the Advancement of Cognitive Thinking. I'm aware of the new studies of the sensory and perceptual processes and I speak a number of languages that not a single person on this planet can possibly know but me, not to mention the fact that I'm a fully trained astronomer. Besides, you should take me to your leader."

He says he hasn't had much time to learn things. I think I hurt his pride or his feelings and I'd really like to make up for it somehow. "Well," I tell him, "I'll have to think this out, and in the meantime I may as well make some spaghetti."

He tells me that would be nice and not to forget to make enough for the children but he doesn't say how many there are or give ages and sexes or if I can expect any of them to help me with the dishes.

He says, "Shape up."

It turns out today is Tuesday. Never a very good day on any celestial body.

"There's not only just one way to be a good wife, you know," I tell him. "Besides, where I come from we usually live alone. It's expected. We're brought up for it. Mothers always say, 'When you grow up and go off alone and don't do what I did you'll be single and simple and can live as you please.'"

"Go ahead an' cry. It's O.K.," he says, and he says he's got money enough for dancing lessons if I like that sort of thing.

I tested him surreptitiously and found him wanting though I do admire him in several ways. He wakes me with music he whistles himself. He praises my breasts. He listens when I talk even though he doesn't understand much. He worries about me. He lets me have my way sometimes. He taught me lots of different ways for making love and he keeps asking, "Do you love me? Do you love me?" and I never know quite what to answer. I tell him that I know that the butterfly is a symbol for the female sex organs while the caterpillar, on the other hand, is a symbol for the male. That seems to satisfy him for a little while.

I'll be seeking my fortune behind his back if necessary. I'm going to try to win a trip for two for as far away as I can manage and then take both trips myself consecutively. Also I may send some bottles into space on tiny rockets with calls for help, one to each of the cardinal directions, zenith, nadir, center, etc., with a message saying: Remember me, I'm stuck here in this ordinary solar system, ordinary planet, ordinary back yard (though if the fifth planet goes nova it'll be quite an interesting binary system). You may not recognize me. My uniform is torn and has spaghetti sauce on it. I have a constant ringing in my ears. Be careful when you come. You might turn out to be somebody's wife. He says, "Shape up." I want to know if I should bother trying to make him proud of me. I think I'm pregnant and what about all these other children?

A long message, but to the point, and one that will certainly elicit compassion.

He is Wabb, son of Argg, and I'm drifting into a new role in which I recognize the plight of the overeducated suburban woman being a helpmeet to her hard-working spouse.

But just suppose I really had fallen off a ladder while painting the window sills, why then would I find their language so full of simple sounds and twangs that leave me cold? I'm exhausted with it. There's hardly a combination of sounds that doesn't mean something to them somewhere.

And I have another clue about myself. I heard myself making the cry of an animal. I remember that. Still, *they* are the ones that try to understand everything on an instinctual level and get most of it wrong, at that.

"Hey, no more sittin' around starin' into space."

(I was looking at the sky in hope of rescue.)

"I still think you should take me to your leader."

"Don't be silly."

'Tis the season to be jolly. Down at the south pole the sun's rays slant sideways all day long and night too, or most of it, coming in every window in turn. That's one way to look on the bright side of things and, anyway, you have to trust who you can. After all, I haven't got a cent of their kind of money. What can I do? But speaking of money, if *I* were choosing (and I hope someday I get the chance) I'd bring a better class of people down here who wouldn't always charge what the market will bear.

I tell him it's very likely we will die in an earthquake or tornado. In any case, great winds will come. They will not be man-made. Tides will be higher than ever before. The continents will shrink. Day will be like night. Scientists will scream that the world is tipping and only people with a college degree will be saved.

"Whatta you really want? Beaucoup is too much."

"I would like to be numbered among the survivors and also be on the committee to choose the others that should survive. (You might not be one of them.) I will let myself be guided by my innermost feelings, my second sight, so to speak." I tell him this, all the time thinking that when archetypal woman meets archetypal man I'll know it instantly (by my innermost feelings) and I'll have a lot more to say about it all then. But right now, as I mentioned, I haven't any money.

Meanwhile we have been walking barefoot in the silence of the suburbs at eleven-thirty A.M. and I've already called him darling twice without thinking what I was saying. Oh, I would have so much preferred a Renaissance man of some sort and one a little less thick at the waist. This morning, though, I thought I saw a faint spark of understanding in his eyes just as I was explaining that I may have been, figuratively speaking, tearing out the pages of a book I wrote myself. There may be some hope after all.

I am no ordinary woman. At least I don't *think* so. Sometimes I'm mistaken for a boy and they say I will soon give birth to twins. Not something everyone does. (If I don't command attention, perhaps they will soon command respect. For this reason I hope they are both male. Also I would like a couple of little penises to look at when I feel like it.) These twins will not be ordinary babies, and it's true, they're not. Time has gone by so fast that I have given birth to them already and they *are* male, faintly mongoloid, blue . . . but all babies have blue eyes. Born with full heads of hair which certainly means something. Both are blond even though one must symbolize the dark side of life and the other the light side. One of them, either the good one or the bad one, is going to get himself into a lot of trouble by being either too good or too bad. As soon as they are old enough to call me Muth-uh I'll tell them my own story: that I come from a strange place in the sky, invisible to the naked eye. Something called a planet where life goes on much as it does here except that the policy making is left to those who can handle it.

Just then I thought I heard the archetypal man's deep bass voice, but it was only him, Wabb son of Argg, calling the neighbors to celebrate the birth of twins.

It's my unique past, I'll tell them . . . "It's Muth-uh's unique past that has made her what she is today."

But now *he's* calling me Muth-uh, too. I sputter and try to reply in kind: "Daddy . . . uh . . . Duh . . . Da . . . Pop."

"Come to muh big, fat arms, ya bastid," he says.

I wish he would enunciate more clearly. I'm not really sure that's what he said at all, but I come anyway. It doesn't matter how close I get because I had garlic for lunch. He puts his arms around me. (He thinks he knows what sex I am just by looking.) "Dream girl, yup, take a break now." I feel his big lips below my ear, then down on my neck and I'm thinking there are a lot of ways of being sophisticated.

But I believe I have made a tragic mistake. I should have been concentrating my efforts in entirely different areas (in spite of not having any money). I could have invented for them not only the wheel (that's easy) but (more important) the axle and axle grease. But, I'm wondering, how could I have brought them fire so that they wouldn't have burned themselves with it? But perhaps these are not the real people of this planet at all, but descendants of Neanderthalers or abominable snowmen, here in the primitive outer reaches of society, living on the slopes of mountains and at the edges of the deserts. (No wonder they're hairy.)

Time is still passing right here and now, however, and quite rapidly, as before. The twins' rate of growth is disappointing. (Hosay One and Hosay Two. He named them. That doesn't mean I love them any less.) They still don't say Muth-uh very well yet and sometimes I wonder if they ever will, and they are looking much more like him than like me. But the way the minds here are growing weaker every generation (not to mention the political situation here) I suppose they will seem quite normal when they are sixty-five or so. Until that time, I will feign a gay insouciance (all the while awaiting either talent scouts, rescue from the skies or archetypal man, whichever comes first.)

But quickly, before he says I'm up to my old tricks again, let me ask why can't I make as much money as a good whore? "You think this is all just science fiction," I say. "Why, you still believe in the old sawing-a-woman-in-half trick and the disappearing ten of diamonds. What can I say to you?"

I don't tell him, but I'm afraid that, rather than continuing my journey through space and time, I will have to continue it only through time, and (usually) there's something to look at out the window every day. And one isn't much sadder up there in the sky watching galaxies fade by. Why should I worry? Why should I talk so much and so loud? Why should I stay alert to the differences between us, them and me? And then, why shouldn't I croak and groan now and then, dizzy, having fallen down?

FEMININE DEMYSTIFICATION

Jo Ann Harper

Whether you know it or not, the first skirmishes of the Biological Revolution are already behind us. Consider the sophistication of a modern hog farm outside Columbus, Nebraska. Intended to be pathogen-free, the facilities resemble sets from *The Andromeda Strain*. Prize blood-line sows are artificially inseminated; after an appropriate time, the pig foetuses are transplanted to the wombs of cheap and expendable host sows. Shortly prior to the time for "natural" birth, the litters are delivered by hysterectomy, limiting exposure to the endemic diseases that plague pigs. The host-mothers die In the process. The donor-mothers, meanwhile, are again impregnated; and so the system is perpetuated.

That is only the crudest beginning for ectogenesis . . .

FEMININE DEMYSTIFICATION

White light of the lab
    instead of
the labia spread wide;
waiting for their tubes
    rather than your touch.

"Come for me," you would demand
while I waited within myself
    (my thighs taut as rope
    wound round a fence)
for the dim beginnings/deep in the wet flesh
        which signal the final dark convulsion.

This, a convocation instead.
Air, clear as the breath of a child,
    fills the room.
Their machines gleam while I brood on your
    fantasy,
    that fine and shining scene
Which brought me to this place.

I'm an old-fashioned girl: I carry
the cross, thorns of humanism
wrap around my head like a migraine.
It's your gain—gifted with a baby.
My body reluctantly yielding
    what yours will receive,
    sheathed in its sac.

You, in your separate lab, asleep,
    deep in the peace of their
    silent science. Alone and unprotected,

But prepared—prepped for the process which will
    emasculate you.
Your masculinity soon to be submerged
    in the thousand secret thrills
    of maternity.

And me? If I could have climbed like a vine
    around your masculinity,
    I would have.
But you, with your long brown hair
    and pierced ear—gold lobe shining through,
    would have none of that.
My lover, an atavistic mother.

THE DUST OF EVENING
Robert Crais

There's something particularly American about the mystique of the open road. Cite Kesey and Kerouac, *Vanishing Point* and *Easy Rider;* it's an important fragment of the American Dream dating back before even Whitman and James Fenimore Cooper. There is no reason to suppose it won't extend into our American future.

Robert Crais is a native Louisianan and graduate of the Clarion Workshop in Science Fiction and Fantasy. This story was his second sale.

THE DUST OF EVENING

Jackson crawled to the mouth of the cave. Outside, the stars and moon hidden behind thick ash clouds, there was only darkness. As he moved, the scraping of cloth against rock shattered the silence of the cave which, itself, seemed filled with black liquid of no dimensions. His guardmate, Carol, said, "You make too much noise when you move."

He smiled to himself, then pushed away from the opening. "He's down there."

"Who?"

"You know 'who'—Maxie."

Carol's voice came back tight, unamused. "You can't even see *me*. How the hell do you know he's down there?"

Jackson settled against a piece of the wall well away from the cave's mouth, careful to place his left leg gently before himself. "My knee hurts."

"How do you *know* he's there?"

"Maybe because my knee hurts." He was sorry he had mentioned it.

"But your knee always hurts."

He kept silent, then, "No, not always."

Jackson heard her draw breath sharply as if she were going to speak, then hesitate, and finally sigh as if she had decided to say nothing.

Words came from him suddenly then, as if there had never been an uneasy lag in their exchange. "What does an out-of-work skydiver do?"

"What?" Her voice was normal and clear and maybe tinted by a smile, spoken not at all in the muted tones usually reserved for the dog watch.

He didn't answer.

"Well, what did you say?"

Jackson pressed a hand against the ground. The cool

coarse texture contained nothing to trigger his emotions. "I said, 'What does an out-of-work skydiver do?' "

"Is that a joke?"

He thought about it. "Yeah, it's a joke."

"OK, I give up. What's the answer?"

"He goes insane."

She paused, waiting for more, then said, "You bring me down. Man, *really* poor. If that's the best—" She stopped, whispered, "Listen, you hear something?"

The cave was quiet again. Jackson strained his head toward the mouth, held his breath to search for any possible sound. Nothing at first, but finally the clicking noise of chain over sprocket drifted up from far down the slope.

He said quietly, "I told you: Maxie."

The noise stopped. Carol shifted; her sounds of movement were enormous in the taut silence.

From the base of the slope, at the edge of the road—existing only during the day, a nonplace at night where only sounds could live—now, half noises: heavy rubber on small gravel, leather against metal, the deformation noises of compressing springs. Then, a noise both complete and contained: a voice. "I know it's your watch, Jackson."

The cave filled with the sounds of two people moving. Jackson felt his way to the cave's mouth, then squinted futilely, trying to pick out Maxie's form.

Maxie spoke again. "Yeah, bastard, I know you're up there." An ellipse of light appeared far below the cave. It began to inscribe an arc accompanied by a metal-on-metal squeak. "I just wanted you to know I was here, motherfucker." Jackson felt awed at the way Maxie's voice sounded low and dissociated, its source merely light on the rocks. "I'll be back after sunup. You got me, suckass? It's me and you after sunup."

Why always me, thought Jackson, why the hell always me?

There came a grunt, four springs suddenly slammed down, the snapping in place of metal rods, a two-cylinder motor suddenly turned over, a catching blast and the motor exploded to life. The voice yelled, "LATER," which was partially obscured by the motorcycle swinging around. The ellipse of light presaged the motorcycle's path: a spray of pebbles rained sounds along the slope. The roar and light grew smaller until finally they were gone.

"What is it with you and him?" Carol asked, her voice a whisper.

Jackson shook his head, then realized she couldn't see him. "I don't know. Maybe from before. You know, we kinda knew each other. A long time ago. But . . . not for anything like this."

She spoke gently. "Does he scare you?"

"Yes." Jackson didn't hesitate. "Yeah, I don't understand this and I guess he scares me."

"Hey," she said, her voice in a brighter tone, "we've done what, a dozen watches together? Something like that?"

"Yeah. Something like that."

"So, Maxie's like the entertainment, right? The watch is boring, then Maxie shows up, does his song-and-dance, then leaves. Maxie's the clown. Entertaining to the last, to when we're all so much sulphurized, canceritic garbage."

Jackson knew from her voice that she would be smiling. She had a nice smile. "Maxie isn't 'the clown,'" he said. "Sometimes I think he's . . . well, I was reading one of your books on psychology. And I found this thing called 'depersonalization'. . . ."

"OK," she picked up, "a neurosis. It's a syndrome dominated by a feeling of unreality and of estrangement from the self, body, or surroundings."

"Yeah," Jackson said. "Sometimes I feel that way: not here. And Maxie is just the shadow image of me, the part that isn't here. Dissociated."

Carol's voice was concerned. "You'd better slow down, Jackson. Don't dwell on this thing too much. Don't let it get to be a part of you."

Jackson shifted into a comfortable position, rubbed his stiff left knee and placed his mind far away from this cave, this time. "It's going to be a cold watch," he said, buttoning his Army parka. "And a long one."

He heard Carol pulling zippers and wrapping blankets about herself. He closed his eyes against the darkness and thought about the long wait until daybreak. There was quiet for several minutes, then Carol asked softly, "What did you mean about that parachutist?"

"Nothing."

"Did you used to be a parachutist, Jackson?"

He smiled to himself and touched his knee. Then the smile faded. The air was cold and the rocks were hard and nobody here knew what freedom could be and he wished he wasn't there at all. "No," he said, "I've always been a cavedweller."

The cave had grown lighter. Shadows and highlights now gave visual texture to what had been, hours before, merely boundaries of the mind. Jackson's muscles were cramped from lying so long in one position. His left knee throbbed and had grown stiffer. He kneaded the sensitive area and slowly worked the leg until it could be bent without much effort. He glanced at Carol—bits of ash had drifted into the cave and flecked her loose brown hair, giving it a salt and pepper appearance—then out the mouth of the cave.

From north to south, the striations of the high volcanic ash clouds moved across the sky like red ocean waves. He could only sigh as he watched them. Perhaps that was why he always volunteered for night guard, to see the rich, crimson glow visible only through a veil of ash and aerosol as dawn approached.

He felt Carol move, her knee brush his arm. In the dark, he thought, they were the same size and colorless, but now she was small against him, her hair and eyes, like his, stained scarlet by the sun.

Her voice held the hoarseness of sleep. "What are you going to do when Maxie comes back?"

Jackson tried to discern the defined ash patterns near the horizon. "I guess that depends on Maxie. Maybe he won't come back." He walked a few yards out of the cave's mouth, and followed the drifting patterns of the clouds, silver in the early morning crimson of the sky. An illusion, he knew, but he marveled as they seemed to roll toward him, born at the horizon. This is great, he thought. They move from there to here and just keep on going. Always moving, in the most beautiful sky there ever was. Man, to be up there *now!*

He turned to the cliff-face and stretched, arching his back till the small bones in his shoulders and neck snapped. He frowned. Looking at the cliff, Jackson imagined the six hundred people of the colony moving through the catacomb of tunnels and caverns in the rock—buried—keeping busy; walking and talking and moving their hands in worthless motion, and working and building and trying like hell to find something before it was too late. Something that they could never find in there. Never. "Not in there," he said.

Carol moved to the cave's mouth, stopping before she was fully exposed to the morning light. "Did you say something?"

Jackson shook his head. "Maybe Maxie's got the right idea."

She tossed a pebble toward him, then another because the first one missed. "If you think that, then why don't you leave? It's real easy to do it Maxie's way: just leave."

He returned to the cave, letting his breath escape in a gradual, low whistle.

"Well?" she said.

"Well what?"

She smiled, then said suddenly, "Hey, you know I don't even smell the sulphur anymore. I think I'm getting used to it, like it's becoming thinner and thinner. Maybe it's being absorbed or something."

Jackson laughed as he dropped to the cave's floor, careful of his left knee. "No, I doubt it. It's like you said at first: you're getting used to it. But you know what I haven't been able to get over? The way the sky is rippled with stripes in the morning and at sunset. Jesus, there has *never* been a more beautiful sky."

She nodded. "Some nights I lay awake and think this really isn't the way it should happen. You know, when the world dies everything is supposed to be torture and pain, a lot of misery and moaning. But this isn't it. After the smell goes, there will only be the sky. And like you said, it's *beautiful*."

Jackson arranged himself into a more comfortable position. "You're being a little overly dramatic, aren't you? The world isn't exactly dying."

"Jesus, a sixty-five to seventy per cent mortality rate isn't *dead?*"

He shrugged. "For us—probably. The ash clouds seem to prefer resting over deserts. Aren't you glad you fell for the ad to 'come live in sunny, healthful Arizona'?"

Carol yawned, stretched her arms. "Yeah. But doesn't it seem to you kind of funny that all those things are missing?"

"The pain will come. Sure as hell the pain will come. How many of us and the kids have already begun to cough? How many of the older people have become bedridden? So don't worry, the pain is gonna get here." He laughed, watching the shimmering sky slowly changing to the colors of day. "Yeah, we're gonna get it *good!*"

Carol pursed her lips. Her brow furrowed an instant, then was smooth. "Sometimes you sound like you don't even give a damn."

He snorted, running his fingers about each eye. "Sometimes . . . ah, hell. I care more than you know about." He coughed, cleared his throat. "You know, most people—*most* of 'em—piss away their lives and are never really *alive*. Well, they're nothing—"

"Christ, Jackson."

"—but it's the ones who've known *life*, who were *alive* during their times, that this is hard on. The guys who were *free.*"

"Finished your sermon?"

Sighing, he lolled his head against gritty rock, massaged the bridge of his nose with thumb and forefinger. "Ain't this some shit."

"Wake up!" His foot was being moved, twisted from side to side. "Wake up, Jackson!" There was pressure there at his foot. No! Not there, his chest! Something on his chest. Coming from the light. The light? The bands. "Jackson . . . dammit, wake up. I can hear Maxie's bike. Wake up, stupid."

The cough began before he came awake, his diaphragm heaving in static rhythms, trying to tear loose from the pressure in his lungs. He convulsed four times, then again, his face scarlet and creased, till bits of matter came into his mouth. He spat them into the rocks down the path.

From where he knelt—both knees, his left hand, the right at his mouth—Jackson glanced from beneath his brows at her, his voice hoarse. "Yeah, baby, the pain is coming."

Carol moved closer, her voice soft. "I didn't know you had it so bad. Maybe you should give up post watching. Henda will understand. Really."

He nodded, his face pale, eyes dull. "Thanks. But it's no worse than anyone else's. Just my fucking bronchitis makes it bad sometimes. It's no big thing; it'll pass. Forget that. What about Maxie?"

"Listen . . . hear it? I can hear his chopper."

The grind of Maxie's motorcycle sifted through the passes and channels of the mountains, giving the impression of many bikers arriving from as many directions. The sounds triggered a flow of sour juices into Jackson's throat and stomach.

"You want me to go tell Henda?" Carol asked.

He pushed to his feet, glanced to her, trying desperately to speak with his eyes, but failed. "No. Uh, why don't you stay."

Maxie snuffed the engine and lounged back against the sissy bar of the chopped Triumph to glare at the dark hole above him. His once black vest and jeans were grey with road dust, his hands were the dark color of grease. His skin showed the flush of excessive ultraviolet. "Hey, Jackson. Fuck you, Jackson. Fuck you in the ass, you bastard."

Jackson's gut felt buoyant, yet he smiled, whispered to Carol, "And would you believe that is not an insane man?"

Maxie flicked the butt of his cigarette into the rocks. "You eat some shit, Jackson. Hear? Fuck you." Maxie didn't shout, but his voice carried clearly to the cave.

Carol pushed away from the cave's mouth and the sunlight, wrapping herself in shadow. "Why do you feel he just sits there and curses you? That's all he ever does."

Jackson propped himself against the tunnel wall so he could watch Maxie. "Dunno." Then he smiled. "I'll bet you he does it because it's fun. Let's ask him." Jackson shouted down to the denim-clad figure, "Say, Maxie, why are you doing this, man?"

"Fuck you, Jackson." Maxie waved his middle finger in looping circles.

"See, he's having a good time."

A smile touched the corners of her mouth, then faded. "I think he's waiting for something. He's got something on his mind."

"Yeah, he's waiting all right. Like everyone else."

"Hey, Jackson, you shit, I'm going away now, but I'll be back. This is for you till I get back, Jackson, you cocksucker." Maxie swung his legs away from the bike, straddled a piece of rock, and began to urinate. Finished, he made the motions of an exaggerated masturbation, then swung back on his motorcycle. "You remember that, Jackson. Fuck you." Maxie kicked the starter once; the engine caught then died, its cough as rasping as Jackson's. Kicked again, the engine exploded to life, filling the rocky area with fading echoes as Maxie wheeled away.

Carol again moved next to him, and Jackson found himself listening carefully to the sounds that were made as she moved, sat, encircled her thighs with her arms, then spoke. "The sky's always clearer when Maxie leaves."

"What do you mean?"

"I mean the sky's always clearer when Maxie leaves." Carol's chin resting on her knees, Jackson thought her words sounded as if the tops and bottoms of each were clipped away. "The times during the day, I mean. It works like a smooth machine: he comes, he goes, and the sky seems less heavy, the blue not quite so ashen."

Jackson stared into the high umbrella of ash, no longer delicate striations, now merged into tight bands, and tried to discern some difference. "You're going as nuts as everyone else."

She smiled. "Why shouldn't I?"

Jackson nodded, reached out a hand to rub his sore knee, but diverted the hand to rest on the floor. He glanced into the cave, then outward toward the sky. "He doesn't shout at any of the others."

"Well, he knew you, right?"

"Yeah. Yeah . . ." He trailed the answer off and stayed silent, his eyes staring at something far away.

"How . . . look, I know it's none of my business, but how did you know him . . . before, I mean."

Jackson shifted position uncomfortably. "Before." He lapsed into thought. "Before, Maxie and I were alive together. That's it: we both were alive."

Carol leaned toward him. "You were close?" Her voice was incredulous.

"What's close? No, we hardly knew each other, but, well, you know." He watched her stare at him and thought that perhaps he should say more. But somehow, it all seemed too meaningless to continue.

"Was he the parachutist?"

Jackson looked at her and grinned. "We all were the skydivers. Some of us just more literally than others."

From behind them came the muffled sounds of crepe soles on rock. A figure caught up to the sounds, trapped them, then allowed them to follow. The man was past middle age and balding above each temple. His skin about the neck and elbows resembled weathered oak bark and complemented the smoother surfaces of his face. He carried a flask and small cloth pouch.

"Was that Maxie again?" he asked.

Carol stood, rolled her head about her shoulders, stretching tired neck muscles. "Hi, Dr. Henda. Yeah, that was old Maxie again. Still after Jackson." She lightly kicked Jackson's good leg.

Dr. Henda frowned. "Did he try to come up here, Jackson?"

Jackson shook his head. "No, sir. He just stood down there and screamed like always."

Dr. Henda wet his lips, tightened the muscles along his cheeks. "Well . . . so long as he doesn't try to get in." Henda walked a few yards into the sunlight and glanced across the sky. "The new filters we've installed uptop in Research are working fine, really reducing the ultraviolet. You can get tanned now without having to worry about cancer." Jackson watched the doctor as he took several deep breaths, turned to face a slight breeze coming from the base of the rise. Henda seemed to be appreciating those few moments in the open air, Jackson thought. Then the older man turned, grinning, and said, "Well, Carol, I guess you'd better come on in early if you're going to help Dr. Fourrier with those psych profiles. We need them by this evening." He unslung the water and food containers, placing them in the space between Jackson's crossed legs. "Stay awake for another couple of hours, will you, Jackson? Rotolo and Knight have the next shift."

Jackson uncorked the jug, took a deep draught. "Sure, Doctor. No problem." He placed the food and water against the oilcloth wrapping of the rifle, drawing Henda's eye there.

"Oh . . . and Jackson, maybe you should unwrap that thing. In case Maxie comes back." Henda rubbed a palm against his shorts. He looked worried. "Maybe Rotolo and Knight would come on early."

Jackson shook his head. "Hey, thanks, but this is no sweat. Really. Just make sure those two bums don't show up late, OK?"

The doctor's face remained serious and concerned. The gossamer webbing about his eyes grew deeper, causing the slight shadows of his face to darken. "All right. But be careful." He looked out onto the desert. "Dammit! Just be careful." Henda turned without waiting for Carol and headed down into the cave. She called after him, "I'll be along in a few minutes." Jackson watched the creases of his khaki shirt shift angles with each step until the darkness of the hole engulfed him.

"Jesus," he said, shaking his head.

"What are you shaking your head about?" she asked, standing above him.

Jackson shrugged, then looked up, smiling. "Nothing."

She frowned. "Come on, man, he's got reason to be worried. He's got all that to think of." She gestured into the cave.

" 'Nothing,' I said," Jackson snapped, ice ridges in his voice. He felt his face flush, then, and quickly said, "Nothing," but this time much softer. He paused and reached for a food package.

He could feel her studying his face. She asked, "You aren't thinking about leaving, are you?"

Jackson watched the way his hands peeled at the gummed wax paper of his food package and answered slowly. " 'Course not. If the sulphur don't getcha, then the UV will."

She smiled, prodded his leg with her toe. "Well, I'll kick Rotolo's ass to hurry him along, right!"

"Kick it just for fun," he told her, freeing the food from its container, glancing up to grin a goodbye, then returning to the sticky wrapping.

She started to follow Henda, then turned. "Jackson, grounded parachutists don't *always* go over the edge, do they?"

"Nope. Now take off. Henda's waiting."

As she left he sipped from the water flask, small trickles tracing creases from mouth corners to jaw, branching there to track over his throat in smaller paths. The last sounds of Carol's footsteps faded from his reach, and he was alone. "But skydivers . . . maybe skydivers do."

Jackson grasped the wax wrapper with thumb and forefinger, pressing the center toward him with his middle fingers to lick the final few particles of jellied beef from the last meat package. He wadded the paper into a tight ball and placed it with the others.

The sky was near-blue grey, becoming brighter as the sun arced toward its noon zenith. The heat of the day drew heavy beads of sweat from forehead, nose, and neck. He blew air loudly from his mouth, the stream pulling small droplets from his lips; then brushed away the pathways of sweat where they made his neck itch.

The rumble of Maxie's motorcycle was first soft, then grew louder, fouling the silence. Jackson went to the edge of the cave, standing in the sunlight, waiting for Maxie to round the final curve. His stomach held the same dropsick feeling that coursed through his system each time Maxie arrived.

The man and motorcycle appeared from the brown rocks, the bike suddenly angling the sun into Jackson's eyes, making him blink before the brightest rays of light were channeled to another direction. Maxie pulled the bike around, coming smoothly to a stop at the juncture of road and hillside. He allowed the motor to continue its low, burping noises, shouting above them to the cave mouth where Jackson stood.

"Jackson, you asshole, I told you I'd be back today, didn't I? And I got something for you, too, you bastard!" Maxie pulled a glinting shape from his boot, waved it around his head, the steel blade of the stiletto picking up pieces of light, hurling them toward Jackson. "I'm coming today, you sonuvabitch."

Jackson was momentarily unsure of whether Maxie was serious, but then he moved to the gun, pushed the oilcloth from the walnut stock. Maxie's words followed him there and seemed to act as a buffer that prevented his feeling the rifle. He grasped the stock; his index finger touched the metal of the trigger guard and lent sudden reality to the weapon. The polished wood felt slick against his palm. He lifted the gun to the sound of Maxie revving his engine.

"You hear me, Jackson. You can go in there if you want, but I'm still coming, you bastard. You hear me . . ."

The engine noises increased, peaked, suddenly went lower as Maxie engaged the gear, the smooth screech of the street-spinning tire changing to the digging sounds of rubber slipping on dusty rock.

Jackson watched him drive, watched the bike buck and weave and grow larger. Dust roostertailed from the rear wheel, sprayed in sweeping angles as the motorcycle wound from smooth place to smooth place, Maxie guiding the extended front wheel past outcroppings and fork-busting ruts.

Jackson rubbed sweat from his forehead and eyes with a gritty forearm. He raised the rifle to his shoulder, thought how different these actions were from the way he had imagined. There had always been indecision, disgust, the repulsion of taking human life. Now, in reality, there was nothing. He couldn't even see Maxie's eyes; Maxie was watching the ground.

The bullet pulled Maxie backward, past the sissy bar, freeing the bike from control. It crashed into the incline, then slid backward, across Maxie's legs, and finally to the smooth concrete of the highway. Jackson watched Maxie's body twist, bounce against the stones, then roll limply to a stop.

Jackson made his way to Maxie, turned the body over to see the small, bruised hole high on its chest. He felt the area, withdrew bloodied fingers.

He stumbled the rest of the way down the slope and stood over the motorcycle, examining the scratches and pits that marred its ebony fuel tank. There seemed a wild peace about the machine; the thought caused him to right the motorcycle, run his fingers along its seat and frame. Touching the handles, swiveling the front wheel in a spherical arc, Jackson heaved his bad leg across the seat and tested his weight and balance. A footpeg was bent, but other than that, the machine seemed undamaged by its crash and slide. He rested his heel over the kick starter and plunged it down. The motor caught and snapped to life. He felt for the lowest gear, engaged the clutch slowly and savored the strengthening wind against his face.

The heavier winds of high speed raised his hair back, looping the tiny strands of his sideburns to tickle his ears. His eyes watered, washing the ash away. The raw sun felt good against his skin. UV or no UV, it felt good. Jackson opened his mouth; the cool, rough air was exhilarating against the tender tissues there. This isn't bad, he thought. He squinted along the winding highway, and soon his knee no longer ached.

THE DEATH OF SAPPHO

Marge Piercy

One can hope that America's future will be not only less sexist, but also less age-ist, not to mention more accepting of death as a natural process. "The Death of Sappho" is a freestanding excerpt from Marge Piercy's recent novel *Woman on the Edge of Time*. Known as a writer of both feminist fiction and poetry, Piercy's previous books include *Dance the Eagle to Sleep* and *Small Changes*.

THE DEATH OF SAPPHO

That Monday one of Dr. Redding's attendants, a stooped paunchy man with the burst capillaries in his nose that marked an alcoholic, came to fetch Connie. As the nurse shuffled the papers to sign her out to the attendant, she could feel the palpable envy around her. It did not matter what she was going to: she was going off ward. Nurse Wright started to grab a coat for her but the attendant said, "Don't bother. It's raining cats and dogs. I'll take 'em through the tunnel."

Nurse Wright pursed her lips. "You'd better take a coat anyhow. Somebody else might have to bring the patient back."

The coat was so long it hung to her mid-calves and the sleeves concealed her hands, but she knew better than to complain. She plodded after the attendant, folding the sleeves back so that she could use her hands on the two surviving buttons.

All the old buildings were joined by tunnels through which equipment, supplies and sometimes patients were shipped back and forth. Occasionally patients with grounds privileges hung out in the tunnels smoking, talking, flirting, finding a dark place to sleep. No one on staff with the rank above attendant ever seemed to use them.

"Hi, Mack, Tomo. How ya doing?" Her attendant stopped to greet two men wheeling a covered cart.

"Hokay, hokay," the short one said briskly. "How goes with you?"

"Hi, Fats. Man, this place is creepy today," the younger said. "If it keeps on raining like this, the whole damn place is going to grow two inches of mold."

"I hate it when it rains every day," Fats said. "Hey, you got something nice this week?"

"Everything, man. Red devils, yellow jackets, rainbows.

85

The stiffest coke you ever snorted. You don't go for ups . . . how about sopors? You dig on them, don't you, Fats?"

The man with the accent blinked at them with faint contempt and began reading what looked like a sports magazine in Japanese, pulled from his pocket under the white coat. As they bargained she stood in her huge coat waiting. The mad are invisible. Neither had any fear she could damage him. Indeed if she cared to try, she would only hurt herself. Revenge came easily to staff.

"What's under the tablecloth?" Fats poked the bundle on the cart.

"Old geezer from chronic service." Mack cast back the sheet. Sharp gaunt face of an old woman, her dark flinty eyes in death stared straight up with a look of rage. Mack flipped the sheet over her again but it caught on her hooked nose. He had to free it. "Kicked off last night. Got to truck it down to the meat department."

"See you around, man." Mack started pushing the cart and Tomo hastened to take his position, although the cart was obviously light enough for one to handle.

The last time she had been summoned, they had given her the most thorough physical of her life, and as a side effect treated her old burn and sent her to the dentist for work on her battered teeth. As she was thrust in, she looked at the patients lined up on the chairs as usual: the graceful West Indian, the tiny black woman, Captain Cream; Miss Green; Orville and Alice; Alvin, who was white, forty-two, and perhaps the closest of those she had met in the hall here to being really mad; Mrs. Ortiz, a thin bouncy Puerto Rican woman who winked at her; and Skip, who had saved her a place beside him.

"What's coming down today?" she asked him.

"What they fondly call a battery of tests. Rorschachs, Draw-a-person, sentence completion, WAIS, Wechsler Memory Scale, MMPI . . ."

She clutched her shoulders. "What do they do to us? Does it hurt?"

"Only when you laugh. I don't believe it! I've been tested since I was eleven. You've never had these mothers play with you?"

She shook her head. "What will happen?"

"Oh, like they ask you would you rather fly a plane or play with dolls. Follow the stereotypes. But why should I have to pretend I'd rather watch a football game than a

ballet in order not to be labeled queer? The first man I
ever had sex with was an attendant at Wynmont—that's a
private buzz farm they sent me to when I was thirteen."

"So young. Why did they do that?"

"My parents thought I didn't work right, so they sent me
to be fixed. You know, you send the riding mower back
to the factory to be fixed if you get a lemon. Why not a
son?"

"Did you figure out yet what this whole thing is?"

"Some research project with us as the guinea pigs. But
I'm on the case. I'll break their game soon. Fats is queer on
me."

A woman was dumped beside her, a tall lean satin black
woman with her hair in a big wild Afro.

"I guess we're the final winners of their screening," Connie said to her. "I saw you when they were X-raying us,
but we never met. I'm Connie Ramos."

"Alice Blue Bottom, honey. You Puerto Rican?"

"No, Chicana. I was born in Texas."

"No lie? You don't sound like it. Me, I got myself born
in Biloxi, Mississippi. You ever been there?"

She shook her head. "I grew up in Chicago from when I
was seven."

"You know what, girl? I put in five years on the South
Side of Chicago working as a cocktail waitress in the Kit
Kat Club. Left and come to Harlem with a man I stupid to
cross the street with."

"How come you call yourself Alice Blue Bottom?" Skip
asked, smiling from under his long lashes.

"Long skinny white boy, don't you wish you know that?"
She tilted back her tower of a neck and laughed with her
breasts freely jiggling against the red dress. She had her
own clothing, for sure. Some attendant had made her sew
up the front a couple of inches with the wrong color thread,
but the dress was still shorter and fit better than anything
else around. " 'Cause I'm so black, I'm blue. Maybe . . . No
way you gonna find out."

"That's Skip," Connie said. "Do you know anything
about this project they're using us for?"

"Papermaking. That's all. That's all they ever doing.
You know time you be sitting in that jiveassed group
therapy, those doctors thinking how they going to write it
all up. How they going to tell it on the mountain at they
next staff session. Bullshit!"

Alice's name was called and she strolled after the nurse, swinging her broad high ass across the waiting room. An attendant brought Sybil out of the office, and Connie half rose. Sybil saw her at once and their eyes exchanged messages of hope. Fats placed Sybil in a chair far down the line. As soon as Fats turned his back, Sybil hopped up and quietly slid into the seat Alice had just left.

"Sybil, it's good to see you! I heard they were shocking you?"

Sybil raised an elegant bony hand to her forehead. "I have dreadful headaches. I have trouble remembering words, the names of objects. Yesterday I could not think what one calls the wood around a door! I nearly wept with rage. What ward are you on?"

"G-2. Not so bad. Are you still on L-6?"

"No, D-5. I wish we were on the same ward. Do you have grounds privileges?"

"Not yet. I'm trying."

"Hey, you." Fats marched over to Sybil. "I put you down at the end. Don't go sneaking away on me."

"We know each other," Connie pleaded. Her voice fawned. "We were just talking. Isn't it good for us to relate?"

"Don't sweet-talk me," Fats said. "You're all violent or you wouldn't be here. You do what I say and we'll get along. Otherwise you'll be eating dirt." He marched Sybil down to the chair where he had parked her.

"Are you lovers with each other?" Skip asked her softly.

"No, we're real good friends. I know her from last time in." She did not mind his asking, really. Better than thinking it and never asking.

"They almost didn't include her. I think Dr. Morgan's scared of big women. But Dr. Redding said he can handle any of us and have us standing on our heads. That's what he said, that dear man."

"Ummmm." She smiled. "I bet he's never seen Sybil when she's fighting mad. It takes two attendants to hold her down."

"I like to fantasize about that. But all I seem to hurt is myself."

"Me too. Except for what got me in here. Listen, Skip, if you entirely hated yourself, you'd be dead by now, right? So part of you does love you."

He giggled wildly. "What a valentine. Part of me loves

me. Signed, some love, Skip." He unfolded to his feet as
Fats came for him.

The next day rain still blew in gusts across the grounds
and the porch was too wet to sit on. Sleepy with thorazine
she went into the dayroom. The set flickered, giving a cover
to sitting. She took a chair and nodded out. They weren't
allowed to sleep, but if she dozed sitting up, the attendants
wouldn't bother her. She was sinking into the stuffy sleep
of thorazine when she felt Luciente's presence touching her
mind.

That woke her. In the two months she had been in contact with Luciente, she had not learned to take her approach
for granted.

"Should I bring you over?" Luciente asked.

In a few minutes she was standing in Mattapoisett again,
in what Luciente told her was 2137. "It's raining here
too," she said with disappointment in her thickened voice.

"You don't farm, Connie, or you wouldn't feel bad about
rain." Luciente peered into her face. "You're so drugged
you're not quite with me. May I help you?" Luciente put
her warm dry calloused hands beside Connie's temple and
pressed. She began a series of exploratory pressures over
Connie's head. "Here, sit on the bench." Luciente spoke to
her in a low compelling tone. "Relax. Relax. Yes. Open up.
Yes. Flow with me. Relax."

She knew she was being hypnotized and that the iron
cage around her brain was lifting. The heaviness slid from
her.

"Zo. Better?" Luciente handed her a closely woven hat
to keep off the rain, broad enough to protect her shoulders
and unlike an umbrella, not requiring a hand to hold it. Off
they started along the wet paths of the village. "Come, we'll
bike to the Grange—beautiful three-hundred-year-old
wooden building!" At the end of the village beyond the fish
breeding tanks stood racks of bicycles.

"But I haven't been on a bike in years! I can't!"

"Good. We'll take a two-seater. I'll pedal and you'll do
what you can."

"I've seen lots of wooden buildings, Luciente! I've seen
buildings a lot older than that in Texas."

"You wanted to see 'Government.' It's working today!"

"The town government? Like a mayor? A council?"

Luciente made a face, throwing her slack-clad leg over

the bike. "Look at it and then we'll figure out what it's like, okay?" They set out along a narrow paved way wandering a pleasant route over a high curved bridge across the river, under big and little trees, past roses drooping under the load of the rain, past willows, past boats and corn patches with pole beans and pumpkins interplanted, past the edge of another village marked by a bike rack.

"This is Cranberry," Luciente said, hitting the brakes so they squeaked to a stop. "Everybody's always making lists of what I ought to show you. Every lug in my base, my mems, everybody at council. Even my defense squad, I'm practicing on my belly and everybody's giving me lists of what I should show you. Afro-Carib flavor village."

"I see gardens. Windmills. People. Greenhouses. Where are the huts?"

"Below." Luciente left the bike by a big maple and helped her off. "We'll stop by Erzulia." She used her kenner. "Zuli! It's Luci. I brought the woman from the past. Meet us at your space to show a Cranberry dwelling, favor?"

"No such," said a voice that sounded much more like a black from her own time than anybody she'd heard here. "Got a mean pelvic fracture, old person from Fall River. You drop right by my space and show it your own self."

"Erzulia and Bee are sweet friends," Luciente said. "Erzulia has tens of lovers. Person never stales on anybody, just adds on. Over there!" She pointed to a two-story building. "The hospital where Zuli works—hospital for our township. That great big greenhouse is the one where they breed the spinners—those single-celled creatures we use for fences and barriers."

"Creatures! They're alive?"

"Fasure. They mend themselves."

As they walked, she saw that courtyards were dug into the earth the level of an ample story, surrounded by dense, often thorny hedges—blackberries, raspberries—an animal or a child couldn't push through. At ground level trees grew, gardens flourished, paths wound, swings hung from trees and people trotted and biked by. Goats and cows grazed, chickens ran pecking, a cat played with a dying baby rabbit. The solar heat collectors and the intakes for rainwater cisterns studded the surface like sculpture, some of them decorated with carved masks, others scalloped, inlaid with shell and glass mosaics.

Luciente led her by the hand down wide steps curving into a submerged courtyard. The yard itself was paved and had in the center a big weatherbeaten table with benches all around and a scattering of chairs. A chess game sat on the table half played under a clear cover like ones Connie had seen put over big cakes. The four walls around the court were glass threaded with spidery lines almost too fine to focus on.

"The glass can be opaqued or made one-way," Luciente explained.

"This whole house belongs to Erzulia?" Maybe they were richer here.

"No! They live in families. Everybody has private space but they have common space too for family. For eating, playing, watching holies. The walls are plenty thick for quiet."

Individual rooms opened onto courts and the courts served partly as hallways and partly as common space. Halls joined rooms on other courts. Luciente guided her through the maze, occasionally consulting her kenner to ask permission to open a door. They cut through a kitchen where Luciente begged a taste of a hot spicy seafood stew. Only two private rooms were occupied at this time of day. In one Luciente said person was meditating. On the door was hung a paper hand with the fingers held up.

"That's what they use when they don't want you to enter. I say meditating—of course they may be coupling, reading, sleeping or just pouting."

Erzulia's room faced west. It was spacious with walls entirely covered in woven and embroidered hangings, texture upon texture and color upon color. Her bed was a high platform reached by a ladder, the space underneath closed in with hangings to make a dark cave of cushions, a small altar, shelves of herbs in bottles. The furniture was of a dark knobbly substance that reminded her of bamboo. On the bed a strange blue costume was laid out.

"We should not stay here. That's Erzulia's raiment." Luciente used the old formal word.

"Is she a mother getting ready for a naming?"

"Zuli's never been a mother. Sappho is dying and Erzulia is per friend. They share a sense of old rites. Zuli follows voodoo as a discipline, as do many in Cranberry, while Sappho is an Indian old believer. But they share a closeness to . . . myths, archetypes."

"Sappho? That old woman who was telling stories to the kids?"

"The same. A great shaper of tales. Now person is very old. It's time for per to die."

"Oh?" She saw the sharp face of the corpse in the tunnel. "I wonder if she's so sure it's time?"

"Per body has weakened since Wednesday. Time comes for any fruit to fall. It's a good death that arrives when you're ready for it, no?"

They climbed another broad stair to the ground where the rain was easing and dark clouds scudded over, rapidly going out toward the Sound. The air smelled clean and cottony.

In the old white Grange Hall with its octagonal tower, twenty-five or thirty people sat around an oblong table arguing about cement, zinc, tin, copper, platinum, steel, gravel, limestone and things she could not identify. Many of them seemed to be women, although she often found when she heard a voice that she had guessed wrong. They ranged from sixteen to extreme old age. Few of them looked entirely white, although their being tanned by the sun made that harder to judge than it might have been in the middle of the winter. They spoke in ordinary voices and did not seem to be speechifying. Behind some seated at the table sat others listening closely and at times putting in their comments and questions.

"We have a five-minute limit on speeches. We figure that anything person can't say in five minutes, person is better off not saying." Luciente and she pulled up chairs to sit behind Otter, whom she had not at first recognized with her black hair in a single braid and her body in overalls splashed with mud and salt. Otter flashed them a smile before turning back to the display set in the table between every other delegate that showed figures, allotments, graphs they were discussing.

"This is your government?"

"It's the planning council for our township."

"Are they elected?"

"Chosen by lot. You do it for a year: three-month with the rep before you and three with the person replacing you and six alone."

"We want to clear some of the woods on Goat Hill." A map flashed on the displays set in the table. The person speaking, with sideburns and a bristling moustache, somehow drew on the map indicating the section he referred to. "We would like to increase our buckwheat crop."

Luciente murmured, "Rep from Goat Hill, Cape Verde flavor village upriver."

"Seems to me that cuts into the catchment area for rainwater. We have none too much water, people," a person with green hair said.

"We are only thinking of a matter of fifty, sixty acres of second growth woods and scrub. Our region imports too much grain, we have all agreed on that," the moustache argued.

"Without water we can grow nothing. Our ancestors destroyed water as if there were an infinite amount of it, sucking it out of the earth and dirtying and poisoning it as it flowed," Otter said indignantly. "Let us not be cavalier about water. What does the soil bank say?"

"I'll direct the question."

Luciente leaned close. "That's the rep from Cranberry. That person is chair today."

"Who is that with green hair?"

"Earth Advocate—speaks for rights of the total environment. Beside per is the Animal Advocate. Those positions are not chosen strictly by lot, but by dream. Every spring some person dreams they are the new Animal Advocate or Earth Advocate. Those who feel this come together and the choice among them falls by lot."

The computer was flashing figures and more figures on the displays. After everyone had stared at the display, the Ned's Point rep spoke. "The woods in question are fasure catchment. To take these acres from forest would cut our capacity to hold our water table."

"How can we up our grain output if we can't pull land from scrubby woods to farming?" the Cranberry rep asked.

"Then we must up the output of the land we have," the Earth Advocate said. "We're only starting to find ways of intensively farming, so the soil is build more fertile instead of bled to dust."

Otter was still studying the display, her fat braid hanging over one shoulder. "These woods are birch, cherry, aspen, but with white pines growing up. Will be white pine forest in ten years. Its history as we have it is: climax forest, cleared for farming, abandoned, scrub to climax again, bulldozed for housing, burned over, now returning to forest."

At her ear Luciente murmured, "We arrive with the needs of each village and try to divide scarce resources justly. Often we must visit the spot. Next level is regional planning. Reps chosen by lot from township level go to the regional to discuss gross decisions. The needs go up and the possibilities come down. If people are chilled by a decision, they go and argue. Or they barter directly with places needing the same resources, and compromise."

A vote was taken and the Goat Hill was turned down. The Marion rep suggested, "Let's ask for a graingrower from Springfield to come to Goat Hill and see if they can suggest how to grow buckwheat without clearing more land. We in Marion would be feathered to feast the guest."

Luciente's kenner called. "How long?" Connie heard her say and then, "We'll come soon."

"The old bridge is beautiful," a middle-aged man was arguing. "Three hundred years old, of real wrought iron. We have a skilled crafter to top shape it."

"Nobody in your village has bled from the old bridge being out. We need ore for jizers," an old woman said. "The bridge is pretty, but our freedom may depend on jizers. Head before tail!"

"Weren't you advised last year to look out for alloys that use up less ore?" the rep from Cranberry said.

"We're working on it. So is everybody else!"

The Goat Hill rep suggested, "For the bridge, why not use a biological? It'd corrode less. Repair itself."

"We must scamp now," Luciente said, pulling her up. "Fast. We'll hop the dipper."

"What about the bike?"

Luciente looked at her blankly. "Somebody will use it."

The dipper turned out to be a bus-train object that rode on a cushion of air about a foot off the ground until it stopped, when it settled with a great sigh. It moved along at moderate speed stopping at every village, and people got on and off with packages and babies and animals and once with a huge swordfish wrapped in leaves. They sat down in a compartment with an old man facing them, wizened up like a sultana, fiddling constantly with a satisfied air with the blanket wrapped around his baby.

"Why do you have the bus cut up in little rooms this way? You'd get more people in if it was like we used to have, just one big space inside."

"It's easier to talk this way," Luciente said. "Warmer."

"You're a guest?" the old man said. "From where? Or are you a drifter?"

"From the past," Luciente explained.

"Ah, I heard, I heard. So . . ." He peered at her curiously.

"Where do you live?" Luciente asked.

"Ned's Point, where I just got on, where else? We're Ashkenazi," he told Connie.

"I don't know what that is."

"We're the flavor of Eastern European Jewry. Freud, Marx, Trotsky, Singer, Meleichem, Reich, Luxembourg, Wassermann, Vitova, all these were Ashkenazi!"

"They build the kenners," Luciente said. "We were just visiting the planners."

"Look, I don't understand," Connie said. "If workers in a factory, say the kenner factory, want to make more kenners and the planners decide to give them less stuff, who wins?"

"We argue," the man said. "How else?"

"There's no final authority, Connie," Luciente said.

"There's got to be. Who finally says yes or no?"

"We argue till we close to agree. We just continue. Oh, it's disgusting sometimes. It bottoms you."

"After a big political fight, we guest each other," the man said. "The winners have to feed the losers and give presents. Have you been to a town meeting?"

When Connie shook her head he clucked and shook a finger at Luciente. "You must take per. How will person learn about us?"

"Fasure," Luciente said sourly. "I'm trying! Grasp, political decisions—like whether to raise or lower population—go a different route. We talk locally and then choose a rep to speak our posit on area hookup. Then we all sit in holi simulcast and the rep from each group speaks their village posit. Then we go back into local meeting to fuse our final word. Then the reps argue once more before everybody. Then we vote."

"You must spend an awful lot of time in meetings."

"Shalom. I get off here," the old man said. "Make per bring you to Ned's Point. I'm Rebekah and I live by the east side the shul."

Luciente waved goodbye. "How can people control their lives without spending a lot of time in meetings?"

"Don't you get sick of each other?"

"Staling usually has a reason. But you can always leave, wander awhile, or find a new village."

"All right, suppose I don't want to go to meetings."

"Who could force you? People would ask why you no longer care. Friends might suggest you take a retreat or talk to a healer. If your mems felt you'd cut them off, they might ask you to leave. If too many in a village cut off, the neighboring villages send for a team of involvers."

"Years ago I was living in Chicago. I got involved that way. Meetings, meetings, meetings! My life was so busy, my head was boiling! I felt such hope. It was after my husband Martín . . . he got killed. I was young and naive and it was supposed to be a War on Poverty . . . but it was just the same political machine and us stupid poor people, us . . . idiots who thought we were running things for a change . . . we ended up right back where we were. They gave some paying jobs to so-called neighborhood leaders. All those meetings. I ended up with nothing but feeling sore and ripped off."

"You lose until you win—that's a saying those who changed our world left us. Poor people did get together." Luciente rose and made ready to get out as the dipper settled into the grass. She spoke to her kenner. "Locate Sappho."

"Sappho is located in tent near mill," the kenner said.

They walked the river path to the south end of the village where a big tent had been set up. The rain slowed to a fine drizzle and the wind came fresh down the stream. The river was eddying at the turn of the tide, not quite flowing in or out. On a cot under a low roof of canvas, the old woman Sappho lay. She wore deerskin leggings and tunic, large on her and aged though beautifully decorated with quill work in soft colors. Gaunter than ever, her face seemed to draw back from the beak of her Indian nose. Her lips were thinned almost away. The skull stood out through the scant hair, pressing the withered skin of her forehead and cheeks. Sappho's black eyes were dull and Connie was not sure she could see, but still she turned her head from side to side to follow conversations, the heavy head turning wearily on the tiny neck like a seed head on a dried stalk.

"Sappho, here I am, Luciente, come to be with you. I've brought the woman from the past."

"Luciente, child of earth and fire like a good pot. The other I do not know. Leave it."

"Does she want me to leave?" Connie whispered.

"No, no," Luciente said in her normal loud voice. "Person only wants not to be made to remember who you are."

"Has Swallow come? Where is my child?" Her thin voice scratched the ear.

Squatting near the cot, Jackrabbit spoke to his kenner. Then he answered her. "Bolivar is in a floater forty minutes distant. Person is hurrying, Sappho."

"I go with the tide. Swallow should hasten."

"Bolivar, hurry up! This is Jackrabbit. Sappho wishes to die soon. Can't you push yourself?"

"Ram it, my love, I'm coming faster than I can already!" The male voice sounded irritated. "You tell Sappho to wait. Person has no patience. I'm in heavy turbulence, I'm bucking the wind, and I have to keep climbing. Are you so sick of my sleek body you want me to scatter it all over the Berkshires?"

"Swallow is always late." Sappho smiled into the ceiling of the tent. "Swallow believes nothing will happen without per."

A young woman with a heart-shaped ivory face and long straight brown hair to her buttocks moved forward suddenly from her position kneeling by the cot. Laying her cheek against Sappho's scarcely moving chest, she began to weep.

"Louise-Michel?"

"No, no, it's Aspen! Can't you recognize me?"

"Aspen? But I remember Louise-Michel and so many I loved . . . Aspen, do not weep on me. I want to go out with the waters quietly."

"Don't die! Wait. If you love me, wait!"

A flick of temper crossed Sappho's face. "If you love me, cut off your hair. Yes, I'll be buried with your hair."

Aspen rose and said more composedly, "I'll go at once and cut it." She trotted off.

"Why did you do that, you witch?" Jackrabbit said. "That was mean."

"Person was bothering me. It's my dying." Sappho lay breathing hoarsely. "Besides, will make per feel better. You'll see."

"Who was Louise-Michel?"

"Second lover. Good friend. Person had long hair too,

but person was strong . . . Died diving accident. I should not have taken a pillow friend so late. It was vanity. Had little to give . . . Same with Swallow. Too late to put in for another child . . . Vanity."

"Not true," Jackrabbit said. "The power in you has stayed strong. Bolivar has much of you inside that I love."

"I have made some good tales, no?"

"They will outlive you many generations," White Oak said from the foot of the cot.

"Luciente!" Connie tugged at her elbow. "If she's dying, why is she out in the rain?"

"But Sappho is under a tent. Person wants to die beside the river."

"But why isn't there a doctor? If she was in a hospital, she might not die, Luciente. She might live longer."

"But why not die?" Luciente stared at her with incomprehension on her broad peasant face. "Sappho is eighty-two. A good time to give back."

"You're just going to let her lie here in the chilly air until she dies?"

"But why not?" Luciente scowled with confusion. "Everybody gives back. We all carry our death at the core—if you don't inknow that, your life is hollow, no? This is a good death. I hope Swallow gets—now Sappho's got me doing that. Person's so wicked and mischievous! Sappho insists today on using Bolivar's childhood name!"

"Auntie Sappho!" A little kid was tugging at her slack hand. "I come to say goodbye."

"Who is it?" Sappho's eyes were shut and she did not open them. "What chipmunk nibbles at my hand?"

"It's me, Luna. Won't you tell us stories anymore?"

"Never! Somebody else. But not like me!" A light spasm shook her and left her with her mouth slightly opened.

"In hundreds, in thousands of children your stories have made strong patterns," White Oak said. "Your stories have altered our dreams."

Sappho did not speak for a long time. Then she said, "Take me nearer the river. I can't hear it."

Jackrabbit and White Oak carried her cot between them. White Oak asked, "Sappho, old darling, is this near enough?"

Sappho did not answer directly but twisted her head. "Take me nearer. I can't hear it."

They carried her cot as near as they dared, but still she

complained. "Per hearing is gone," White Oak said. "Lift Sappho carefully and we'll dip per fingers in. Person will understand."

Jackrabbit picked her up gently, with grave care, and then slowly knelt still holding her, while White Oak brought Sappho's hand down to the water and held it in the current. The fingers unclenched, the hand slowly opened. "Ah," she muttered. "The tide is going out."

"Bolivar's not going to make it," White Oak said softly, although Sappho could no longer hear.

Jackrabbit sputtered into his kenner, "Bolivar! Sappho is dying now!"

"Ten minutes, comrade, ten lousy minutes!"

Aspen returned with her hair cut off. She knelt beside the cot where Jackrabbit had stretched Sappho's husk of body. Understanding after a moment that Sappho could no longer hear her, she pressed her shorn hair into the old woman's lax hand. Sappho's hand clasped about the hair and again her mouth twitched in a faint grimace of smile. "Aspen, child, plant a mulberry tree for the birds that love fruit."

"Sappho's not gonna last till Bolivar comes." A woman's low voice with the penetration of something worked to a lethal point. "Aspen, sit by that pole. Hush your crying—you cloud my core."

"Erzulia, you should have come sooner!" Luciente spoke with reproach. "You're not in regalia?"

"Person did not send for me. I come only for the death. In respect. Sappho's far, far into the past, the old loving."

White Oak said, "Erzulia, can you hold her till Bolivar comes?"

"Scamp to the floater pad. Put out a speed warning and bring Bolivar by zoomer. I gonna core hard and try." Erzulia did not watch to see if she were obeyed but sat on the cot's edge and took Sappho's fragile head in her long-fingered black hands. Erzulia's hair was put up in dozens of narrow braids woven into a beehive on her highdomed head. She dressed in a long-folded overskirt of a blue cloth batiked into a pattern of snakes and flowers, leaving her breasts and lithe powerful shoulders bare. Her large eyes glazed over as she grasped Sappho and sweat ran over her long conical outpointing breasts, sweat rose from her in a heat shimmer as if from the body of a long-distance runner.

Luciente spoke softly to her kenner. "Bee, you should come to the tent. Erzulia holds Sappho by mind lock till Bolivar comes."

Bee's voice said, "Can't come now. In the middle of a test run. I'll set my kenner for alert when Bolivar lands and run all the way."

"Watch out, then! Bolivar always overschedules. To do too much oneself all the time is some kind of arrogance. That's why person is late again."

"Luciente! If person were early, you'd read arrogance into that, Bolivar thinking Sappho could not die without per? Till when."

"It all seems . . . peculiar to me," Connie said. "A bunch of amateurs."

"Who's professional at dying? We each get only one turn, no practice." Luciente put an arm around her waist.

"In my family in Mexico, people died this way. But in the city poor people die in hospitals. The attendants put up a screen. The nurse keeps an eye on you if she isn't too hassled. My mother died in the hospital in Chicago . . . so scared. Before when she was in the hospital, they took out her womb."

"We don't do much taking out. When we do, we regrow. We program the local cells. Slow healing but better after."

"I haven't met any doctors. How come there's no doctor?"

Luciente laughed. "Look! Erzulia is a healer."

"A witch doctor!"

"You mean that as an insult? Erzulia works in the hospital in Cranberry. They have the hospital for this township."

"What does she do in the hospital?"

"Oh, person teaches people to heal themselves. Does surgery. Manipulating, pain easing, bone knitting. Erzulia's skilled! Person has trained hundreds of healers and pioneered new methods of bone knitting and pain easing. There's a way of setting pelvic fractures in the aged named after per."

She looked at the tall black woman sitting crosslegged on the cot with sweat pouring down her muscular arms and big breasts and she could not see her as a doctor in a white coat in a big hospital. "How can anybody be into voodoo and medicine? It doesn't make sense!"

"Each makes a different kind of sense, no? How not?"

She was lying in bed, with the doctor doing rounds and cracking jokes for the amusement of his residents over the bodies of the women patients, mostly black and Puerto Rican whom some female troubles had cast up on this hard white beach, this glaring sterile reef. They were handed releases to sign carefully vague, so that the residents could get practice on the type of operations they needed. In the bed next to her was a nineteen-year-old black woman on welfare who had been admitted for an abortion in the fourteenth week and had been given a hysterectomy instead of a saline abortion. The woman had gone into a withdrawn shock that made her a quiet patient. Nobody bothered about her as she stared at the ceiling. The women with syphilis were treated to obscene jokes. All the doctors ever said to any complaint was, "We're giving you some medicine that will take care of that." They did pelvics and rectals seven or eight times in a row on interesting cases, so all the doctors and residents could get a look, all the time explaining nothing. "You're a very sick little girl," the doctor said to a forty-year-old woman whose intestines they had accidentally perforated removing an embedded IUD.

Anger began to blur the scene and she moved closer to Luciente for support, feeling the ground solidify again beneath her. Suddenly she felt excitement rise like a wind through the tent. "Bolivar is down," Jackrabbit cried out. A bell began to toll.

"What's the bell?" she asked.

"For death," Luciente said.

"But she isn't dead yet!"

"But person soon will be." Jackrabbit frowned. "Pepper-and-salt, it's not always bad to die, is it? Who'd want to be built of steel and go on living after all the people born in your breeder in your time, all your mems and mates and mothers, all your sweet friends had long gone down? Sappho's body is frail as a ripe milkweed pod ready to spill its seed on the air."

Connie snorted and turned away. The bell tolled through the damp air in waves of heavy sound. Slowly more people began to drift into the tent, keeping away from the side toward the floater pad. Finally she heard a high-pitched warning siren and a fast-moving vehicle flashing red lights came shrieking toward them about a foot off the ground. It came to an abrupt halt right outside the tent and settled with a hiss. White Oak hopped out and a person—the voice

had been male, she thought—about five feet nine, compact-
ly built, slid out the right and strode with quick slithery
grace toward the tent. Bolivar, she supposed, had kinky
hair worn in braids fully as elaborate as Erzulia's, but his
skin was fair and heavily freckled with the sun. He wore
knee-length . . . she could not call it anything but a dress,
with stripes on the bias.

Luciente nodded curtly as he swept by. "Erzulia has been
holding Sappho for you."

"Why not you? You could have!" he rapped out.

"Not with the woman from the past in tow."

"Umm." Briefly he glanced at her, his skeptical eyes pale
gray and cold as rock. Then he rushed to the cot, embraced
Jackrabbit briefly and then put his hands on Sappho's head
beside Erzulia's hands. After a moment Erzulia seemed to
come to and slowly her grip loosened. She rolled off the cot
onto the ground. As Aspen supported her, Bee came forward.

"I'll take Zuli now. Person's weary and must sleep."
Gently Bee rose with her slung over his shoulder and
carried her off along the river path toward the bridge down-
stream, whistling softly as he padded off.

Everyone had drawn back to leave Bolivar with Sappho.
He held her head with his fingers flexing, moving, and for
the first time in a quarter of an hour, her lips groped to
form words. "Good . . . Here! Good," was all she said and
then in a hoarse shudder she expelled her breath and was
still.

Bolivar rose. "The person who was Sappho is dead."

Jackrabbit spoke to his kenner, ceremoniously repeating,
"The person who was Sappho is dead."

The bell tolled more slowly. Barbarossa dodged through
the gathering people carrying a plank. He laid it on the
ground and Luciente moved forward to help Jackrabbit and
Bolivar lift Sappho from the cot and place her on the plank.
White Oak and Aspen, shaken with weeping, turned to each
other to embrace. Bolivar's knuckles were clenched white
on Jackrabbit's arm. The freckles on his hand stood out like
the blotches on aged skin. White Oak wept too, steadily
stroking Aspen's cropped head.

Jackrabbit was one of the four people who lifted a corner
of the plank and began to carry Sappho into the filmy
strands of rain. Aspen's thick brown hair lay like a bouquet
of shiny grasses wedged under the small claw-hands, folded

on Sappho's narrow chest. Aspen, White Oak and Bolivar stumbled along behind the body, White Oak walking with her arm around Aspen, Bolivar going along ahead of them in stiff dignity, as if the only joints in his body were in his bare knees. Luciente fell in behind them with Connie. "Where are we going? In my time, the undertaker would get the body."

"The family, the lovers, the closest friends sit with the body to loosen their first grief. After supper everybody in the village will gather for a wake in the big meeting hall where we politic, watch holies, hold indoor rituals."

"When is the funeral?"

"Funeral?" Luciente consulted the kenner. "We have no such. All night we stay up together speaking of Sappho. Then at dawn we dig a grave and lay the body in. Then we plant the mulberry tree Sappho wanted. Someone will go to the tree-nursery in Marion for one. Then before we go to bed, we visit the breeder and signal the intent to begin a baby."

"Right away? That's heartless. One in, one out!"

"Why heartless? In a week traditionally, when we are caught up on work and sleep, we discuss into which family the child should be born and who are to be mothers. We begin by meditating on the dead."

"It just seems . . . barbaric somehow. No funeral, no undertaker. Just shovel them in."

"Connie, your old way appears barbaric to us, trying to keep the rotting body. To pretend we are not made of elements ancient as the earth, that we do not owe those elements back to the web of all living. For us a good death is one come in the fullness of age, without much pain and in clear mind. A full life is a used life! . . . Person should be tired. You should sit in on the wake with us! You'll see. It feels beautiful, it feels good. You'll see what beauty Jackrabbit makes—he and Bolivar spectacle together. Bolivar is a ritual maker. I myself will perform tonight with my drums—which we should scamp over and get after we set up at the meetinghouse."

"Something is wrong!" She felt a threat shaking her. "Let go, Luciente. Let me go!"

"With haste, Connie!" Luciente stepped back and Connie faded through into the chair in the dim daydream. Nurse Wright was slapping her to and fro till her jaw ached.

"Please . . . don't!"

"Thought you'd . . . withdrawn."

"I feel real funny today, I think I slept or passed out. The medication . . . I felt real funny after I took it today."

Nurse Wright was a motherly woman in her fifties but overworked. She had given up and just drifted along in the ward, leaning heavily on her attendants. Connie liked her but felt she couldn't be relied on. Nurse Wright peered in her eyes. "Ummm. I'll mention it to the doctor. Maybe you're on the wrong dosage."

"I think I'm kind of sensitive to drugs, maybe," she said, meekly. She was still shuddering with the force of the transition. Her heart pounded wildly and Nurse Wright, taking her by the wrist, pursed her lips at the pulse.

"I'll mention it to the doctor. You may be on too high a dosage, or maybe not. He'll say in the end. Now, on your feet."

She rose shakily. "I feel funny."

"Come along, now. It's time to get in line for your supper."

LIKE SNOW-HUMPED FIELDS AFRAID OF RAIN
William Jon Watkins

How many of you reading this book realistically expect to be alive to see the **actual** Tricentennial? Possibly more than one might think. Thanks to Robert Ettinger and his colleagues, the relatively new field of cryobiology flourishes. Steady streams of optimists elect to have their bodies cryonically frozen upon "death" and preserved by liquid nitrogen with the hope of being ultimately repaired and revived. William Jon Watkins, in five short poems, wryly depicts the quickfrozen legacy we're leaving our descendants. Watkins, 34, is an Associate Professor of English at Brookdale Community College in New Jersey. He has published four novels, three stories in *Cosmopolitan* and a considerable number of poems both in and out of SF.

LIKE SNOW-HUMPED FIELDS AFRAID OF RAIN

AS SOON AS YOU CALL ...

The man from the Cryolab comes down
in his white potholder gloves,
and his segmented hose
all furred with frost,
in his white pajamas complete with feet,
and his visored hat of sparkling ice
to stiffen your blood
and brain
and bones
and carry you off
in his snowwhite truck
with its capsuled sides
to where the bodies lie
like snow-humped fields afraid of rain.

TIMECRAWLER

Timecrawler,
going the snail's road
to eternity
in your ice body,
your cells tick once a decade
like feeler hairs
on the feet of caterpillars
caught in the quickfreeze
of New Jersey spring.
Timecrawler,
going slug slow
across the timespan,
between the wheels
of passing dynasties,
do you really hope
for butterfly resurrection
in the permanent summer
of some medical tomorrow?

MOMENTO MORI

They went to sleep
like dormant insects
in a hive backed by the Government,
a horrorshow of internal deformities,
like a medical student's nightmare
preserved in ice.
In the third decade of their stillness
ice was repudiated
and the last of their relatives
went into the flames.
They became an Official Anomaly.
In the fifth decade
their culture went critical
and barely survived.
Everything was rearranged.
The New Government
sold them for surplus
as Official Miscellaneous.
An eccentric bought them up
like paperweights
and displays them now
like bugs in amber
to whoever comes around.

WHEN THE VIKINGS OWNED THE MYTHOLOGY

When the Vikings owned the mythology,
only giants were made of ice.
Now, dwarves, cretins, even politicians
can be quickfrozen
like bags of bacteria wrapped for storage.
No doubt,
when they come out of the cold,
like divine retribution,
they will be greeted as celebrities
and lionized like
Watergate criminals on a lecture tour.
When the Vikings owned the mythology,
the frost giants came out of Nilfheim
at the end of the world
and killed everything
that had been brave, or noble, or good.
Maybe the Vikings were right.

IF FREEZING IS A ONE-WAY STREET

In winters of Freon,
cells more delicate than orchids
are turning slowly
permanently
into ice.
Ropes of blood
brittle as icicles
distend the veins
beyond their limits.
The ear drums
rattle like sheets of ice
plucked from puddles,
ready to shatter
at the slightest sound.
The jelly of the eye
is hard as cemetery stone
tormented by January.
In the crevices of the brain
permanent glaciers are forming
that will retreat
from no equatorial sun.
Deep under the Pons,
like a tiny Neanderthal,
the Pineal
sits around the fire of the personality
dreaming of summer

                    perhaps forever.

AND I FOR AN EYE

James Stevens

James Stevens, 31, is bilingual (English and Spanish), bi-cultural (father from Illinois, mother from Puerto Rico), and Bicentennial (first child, a boy named Ian James, born January 15, 1976). He is also the Director of Radio and Television Production for Foote, Cone & Belding Advertising, Caribbean. In my letter of acceptance, I mentioned that my associate editor had thought Stevens' stories read as though Georgette Heyer were still alive and writing and very, very decadent. Jim Stevens wrote back: "Who is Georgette Heyer?" So much for the presumed universality of Regency romances.

The cosmetic surgery industry continues to grow as people with unsatisfying (at least to themselves) physiognomies seek to augment, diminish or otherwise alter their noses, rumps, wrinkles, breasts and other parts of their bodies. Even tiny Trinidad, Colorado (population: 10,000), has a flourishing sex-change clinic. Given another hundred years—

AND I FOR AN EYE

One gay May morning Coal sent Marquesa a lavender-scented note offering to trade legs if Marquesa would acquiesce to trade eyes.

Marquesa's reaction was classically in keeping with her persona. She tore the note into minute shreds. She cursed Coal in seven languages—three Romance, one Slavic, two Oriental, one Dead. She incinerated insulting portions of Coal's portrait and ordered the charred oilphoto removed from its place of honor near the likeness of Don R. and mounted very obviously opposite the servants' bidet.

Then she considered the offer.

"Her eyes are like living things, don't you think?"

"I've observed that, yes. They seem . . . 'furred' isn't the word . . . ."

"There's a *texture* to them."

"Yes, a *texture.*"

"Like velvet?"

"Not exactly, no . . . but that's very close, I should think."

"Pre-Columbian eyes . . ."

"Yes . . . ?"

"Like mummified children bound in leather."

"Yes! That's it exactly. Suede! Her eyes are suede."

"One feels one could rub them gently between thumb and forefinger."

"Sensual thought."

"Can you imagine holding them drily in your mouth?"

Within Marquesa dwelt a tall willowy lass, a lass with limbs like silver birches.

Oh, she was far from ugly, our Marquesa, only short, but that was ugliness enough for her. Given the full freedom of her free will, she would have chosen to be taller. The choice had not fallen to her and so she wore everywhere great platform shoes like ancient cothurni.

They were her insignia, though she hid them under skirts whose embroidered hems brushed the floor like tulips, and this secrecy enhanced the value of the insignia, for only the most knowledgeable even suspected its existence.

"She's strutting magenta heels tonight."

"With that glowgreen chinstripe? How *outré.*"

"Au contraire, mon cher. Charmante. The clash is invisible and thus exists only in your mind. And then only since the moment I made you aware of it."

"Delicious! How did you find her out?"

"Peeked."

"No!"

"Oh yes."

"Where?"

"There's a peephole to the . . . facility."

"How very . . ."

". . . *au courant?*"

"Precisely. She still there?"

"Could well be. They say her bladder is legendary."

An entire wardrobe of cothurni graced her enormous closets, closets which could easily have housed ghetto families in roomy comfort. Even the soles of her slippers were five inches thick. Marquesa loved to start the day out tall.

She dressed always in white. Her skin was the dusty hue of cinnamon; her eyes, enormous and deep brown with black lashes thick as coxcombs. The dresses sheathed her legs and arms and neck and set off her face as a filigreed frame may set off the most delicate cameo. Of finest white linen, her dresses, cool in the summer day sun.

"Her breasts are of finest quality."

"Oh, you've sampled them too?"

"Haven't we all, dear lad?"

"I admit I have been privy to some gossip to that effect. Still . . ."

". . . there's a certain satisfaction in thinking oneself exclusive, *n'est-ce pas?* A luxury of the young. How would you rate them yourself?"

"Her breasts?"

"Yes."

"Oh, of the very first water, most definitely."

"There's no arguing that point."

"Exquisitely shaped."

"True perfection."

"And absolutely impervious to gravity!"

"You noticed that too, did you?"

"Oh yes. With a certain amount of awe I did not deem inappropriate, I might add."

"I had thought at one time that it might be only my imagination. Or perhaps an illusion accomplished with mirrors and other accouterments of prestidigitation and legerdemain."

"Oh, I should think not!"

"Quite. You're not the first to confirm my observation."

"No?"

"There was a young man, formerly employed in a rather important post at Jodrell Banks, his name was Foxx, chap about your age, perhaps you know him?"

"Afraid not."

"He was the first."

"First?"

"To confirm my observation concerning her breasts. He has held them in his hands like ripe melons—his simile, not mine—and found them weightless."

"But firm, no?"

"Oh yes."

"And full."

"Oh yes."

"You say his name was Foxx?"

"I don't much like to discuss him."

"Oh?"

"We had a . . . shortlived friendship, shall we say? Two gentlemen sharing?"

"Oh. Yes."

"Didn't last, though."

"Pity."

"Couldn't possibly have. All we had in common was the weightlessness of her breasts, their brazen defiance of gravity."

"Not enough to build a relationship on, not a lasting one."

"Couldn't possibly have lasted."

"I knew a chap named Foxx. Died penniless."

"That's him."

Her face was delicate and finely sculpted; the bone structure subtly prominent and, like much of her personality, very near the surface.

To be frank, she had a potato nose.

A nice potato nose, a very feminine potato nose, perhaps even a sensual potato nose, but undeniably . . . a potato nose.

Marquesa disguised her nose to the point of invisibility by accentuating her eyes with such finesse that her face seemed merely a repository for those perfect orbs. So lovely were they that no one would have noticed had Marquesa possessed only a raw gaping hole in place of her potato nose.

Marquesa gloried in the beauty of her eyes. Under no circumstances would she have been willing to sell them. Or trade.

"She'd trade her liver in a trice."

"Who could possibly want it? I wouldn't have it, not even as a gift."

"I quite agree. I understand it's thoroughly riddled."

"I wouldn't mind having her spleen."

"Her spleen?"

"Rumor has it she's endowed with a magnificent spleen. I'm something of a connoisseur in that field, you know."

"I had no idea."

"Oh yes, own quite a collection. The Queen's spleen is my *pièce de résistance,* you might say."

"*The* Queen's spleen?!"

"Well . . . not the *present* Queen's, in point of fact. The former's."

"But still, a genuine . . ."

". . . Queen's spleen, yes."

"You must be very proud."

"It affords me some pleasure."

The lines of her collarbone were delicate as a Japanese pen-and-ink; her belly, a silky concavity which strained credibility. Marquesa's was a torso beyond compare.

Yet her legs were stumpy.

Her word, "stumpy," born and nurtured in her heart of hearts, never spoken aloud but ever quivering in those dim inner recesses. In truth, her legs were well knit and firmly muscled and, in fact, of attractive form. They *were* a trifle short, yes, of course, but not grotesquely so. Just not quite long enough for perfect symmetry between torso and legs.

Still, they reached the ground, and that is the essential thing.

And she did have pretty feet.

"Did you know that for years she has fallen asleep, secretly dreaming she would awaken come morning sporting two of the longest, most graceful gams in Christendom?"

"Two regular longstemmed roses, eh?"

"To no avail, of course."

"No, I shouldn't imagine."

"One just doesn't get a new set of legs the way one might get a penny from the Tooth Fairy."

"I should imagine a certain amount of prayer would of necessity be involved. Assuming one harbors ambitions of participating in a miracle."

"*If* one happens to be of a religious nature."

"Pantheist, myself."

"Apostate here."

"Oh really? No chance of . . . repatriation?"

"In a pig's eye."

"I rather like the shortness of her legs, don't you know. Their *comparative* shortness. Find them rather *simpático*."

"Do you?"

"Yes. It's a very human quality, that shortness. Endows her with a great deal of humanity."

"Do you find her nose attractive?"

"I've never noticed it. Does she have one?"

"One presumes . . ."

"I have kissed the dimples of her knee with utmost devotion and worshipped the arch of her small foot."

"Ahm . . . yes. She *has* serviced quite a few of us, hasn't she?"

In an insidious fashion, Coal's offer tempted.

Coal's legs were, after all, the toast of three continents. Entertainment conglomerates had insured them for billions. Coal herself, in her desire to flaunt her perfect pins, had single-handedly inspired the still current pantyhigh fashion.

They were such lovely long legs.

"Has no one ever loved her?"

"Besides myself?"

"You?"

"I."

"Has there been no one, then?"

"There *was* someone once. Reputedly."

"You knew him?"

"No. Slightly."

"Young man?"

"No. Nor old. A rotund man of middling years, florid of face and white of beard. His eyes were green as dragonflies."

"He loved her?"

"Yes."

"And she? Did she . . ."

". . . love him? Why not? I have always believed her capable of the emotion."

"What became of him?"

"He was imprisoned in Mexico."

"The charge?"

"Who knows? It was a mistake, anyroad. He'd done nothing. Nothing illegal. One of those Latin mistakes. Hereditary sort of thing."

"Yes. No *Magna Carta*."

"Exactly. They say he's there yet."

"Alive?"

"Presumably. But sightless."

"Blind?"

"Stone blind. They say he spent his days staring into the sun, tears streaming down his face and soddening his beard. When the tears ceased flowing, he smiled. He smiles all the time now and never weeps."

"Never?"

"Smiles the livelong day."

"Sounds a cheerful chap."

Coal's eyes were blue and backlit; her complexion, a strawberries-and-ice that made her blue eyes a cliché.

But, Marquesa thought, nurturing her temptation, if those selfsame eyes were framed by the raven coxcombs of her own lashes, contrasted against the cinnamon of *her* skin, enfolded in the luxurious shaggy cascades of *her* hair . . .

Marquesa imagined those great luminescent aquamarines encased in the incomparable setting of *her* face and—grandest of all—her face borne aloft like some royal standard by those sinuous, supple, oh-so-very-long, *long* legs . . . and her mind, grown airy with the clarity of Himalayan mornings, made its decision.

"Would you classify her complexion as 'peaches-and-cream'?"

"Why no. More likely 'coffee-and-cream,' I should think."

"You don't think her golden, then?"

"Caramel."

"Have you noticed that her entire body is of a single hue?"

"Oh yes. No tan lines at all."

"Even her nipples."

"Caramel. Every smooth, sweet inch of skin."

"That white wall would be perfect."

"Perfect?"

"To set off her pelt."

"Are you considering making me a gift of it?"

"Of course not. The trophy belongs to the hunter."

"You think me a hunter?"

"Why not? You think me one."

Strutting high atop Coal's stalky limbs, Marquesa danced and sang her way into the hearts of billions. She loved it all: the cheers, the adoration, the money; the unexpected gifts, the flattery, the filthy propositions in the mail. She bared her breasts onstage and crooned lovesongs to them and one critic compared her to a medieval madonna. The world was a newborn kitten mewling for attention in the folds of her palm, weak and adoring and utterly at her mercy.

She performed in *Ciudad México* and Basilio Monteflores, the World's Last Bullfighter, marvelled at her wondrous control over the greater and lesser muscles of her body and fell smitten at her feet. When next he dueled the Last Bull, he vowed to present her with both ears and the tail—symbolic ears and tail, of course, for the Last Bull was invariably pardoned by the mass of *aficionados* who were loath to give up their beloved death in the afternoon, symbolic though it too had become.

It was not, alas, to be, for the Last Bull had grown savvy with experience. Basilio lay gasping on the sand, dark blood staining the delicacy of his ballet slippers while his life leaked from the wound in his groin.

In honor of the occasion, the *orquesta* played *"Silverio Pérez"* and *el Presidente* himself awarded Marquesa the Last Bull in its entirety. The sun had set and a ghost moon risen before the wildly approving crowd regained its composure.

Marquesa stood at the center of the arena—the Last

Bull posing majestically to one side, the Last Bullfighter's body lying in noble repose to the other—surrounded by exuberantly hurled berets, pillows, and wineskins. She blew kisses to the witnesses of the Last *Corrida* and delicately stifled belches inspired by her luncheon tacos.

"Would you call her a heartless wench?"

"Matter of definition."

"Oh?"

"By general standards she'd appear to be, wouldn't she?"

"I'd say."

"By her own, she can be totally faithful. Of course, her faithfulness is strictly mental. 'Spiritual' is her word. I believe she means by that that if she is faithful to you, it is you she thinks of at the moment of orgasm."

"Self-induced or with another man?"

"Either. Or with a woman."

"A woman?!"

"Oh yes. I believe she draws the line at German shepherds and giraffes."

Overcome by charitable impulse, Marquesa ordered the Last Bull and Last Bullfighter chopped into steaks and stewmeat to be distributed to the poor. Overcome in turn by admiration and lust, *el Presidente* offered Marquesa the granting of her greatest desire in exchange for the small favor of allowing *el Presidente* to place his venerable head between the litheness of her thighs.

The release of the loving Don R. from his unjust imprisonment was Marquesa's price.

—Done! cried *el Presidente*.

Don R. sat quietly in an opulent chair across the room while *el Presidente* played out his fantasy. Don R. could not see the Mexican nor his beloved, but he could see that final searing image he had so painstakingly engraved upon both retinas. His eyes forever feasted now on the glory of the sun and in its fiery beauty he sometimes fancied he glimpsed the fleeting smile of Marquesa's exquisite eyes.

Across the room, Marquesa slowly tightened the vise of Coal's fine legs until *el Presidente's* eyes leapt from his head and his skull collapsed like a crushed almond. Coal's eyes shone chill in the heat of Marquesa's face.

Then Marquesa moved to the smiling Don R. and took his index finger tenderly into the warmth of her velvet mouth.

EMISSARY FROM HAMELIN
Harlan Ellison

Harlan Ellison is an admirer of Pablo Neruda and Jorge Luis Borges. A prolific writer, his work includes screenplays, volumes of television criticism, and is noted especially for such short fictions as "The Deathbird" and "Shatterday." One of his current projects is the editing of The Last Dangerous Visions, probably the largest original anthology of speculative fiction ever compiled.

EMISSARY FROM HAMELIN

July 22nd, 2076 . . .
   Exclusive to the Going Nowhere Newsservice . . .
   Mike Strathearn reporting . . .
   My second wife once told me I'd write if I were strapped into a strait jacket in the deepest, moldiest dungeon cell of the most remote lunatic asylum in the world. She said I'd probably write news releases on the insides of my cheeks with my wet tongue-tip. She's probably right, wherever she is. I'm a compulsive. Stranded on the most remote peak of K2 (Mt. Godwin-Austen or Dapsang, 8,475 meters, second highest mountain in the world: in the Himalayas, the Karakorams), I would fold the dispatches in the shape of gliders and skim them off the peak in hopes a Sherpa herdsman or a *yeti* or *some*one would find them. Marooned on a desert island, I would use notes in bottles. No one has ever figured out how someone marooned on a desert island came up with bottles to cast into the sea, but if there weren't a convenient case of empty liquor bottles already there, I'd slip the dispatches into the mouths of dolphins, hoping they had a nice sense of direction. I was born in 2014, little more than a decade after the turn of the century, which makes me sixty-two now, and my mother once ventured that the difficulty she'd had giving birth to me was probably due to my having written all over the walls of her womb. I had a pretty happy childhood and by the time I was . . .
   I'm rambling.
   That's lousy reportage.
   I've always despised personal journalism. I try to be dead-on factual. But there isn't much to do here, and I have this damnable need to *communicate!*
   I'll try to keep to the subject.
   The child. That kid. The emissary from Hamelin.

I got the word he wanted to meet me from the night desk. They called me at home and said, "There's a kid says he's got the biggest story in the history of the world, says he'll only give it to you."

I stared at the face of the guy in the phone. It was a new guy from the Bombay office, wearing a lot of pancake make-up and glitter on his eyelids. I didn't know him except by sight, and I confess I didn't like him. I guess I didn't much like any of the new breed of reporters. Back when I was a kid, back around '27 and '28, I was greatly impressed by all the wacky film comedies of the nineteen-thirties, the ones that took place in the old-style newspaper offices. Wisecracking guys and gals getting the beat on all the other papers, phoning in their leads on phones that just talked, didn't have holo or even sight. Boy, what times those must have been! "Hello, Sharkey? This's Smoke Farnum, hold the presses! I've got a doozy! Gimme rewrite. Hello, rewrite, take a lead for the dead dog final . . ."

I'm rambling again.

This kid. Yeah, I got to stick to telling about that kid.

Well, I looked at this yo-yo from Bombay, and I said, "What the hell are you talking about?"

Glitterlids just stared at me like he wanted to buzz me off, and finally he said, "The cops've got a kid up on a power wand tower out in Westwood. They don't know how he got up there, and they don't much give a damn; but they can't get him down."

"Why not?"

"Says he wants to talk to Strathearn of the Newsservice."

"I asked you why not?"

"Because every time they send up a cop with a flitterpak on, the unit bypasses fail-safe and the cop falls on his ass, that's why not!"

"And what's all this about him having a story?"

"Look, Strathearn," he said, "what the hell am I supposed to be, your grapevine? I've got other things to do; stop annoying me; either take the call or don't. As far as I'm concerned, you can chew mud!" And he buzzed me off before I could ask him why the kid wanted to talk to me and nobody else.

I floated there for a while, just revolving and thinking nothing in particular, just resting. I was half drunk to begin with, and not particularly interested in going out to cover some dumb kid up on a wand. But the more I thought about it, the more curious I got about him, and I must admit my ego was massaged thinking the kid wanted to talk to me and nobody else. It reminded me of the nineteen-twenties, when Haldeman or Manson or Pretty Boy Floyd, one of those mobsters, gave himself up to Walter Winchell. *Hold everything, Sharkey*, I thought. *Stop the presses! I got a five star final for you. Banner headline! Eighty point Railroad Gothic! Crazed killer kid on a wand with the biggest story in the world!*

I had to laugh at myself, but before I knew what I was doing I was peeling the wrapper off a clean suit, blowing it up, putting it on and skitting for Westwood.

What the hell. Maybe it *was* the biggest story in the world. How often does *that* happen?

I can answer that now. I wish I couldn't, but I can. It only happens once. Damn it.

They fitted me out with a flitterpak. I couldn't believe it when the cops said they blamed the kid up there on the power wand tower for the failure of their units. I planned to do something with *that* bit of self-serving alibi when I put together my story. *If* there was a story.

I kicked the unit on, it hummed prettily and I took off. Up I went, without any problem. *What noodles, those cops*, I thought.

I went up, 210 meters. Thank God I'm not afraid of heights. And there he was.

It wasn't a crazed teen-ager. It was a little boy, about ten years old. He was walking around the maintenance platform. Limping. He was dressed in some soft furry kind of jacket and pants, wearing a pointed cap of the same fur, with a feather in it. He had a striped red and yellow scarf around his neck, and at the end of the scarf he had a flute of intricately carved wood attached by a leather thong. I recognized the flute as wood, and the thong as leather. Do you know how long it's been since we had any wood or leather around? Do you know how long it's been since anyone wore fur? Oh, there was a story here, all right.

The kid watched me as I floated up over the guardrails and dropped onto the platform. I kicked off the unit, but I didn't take it off. He was only about a hundred and twenty centimeters tall, but I wasn't taking any chances on his suddenly going wild and doing something unexpected. It was, after all, more than two hundred meters to a messy finish.

And I made a prelim they could edit down when they 'cast it.

"Willy has agreed to give us a demonstration, and for that on-the-scene I transfer you now to our remote in Times Square, New York, state of Manhattan."

I watched the console in the palm of my hand. The screen flickered and I was staring down at 42nd and Broadway. Beside me, the child put the pipe to his lips and began to play.

The song made no sense to me, but it apparently made sense to the cockroaches. If there is a scientific explanation for how a tune played softly on a flute can be heard a continent away by cockroaches, it is an explanation that exists within the bounds of a science we do not yet understand. A science we will probably *never* understand.

But as I watched, the cockroaches of Manhattan began to come out. "And the muttering grew to a grumbling and the grumbling grew to a mighty rumbling and out of the houses the rats came tumbling." Browning would have written it very differently had the Pied Piper called out the cockroaches. At first there was a low twittering sound and the twittering grew to a clittering and the clittering grew to a mighty clattering as their claws skittered and scuttled across the plastic streets and sidewalks. And they came in a trickle and then a mass and then a wash and then a flood. They came from the underground and they came from the walls and they came from the rotting rusting rafters and the garbage-laden hallways and they came out and covered the streets so there was nothing but a carpet of carapaces, a black carpet of evil little shapes.

And the screen showed them heading toward the East River and as I watched they all scrabbled across the island that had been made the state of Manhattan, and they plunged into the East River and were drowned.

Then remote came back to me.

I turned to the child.

"Willy, tell the audience watching us what it is you want them to do."

He turned to me and looked at me, and my sensors held him. "We want everyone to stop what they are doing to make this a bad place, or we will take this place away from you."

And that was all.

He didn't explain it. He clearly didn't feel he should set the method. But it was clear what he intended. Stop paving over the green lands with plastic, stop fighting, stop killing friendship, have courage, don't lie, stop brutalizing each other, value art and wisdom . . . in short, make over the world or lose it.

I was with him all that next week, as he went from town to town and city to city. They laughed at him, of course. They laughed and they ignored him and several times they tried to take him into custody, but the child stopped them.

And yesterday, when time was almost up, we sat on the bank of a filth-filled stream and Willy toyed with the flute as if he wished it were not there, and he said to me, "I am sorry for you."

"You're going to do it, aren't you?"

"Yes," he said. "We have given you seven hundred years. That is enough time. But I am sorry you will go with them. I like you, you are a nice person."

"But not nice enough to spare me."

"You are one with all the others. They did nothing. You did nothing. You are not a bad person; you just did not care enough."

"I wasn't strong enough, Willy. I'm not sure anyone is."

"They should have been. They are not stupid."

And so, today, Willy began walking, and as he walked he played. And this time I heard the song. It was of finer times and cleaner lands, and I followed him. And everyone else followed him. They came out of the houses and the condos, the towers and the undergrounds. They came from far away and from nearby. And they followed him to an empty field where he piped open the air, and it was black inside. As black as a collapsed star, a black hole. And they marched inside, one after another, all the adults in the world. And as I stepped across the threshold I looked at Willy and he was staring at me, even though he did not stop playing his pipe. His eyes were moist again.

And here we are. There is nothing here, but it doesn't seem to matter. Willy and the children of Hamelin meant us no harm, they just couldn't put up with us any longer. We will stay here forever, I'm sure; and perhaps we will die and perhaps this place will keep us as we are now. But here, nonetheless, forever.

And I would tell you what the world is like today, on

July 22nd, 2076, but I don't know. It's out there somewhere. Peopled by children.

I hope Willy is right. I hope they will make a better showing than we did. God knows we had long enough to try.

CORRUPTION OF METALS

Sonya Dorman

It is possible that in another century, Neil Armstrong will be more obscure than such American heroes of the Revolution as Sybil Luddington and Haim Solomon before they got their Bicentennial commemorative stamps. Even now, how many of you can name Armstrong's crewmates? Or the *third* man to walk on the Moon?*

Sonya Dorman is a fine writer of both prose ("Bitching It," "When I Was Miss Dow") and poetry (*Poems, Stretching Fence*). A native New Englander, she presently lives in Connecticut. She raises and shows Akita dogs.

---

* Michael Collins and Edwin Aldrin; the latter accompanied Armstrong to the lunar surface; Collins remained in the orbiter. The third man to walk on the Moon was the *Apollo 12* commander, Pete Conrad.

CORRUPTION OF METALS

miles of glittering
whales   unbuckled bellies
    junked space ships
    lie across hills

    berry bushes twiggle
    along titanium espaliers

the winter solstice lies down
on padded couches   frost enters
    the solar vanes
    with white tentacles

the cameras dream of space
    the way captains
    in black silence
once thought of earth

AZTECS

Vonda N. McIntyre

If America and the rest of the world flipflop contemporary trends and again turn outward toward the stars, then perhaps the coming interstellar culture of Vonda McIntyre's "Aztecs" will have the chance to flourish. This is one answer to those who question the possible failure of society's human software to keep pace with technological innovation.

Vonda McIntyre was once a graduate-level geneticist at the University of Washington. She has now turned to full-time writing in the Pacific Northwest. Some results of that decision are the 1973 Nebula Award-winning novelette "Of Mist, and Grass, and Sand," the recent novel *The Exile Waiting*, and the anthology, coedited with Susan Janice Anderson, *Aurora: Beyond Equality*.

AZTECS

She gave up her heart quite willingly.

After the operation, Laenea Trevelyan lived through what seemed an immense time of semiconsciousness, drugged so she would not feel the pain, kept almost insensible while her healing began. Those who watched her did not know she would have preferred consciousness and an end to her uncertainty. So she slept, shallowly, drifting toward awareness, driven back, existing in a world of nightmare. Her dulled mind suspected danger but could do nothing to protect her. She had been forced too often to sleep through danger. She would have preferred the pain.

Once Laenea almost woke: she glimpsed the sterile white walls and ceiling, blurrily, slowly recognizing what she saw. The green glow of monitoring screens flowed across her shoulder, over the scratchy sheets. Taped down, needles scraped nerves in her arm. She became aware of sounds, and heard the rhythmic thud of a beating heart.

She tried to cry out in anger and despair. Her left hand was heavy, lethargic, insensitive to her commands, but she moved it. It crawled like a spider to her right wrist and fumbled at the needles and tubes.

Air shushed from the room as the door opened. A gentle voice and a gentle touch reproved her, increased the flow of sedative, and cruelly returned her to sleep.

A tear slid back from the corner of her eye and trickled into her hair as she reentered her nightmares, accompanied by the counterpoint of a basic human rhythm, the beating of a heart, that she had hoped never to hear again.

Pastel light was Laenea's first assurance that she would live. It gave her no comfort. Intensive care was stark white, astringent in odor, but yellows and greens brightened this private room. The sedative wore off and she knew she would finally be allowed to wake. She did not fight the continuing drowsiness, but depression prevented anticipation of the return of her senses. She wanted only to live within her own mind, ignoring her body, ignoring failure. She did not even know what she would do in the future; perhaps she had none any more.

Yet the world impinged on her as she grew bored with lying still and sweaty and self-pitying. She had never been able to do simply *nothing*. Stubbornly she kept her eyes closed, but she could not avoid the sounds, the vibrations, for they went through her body in waves, like shudders of cold and fear.

This was my chance, she thought. *But I knew I might fail. It could have been worse, or better: I might have died.*

She slid her hand up her body, from her stomach to her ribs, across the adhesive tape and bandages and the tip of the new scar between her breasts, to her throat. Her fingers rested at the corner of her jaw, just above the carotid artery.

She could not feel a pulse.

Pushing herself up abruptly, Laenea ignored sharp twinges of pain. The vibration of a heartbeat continued beneath her palms, but now she could tell that it did not come from her own body.

The amplifier sat on the bedside table, sending out low frequency thuddings in a steady pattern. Laenea felt laughter bubbling up; she knew it would hurt and she did not care. She lifted the speaker: such a small thing, to cause her so much worry. Its cord ripped from the wall as she flung it across the room, and it smashed in the corner with a satisfying clatter.

She threw aside the stiff starched sheets; she rose, staggered, caught herself. Her breathing was coarse from fluid in her lungs. She coughed, caught her breath, coughed again. Time was a mystery, measured only by weakness: she thought the doctors fools, to force sleep into her, risk her to pneumonia, and play recorded hearts, instead of letting her wake and move and adjust to her new condition.

The tile pressed cool against her bare feet. Laenea walked slowly to a warm patch of sunshine, yellow on the buttercream floor, and gazed out the window. The day was variegated, gray and golden. Clouds moved from the west across the mountains and the Sound while sunlight still spilled over the city. The shadows moved along the water, turning it from shattered silver to slate.

White from the heavy winter snowfall, the Olympic mountains lay between Laenea and the port. The approaching rain hid even the trails of spacecraft escaping the earth, and the bright glints of shuttles returning to their target in the sea. But she would see them soon. She laughed aloud, stretching against the soreness in her chest and the ache of her ribs, throwing back her tangled wavy hair. It tickled the back of her neck, her spine, in the gap between the hospital gown's ties.

Air moved past her as the door opened, as though the room were breathing. Laenea turned and faced the surgeon, a tiny, frail-looking woman with strength like steel wires. The doctor glanced at the shattered amplifier and shook her head.

"Was that necessary?"

"Yes," Laenea said. "For my peace of mind."

"It was here for your peace of mind."

"It has the opposite effect."

"I'll mention that in my report," the surgeon said. "They did it for the first pilots."

"The administrators are known for continuing bad advice."

The doctor laughed. "Well, Pilot, soon you can design your own environment."

"When?"

"Soon. I don't mean to be obscure—I only decide if you can leave the hospital, not if you may. The scar tissue needs time to strengthen. Do you want to go already? I cracked your ribs rather thoroughly."

Laenea grinned. "I know." She was strapped up tight and straight, but she could feel each juncture of rib-end and cartilage.

"It will be a few days at least."

"How long has it been?"

"We kept you asleep almost three days."

"It seemed like weeks."

"Well . . . adjusting to all the changes at once could put you in shock."

"I'm an experiment," Laenea said. "All of us are. With experiments, you should experiment."

"Perhaps. But we would prefer to keep you with us." Her hair was short and iron gray, but when she smiled her face was that of a child. She had long, strong fingers, muscles and tendons sharply defined, nails pared short, good hands for doing any job. Laenea reached out, and they touched each others' wrists, quite gently.

"When I heard the heartbeat," Laenea said, "I thought you'd had to put me back to normal."

"It's meant to be a comforting sound."

"No one else ever complained?"

"Not quite so . . . strongly."

They would have been friends, if they had had time. But Laenea was impatient to progress, as she had been since her first transit, in which life passed without her awareness. "When can I leave?" The hospital was one more place of stasis that she was anxious to escape.

"For now go back to bed. The morning's soon enough to talk about the future."

Laenea turned away without answering. The windows, the walls, the filtered air cut her off from the gray clouds and the city. Rain slipped down the glass. She did not want to sleep any more.

"Pilot—"

Laenea did not answer.

The doctor sighed. "Do something for me, Pilot."

Laenea shrugged.

"I want you to test your control."

Laenea acquiesced with sullen silence.

"Speed your heart up slowly, and pay attention to the results."

Laenea intensified the firing of the nerve.

"What do you feel?"

"Nothing," Laenea said, though the blood rushed through what had been her pulse-points: temples, throat, wrists.

Beside her the surgeon frowned. "Increase a little more, but very slowly."

Laenea obeyed, responding to the abundant supply of oxygen to her brain. Bright lights flashed just behind her vision. Her head hurt in a streak above her right eye to the back of her skull. She felt high and excited. She turned away from the window. "Can't I leave now?"

The surgeon touched her arm at the wrist; Laenea almost laughed aloud at the idea of feeling for *her* pulse. The doctor led her to a chair by the window. "Sit down, Pilot." But Laenea felt she could climb the helix of her dizziness: she felt no need for rest.

"Sit down." The voice was whispery, soft sand slipping across stone. Laenea obeyed.

"Remember the rest of your training, Pilot. Sit back. Relax. Slow the pump. Expand the capillaries. Relax."

Laenea called back her biocontrol. For the first time she was conscious of a presence rather than an absence. Her pulse was gone, but in its place she felt the constant quiet hum of a perfectly balanced rotary machine. It pushed her blood through her body so efficiently that the pressure would destroy her, if she let it. She relaxed and slowed the pump, expanded and contracted the tiny arterial muscles, once, twice, again. The headache, the light-flashes, the ringing in her ears faded and ceased.

She took a deep breath and let it out slowly.

"That's better," the surgeon said. "Don't forget how that feels. You can't go at high speed very long, you'll turn your brain to cheese. You can feel fine for quite a while, you can feel intoxicated. But the hangover is more than I'd care to reckon with." She patted Laenea's hand. "We want to keep you here till we're sure you can regulate the machine. I don't like doing kidney transplants."

Laenea smiled. "I can control it." She began to induce a slow, arhythmic change in the speed of the new pump, in her blood pressure. She found she could do it without thinking, as was necessary to balance the flow. "Can I have the ashes of my heart?"

"Not just yet. Let's be sure, first."

"I'm sure." Somewhere in the winding concrete labyrinth of the hospital, her heart still beat, bathed in warm saline and nutrient solution. As long as it existed, as long as it lived, Laenea would feel threatened in her ambitions. She could not be a pilot and remain a normal human being, with normal human rhythms. Her body still could reject the artificial heart; then she would be made normal again. If she could work at all she would have to remain a crew member, anesthetized and unaware from one end of every journey to the other. She did not think she could stand that any longer. "I'm sure. I won't be back."

Tests and questions and examinations devoured several days in chunks and nibbles. Though she felt strong enough to walk, Laenea was pushed through the halls in a wheelchair. The boredom grew more and more wearing. The pains had faded, and Laenea saw only doctors and attendants and machines: her friends would not come. This was a rite of passage she must survive alone and without guidance.

A day passed in which she did not even see the rain that passed, nor the sunset that was obscured by fog. She asked again when she could leave the hospital, but no one would answer. She allowed herself to become angry, but no one would respond.

Evening, back in her room: Laenea was wide awake. She lay in bed and slid her fingers across her collarbone to the sternum, along the shiny-red line of the tremendous scar. It was still tender, covered with translucent synthetic skin, crossed once just below her breasts with a wide band of adhesive tape to ease her cracked ribs.

The efficient new heart intrigued her. She forced herself consciously to slow its pace, then went through the exercise of constricting and dilating arteries and capillaries. Her biocontrol was excellent. It had to be, or she would not have been passed for surgery.

Slowing the pump should have produced a pleasant lethargy and eventual sleep, but adrenalin from her anger lingered and she did not want to rest. Nor did she want a sleeping pill: she would take no more drugs. Dreamless drug-sleep was the worst kind of all. Fear built up, undischarged by fantasy, producing a great and formless tension.

The twilight was the texture of gray watered silk, opaque and irregular. The hospital's pastels turned cold and mysterious. Laenea threw off the sheet. She was strong again; she was healed. She had undergone months of training, major surgery, and these final capping days of boredom to free herself completely from biological rhythms. There was no reason in the world why she should sleep, like others, when darkness fell.

A civilized hospital: her clothes were in the closet, not squirrelled away in some locked room. She put on black pants, soft leather boots, and a shiny leather vest that laced up the front, leaving her arms and neck bare. The sharp tip of the scar was revealed at her throat and between the laces.

To avoid arguments, she waited until the corridor was deserted. Green paint. meant to be soothing, had gone flat and ugly with age. Her boots were silent on the resilient tile, but in the hollow shaft of the fire stairs the heels clattered against concrete, echoing past her and back. Her legs were tired when she reached bottom. She speeded the flow of blood.

Outside, mist obscured the stars. The moon, just risen, was full and haloed. In the hospital's traffic-eddy, street-lights spread Laenea's shadow out around her like the spokes of a wheel.

A rank of electric cars waited at the corner, tethered like horses in an old movie. She slid her credit key into a lock to release one painted like a turtle, an apt analogy. She got in and drove it toward the waterfront. The little beast rolled slowly along, its motor humming quietly on the flat, straining slightly in low gear on the steep downgrades. Laenea relaxed in the bucket seat and wished she were in a starship, but her imagination would not stretch quite that far. The control stick of a turtle could not become an information and control wall; and the city, while pleasant, was of unrelieved ordinariness compared to the places she had seen. She could not, of course, imagine transit, for it was beyond imagination. Language or mind was insufficient. Transit had never been described.

The waterfront was shabby, dirty, magnetic. Laenea knew she could find acquaintances nearby, but she did not want to stay in the city. She returned the turtle to a stanchion and retrieved her credit key to halt the tally against her account.

The night had grown cold; she noticed the change peripherally in the form of fog and condensation-slick cobblestones. The public market, ramshackle and shored up, littered here and there with wilted vegetables, was deserted. People passed as shadows.

A man moved up behind her while she was in the dim region between two streetlamps. "Hey," he said, "how about—" His tone was belligerent with inexperience or insecurity or fear. Looking down at him, surprised, Laenea laughed. "Poor fool—" He scuttled away like a crab. After a moment of vague pity and amusement, Laenea forgot him. She shivered. Her ears were ringing and her chest ached from the cold.

Small shops nestled between bars and cheap restaurants. Laenea entered one for the warmth. It was very dim, darker than the street, high ceilinged and deep, so narrow she could have touched both side walls by stretching out her arms. She did not. She hunched her shoulders and the ache receded slightly.

"May I help you?"

Like one of the indistinct masses in the back of the shop brought to life, a small ancient man appeared. He was dressed in shabby ill-matched clothes, part of his own wares: Laenea was in a pawnshop or secondhand clothing store. Hung up like trophies, feathers and wide hats and beads covered the walls. Laenea moved farther inside.

"Ah, Pilot," the old man said, "you honor me."

Laenea's delight was childish in its intensity. Only the surgeon had called her "pilot"; to the others in the hospital she had been merely another patient, more troublesome than most.

"It's cold by the water," she said. Some graciousness or apology was due, for she had no intention of buying anything.

"A coat? No, a cloak!" he exclaimed. "A cloak would be set off well by a person of your stature." He turned; his dark form disappeared among the piles and racks of clothes. Laenea saw bright beads and spangles, a quick flash of gold lamé, and wondered uncharitably what dreadful theater costume he would choose. But the garment the small man drew out was dark. He held it up: a long swath of black, lined with scarlet. Laenea had planned to thank him and demur; despite herself she reached out. Velvet-silk outside and smooth satin-silk within caressed her fingers. The cloak had one shoulder cape and a clasp of carved jet. Though heavy, it draped easily and gracefully. She slung it over her shoulders, and it flowed around her almost to her ankles.

"Exquisite," the shopkeeper said. He beckoned and she approached: a dim and pitted full-length mirror stood against the wall beyond him. Bronze patches marred its irregular silver face where the backing had peeled away. Laenea liked the way the cape looked. She folded its edges so the scarlet lining showed, so her throat and the upper curve of her breasts and the tip of the scar were exposed. She shook back her hair.

"Not quite exquisite," she said, smiling. She was too tall and big-boned for that kind of delicacy. She had a widow's peak and high cheekbones, but her jaw was strong and square. Her face laughed well but would not do for coyness.

"It does not please you." He sounded downcast. Laenea could not quite place his faint accent.

"It does," she said. "I'll take it."

He bowed her toward the front of the shop, and she took out her credit key.

"No, no, Pilot," he said. "Not that."

Laenea raised one eyebrow. A few shops on the waterfront accepted only cash, retaining an illicit flavor in a time when almost any activity was legal. But few even of those select establishments would refuse the credit of a crew member or a pilot. "I have no cash," Laenea said. She had not carried any for years, since once finding in various pockets three coins of metal, one of plastic, one of wood, a pleasingly atavistic animal claw (or excellent duplicate), and a boxed bit of organic matter that would have been forbidden on earth fifty years before. Laenea never expected to revisit at least three of the worlds the currency represented.

"Not cash," he said. "It is yours, Pilot. Only—" He glanced up; he looked her in the eyes for the first time. His eyes were very dark and deep, hopeful, expectant. "Only tell me, what is it like? What do you see?"

She pulled back, surprised. She knew people asked the question often. She had asked it herself, wordlessly after the first few times of silence and patient head-shakings. Pilots never answered. Machines could not answer, pilots could not answer. Or would not. The question was answerable only individually. Laenea felt sorry for the shopkeeper and started to say she had not yet been in transit awake, that she was new, that she had only travelled in the crew, drugged near death to stay alive. But, finally, she could not even say that. It was too easy; it would very nearly be a betrayal. It was an untrue truth. It implied she would tell him if she knew, while she did not know if she could or would. She shook her head, she smiled as gently as she could. "I'm sorry."

He nodded sadly. "I should not have asked . . ."

"That's all right."

"I'm too old, you see. Too old for adventure. I came here so long ago . . . but the time, the time disappeared. I never knew what happened. I've dreamed about it. Bad dreams . . ."

"I understand. I was crew for ten years. We never knew what happened either."

"That would be worse, yes. Over and over again, no time between. But now you know."

"Pilots know," Laenea agreed. She handed him the credit key. Though he still tried to refuse it, she insisted on paying.

Hugging the cloak around her, Laenea stepped out into the fog. She fantasized that the shop would now disappear, like all legendary shops dispensing magic and cloaks of invisibility. But she did not look back, for everything a few paces away dissolved into grayness. In a small space around each low streetlamp, heat swirled the fog in wisps toward the sky.

The midnight ferry chuttered across the water, riding the waves on its loud cushion of air. Wrapped in her cloak, Laenea was anonymous. After the island stops, she was the only foot passenger left. With the food counters closed, the drivers on the vehicle deck remained in their trucks, napping or drinking coffee from thermoses. Laenea put her feet on the opposite bench, stretched, and gazed out the window into the darkness. Light from the ferry wavered across the tops of long low swells. Laenea could see both the water and her own reflection, very pale. After a while, she dozed.

The spaceport was a huge, floating, artificial island, anchored far from shore. It gleamed in its own lights. The parabolic solar mirrors looked like the multiple compound eyes of a gigantic water insect. Except for the mirrors and the launching towers, the port's surface was nearly flat, few of its components rising more than a story or two. Tall structures would present saillike faces to the northwest storms.

Beneath the platform, under a vibration-deadening lower layer, under the sea, lay the tripartite city. The roar of shuttles taking off and the scream of their return would drive mad anyone who remained on the surface. Thus the northwest spaceport was far out to sea, away from cities, yet a city in itself, self-protected within the underwater stabilizing shafts.

The ferry climbed a low ramp out of the water and settled onto the loading platform. The hum of electric trucks replaced the growl of huge fans. Laenea moved stiffly down the stairs. She was too tall to sleep comfortably on two-seat benches. Stopping for a moment by the gangway, watching the trucks roll past, she concentrated for a moment and felt the increase in her blood pressure. She could well understand how dangerous it might be, and how easily addictive the higher speed could become, driving her high until like a machine her body was burned out. But for now her energy began returning and the stiffness in her legs and back slowly seeped away.

Except for the trucks, which purred off quickly around the island's perimeters and disappeared, the port was silent so late at night. The passenger shuttle waited empty on its central rail. When Laenea entered, it sensed her, slid its doors shut, and accelerated. A push-button command halted it above Stabilizer Three, which held quarantine, administration, and crew quarters. Laenea was feeling good, warm, and her vision was sparkling bright and clear. She let the velvet cloak flow back across her shoulders, no longer needing its protection. She was alight with the expectation of seeing her friends, in her new avatar.

The elevator led through the center of the stabilizer into the underwater city. Laenea rode it all the way to the bottom of the shaft, one of three that projected into the ocean far below the surface turbulence to hold the platform steady even through the most violent storms. The shafts maintained the island's flotation level as well, pumping sea water in or out of the ballast tanks when a shuttle took off or landed or a ferry crept on board.

The elevator doors opened into the foyer where a spiral staircase reached the lowest level, a bubble at the tip of the main shaft. The lounge was a comfortable cylindrical room, its walls all transparent, gazing out like a continuous eye into the deep sea. Floodlights cast a glow through the cold clear water, picking out the bright speedy forms of fish, large dark predators, scythe-mouthed sharks, the occasional graceful bow of a porpoise, the elegant black-and-white presence of a killer whale. As the radius of visibility increased, the light filtered through bluer and bluer, until finally, in violet, vague shapes eased back and forth with shy curiosity between dim illumination and complete darkness. The lounge, sculpted with plastic foam and carpeted, gave the illusion of being underwater, on the ocean floor itself, a part of the sea. It had not been built originally as a lounge for crew alone, but was taken over by unconscious agreement among the starship people. Outsiders were not rejected, but gently ignored. Feeling unwelcome, they soon departed. Journalists came infrequently, reacting to sensation or disaster. Human pilots had been a sensation, but Laenea was in the second pilot group; the novelty had worn away. She did not mind a bit.

Laenea took off her boots and left them by the stairwell. She recognized one of the other pair: she would have been hard put not to recognize those boots after seeing them once. The scarlet leather was stupendously shined, embroidered with jewels, and inlaid with tiny liquid crystal-filled discs that changed color with the temperature. Laenea smiled. Crew members made up for the dead-time of transit in many different ways; one was to overdo all other aspects of their lives, and the most flamboyant of that group was Minoru.

Walking barefoot in the deep carpet, between the hillocks and hollows of conversation pits, was like walking on the sea floor idealized. Laenea thought that the attraction of the lounge was its relation to the mystery of the sea, for the sea still held mysteries perhaps as deep as any she would encounter in space or in transit. No one but the pilots could even guess at the truth of her assumption, but Laenea had often sat gazing through the shadowed water, dreaming. Soon she too would know; she would not have to imagine any longer.

She moved between small groups of people half-hidden in the recesses of the conversation pits. Near the transparent sea-wall she saw Minoru, his black hair braided with scarlet and silver to his waist; tall Alannai hunched down to be closer to the others, the light on her skin like dark opal, glinting in her close-cropped hair like diamond dust; and pale, quiet Ruth, whose sparkling was rare but nova bright. Holding goblets or mugs, they sat sleepily conversing, and Laenea felt the comfort of a familiar scene.

Minoru, facing her, glanced up. She smiled, expecting him to cry out her name and fling out his arms, as he always did, with his ebullient greeting, showing to advantage the fringe and beadwork on his jacket. But he looked at her, straight on, silent, with an expression so blank that only the unlined long-lived youthfulness of his face could have held it. He whispered her name. Ruth looked over her shoulder and smiled tentatively, as though she were afraid. Alannai unbent, and, head and shoulders above the others, raised her glass solemnly to Laenea. "Pilot," she said, and drank, and hunched back down with her elbows on her sharp knees. Laenea stood above them, outside their circle, looking down on three people whom she had kissed goodbye. Crew always said goodbye, for they slept through their voyages without any certainty that they would wake again. They lived in the cruel childhood prayer: "If I should die before I wake . . ."

Laenea climbed down to them. The circle opened, but she did not enter it. She was as overwhelmed by uncertainty as her friends.

"Sit with us," Ruth said finally. Alannai and Minoru looked uneasy but did not object. Laenea sat down. The triangle between Ruth and Alannai and Minoru did not alter. Each of them was next to the other; Laenea was beside none of them.

Ruth reached out, but her hand trembled. They all waited, and Laenea tried to think of words to reassure them, to affirm that she had not changed.

But she had changed. She realized the surgeon had cut more than skin and muscle and bone.

"I came . . ." But nothing she felt seemed right to tell them. She would not taunt them with her freedom. She took Ruth's outstretched hand. "I came to say goodbye." She embraced them and kissed them and climbed back to the main level. They had all been friends, but they could accept each other no longer.

The first pilots and crew did not mingle, for the responsibility was great, the tensions greater. But Laenea already cared for Ruth and Minoru and Alannai. Her concern would remain when she watched them sleeping and ferried them from one island of light to the next. She understood why she was perpetuating the separation even less than she understood her friends' reserve.

Conversations ebbed and flowed around her like the tides as she moved through the lounge. Seeing people she knew, she avoided them, and she did not try to join an unfamiliar group. Her pride far exceeded her loneliness.

She put aside the pain of her rejection. She felt self-contained and self-assured. When she recognized two pilots, sitting together, isolated, she approached them straightforwardly. She had flown with both of them, but never talked at length with either. They would accept her, or they would not: for the moment, she did not care. She flung back the cloak so they would know her, and realized quite suddenly—with a shock of amused surprise at what she had never noticed consciously before—that all pilots dressed as she had dressed. Laced vest or deeply cut gowns, transparent shirts, halters, all in one way or another revealed the long scar that marked their changes.

Miikala and Ramona-Teresa sat facing each other, elbows on knees, talking together quietly, privately. Even the rhythms of their conversation seemed alien to Laenea, though she could not hear their words. Like other people they communicated as much with their bodies and hands as with speech, but the nods and gestures clashed.

Laenea wondered what pilots talked about. Certainly it could not be the ordinary concerns of ordinary people, the laundry, the shopping, a place to stay, a person, perhaps, to stay with. They would talk about . . . the experiences they alone had; they would talk about what they saw when all others must sleep near death or die.

Human pilots withstood transit better than machine intelligence, but human pilots too were sometimes lost. Miikala and Ramona-Teresa were ten percent of all the pilots who survived from the first generation, ten percent of their own unique, evolving, almost self-contained society. As Laenea stopped on the edge of the pit above them, they fell silent and gazed solemnly up at her.

Ramona-Teresa, a small, heavy-set woman with raven-black hair graying to roan, smiled and lifted her glass. "Pilot!" Miikala, whose eyes were shadowed by heavy brow ridges and an unruly shock of dark brown hair, matched the salute and drank with her.

This toast was a tribute and a welcome, not a farewell. Laenea was a part of the second wave of pilots, one who would follow the original experiment and make it work practically, now that Miikala and Ramona-Teresa and the others had proven time-independence successful by example. Laenea smiled and lowered herself into the pit. Miikala touched her left wrist, Ramona-Teresa her right. Laenea felt, welling up inside her, a bubbling, childish giggle. She could not stop it; it broke free as if filled with helium like a balloon. "Hello," she said, and even her voice was high. She might have been in an Environment on the seafloor, breathing oxy-helium and speaking donaldduck. She felt the blood rushing through the veins in her temples and her throat. Miikala was smiling, saying something in a language with as many liquid vowels as his name; she did not understand a word, yet she knew everything he was saying. Ramona-Teresa hugged her. "Welcome, child."

Laenea could not believe that these lofty, eerie people could accept her with such joy. She realized she had hoped, at best, for a cool and condescending greeting not too destructive of her pride. The embarrassing giggle slipped up and out again, but this time she did not try to stifle it. All three pilots laughed together. Laenea felt high, light, dizzy: excitement pumped adrenalin through her body. She was hot and she could feel tiny beads of perspiration gather on her forehead, just at the hairline.

Quite suddenly the constant dull ache in her chest became a wrenching pain, as though her new heart were being ripped from her, like the old. She could not breathe. She hunched forward, struggling for air, oblivious to the pilots and all the beautiful surroundings. Each time she tried to draw in a breath, the pain drove it out again.

Slowly Miikala's easy voice slipped beyond her panic, and Ramona-Teresa's hands steadied her.

"Relax, relax, remember your training . . ."

Yes: decrease the blood-flow, open up the arteries, dilate all the tiny capillaries, feel the involuntary muscles responding to voluntary control. Slow the pump. Someone bathed her forehead with a cocktail napkin dipped in gin. Laenea welcomed the coolness and even the odor's bitter tang. The pain dissolved gradually until Ramona-Teresa could ease her back on the sitting shelf, onto the cushioned carpet, out of a protective near-fetal position. The jet fastening of the cloak fell away from her throat and the older pilot loosened the laces of her vest.

"It's all right," Ramona-Teresa said. "The adrenalin works as well as ever. We all have to learn more control of that than they think they need to teach. us."

Sitting on his heels beside Laenea, Miikala glanced at the exposed bright scar. "You're out early," he said. "Have they changed the procedure?"

Laenea paled: she had forgotten that her leavetaking of hospitals was something less than official and approved.

"Don't tease her, Miikala," Ramona-Teresa said gruffly. "Or don't you remember how it was when you woke up?"

His heavy eyebrows drew together in a scowl. "I remember."

"Will they make me go back?" Laenea asked. "I'm all right, I just need to get used to it."

"They might try to," Ramona-Teresa said. "They worry so about the money they spend on us. Perhaps they aren't quite so worried any more. We do as well on our own as shut up in their ugly hospitals listening to recorded hearts —do they still do that?"

Laenea shuddered. "It worked for you, they told me— but I broke the speaker."

Miikala laughed with delight. "Causing all other machines to make frantic noises like frightened little mice."

"I thought they hadn't done the operation. I wanted to be one of you so long—" Feeling stronger, Laenea pushed herself up. She left her vest open, glad of the cool air against her skin. "We watched," Miikala said. "We watch you all, but a few are special. We knew you'd come to us. Do you remember this one, Ramona?"

"Yes." She picked up one of the extra glasses, filled it from a shaker, and handed it to Laenea. "You always fought the sleep, my dear. Sometimes I thought you might wake."

"Ahh, Ramona, don't frighten the child."

"Frighten her, this tigress?"

Strangely enough, Laenea was not disturbed by the knowledge that she had been close to waking in transit. She had not, or she would be dead; she would have died quickly of old age, her body bound to normal time and normal space, to the relation between time-dilation and velocity and distance by a billion years of evolution, rhythms planetary, lunar, solar, biological: sub-atomic, for all Laenea or anyone else knew. She was freed of all that now.

She downed half her drink in a single swallow. The air now felt cold against her bare arms and her breasts, so she wrapped her cloak around her shoulders and waited for the satin to warm against her body.

"When do you get your ship?"

"Not for a month." The time seemed a vast expanse of emptiness. She had finished the study and the training; now only her mortal body kept her earthbound.

"They want you completely healed."

"It's too long—how can they expect me to wait until then?"

"For the need."

"I want to know what happens, I have to find out. When's your next flight?"

"Soon," Ramona-Teresa said.

"Take me with you!"

"No, my dear. It would not be proper."

"Proper! We have to make our own rules, not follow theirs. They don't know what's right for us."

Miikala and Ramona-Teresa looked at each other for a long time. Perhaps they spoke to each other with eyes and expressions, but Laenea could not understand.

"No." Ramona's tone invited no argument.

"At least you can tell me—" She saw at once that she had said the wrong thing. The pilots' expressions closed down in silence. But Laenea did not feel guilt or contrition, only anger.

"It isn't because you can't! You talk about it to each other, I know that now at least. You can't tell me you don't."

"No," Miikala said. "We will not say we never speak of it."

"You're selfish and you're cruel." She stood up, momentarily afraid she might stagger again and have to accept their help. But as Ramona and Miikala nodded at each other, with faint, infuriating smiles, Laenea felt the lightness and the silent bells overtaking her.

"She has the need," one of them said, Laenea did not even know which one. She turned her back on them, climbed out of the conversation pit, and stalked away.

The sitting-place she chose nestled her into a steep slope very close to the sea wall. She could feel the coolness of the glass, as though it, not heat, radiated. Grotesque creatures floated past in the spotlights. Laenea relaxed, letting her smooth pulse wax and wane. She wondered, if she sat in this pleasant place long enough, if she would be able to detect the real tides, if the same drifting plant-creatures passed again and again, swept back and forth before the window of the stabilizer by the forces of sun and moon.

Her privacy was marred only slightly, by one man sleeping or lying unconscious nearby. She did not recognize him, but he must be crew. His dark, close-fitting clothes were unremarkably different enough, in design and fabric, that he might be from another world. He must be new. Earth was the hub of commerce; no ship flew long without orbiting it. New crew members always visited at least once. New crew usually visited every world their ships reached at first, if they had the time for quarantine. Laenea had done the same herself. But the quarantines were so severe and so necessary that she, like most other veterans, eventually remained acclimated to one world, stayed on the ship during other planetfalls, and arranged her pattern to intersect her home as frequently as possible.

The sleeping man was a few years younger than Laenea. She thought he must be as tall as she, but that estimation was difficult. He was one of those uncommon people so beautifully proportioned that from any distance at all their height can only be determined by comparison. Nothing about him was exaggerated or attenuated; he gave the impression of strength, but it was the strength of litheness and agility, not violence. Laenea decided he was neither drunk nor drugged but asleep. His face, though relaxed, showed no dissipation. His hair was dark blond and shaggy, a shade lighter than his heavy mustache. He was far from handsome: his features were regular, distinctive, but without beauty. Below the cheekbones his tanned skin was scarred and pitted, as though from some virulent childhood disease. Some of the outer worlds had not yet conquered their epidemics.

Laenea looked away from the new young man. She stared at the dark water-wall at light's-end, letting her vision double and unfocus. She touched her collarbone and slid her fingers to the tip of the smooth scar. Sensation seemed refined across the tissue, as though a wound there would hurt more sharply. Though Laenea was tired and getting hungry she did not force herself to outrun the distractions. For a while her energy should return slowly and naturally. She had pushed herself far enough for one night.

A month would be an eternity; the wait would seem equivalent to all the years she had spent crewing. She was still angry at the other pilots. She felt she had acted like a little puppy, bounding up to them to be welcomed and patted, then, when they grew bored, they had kicked her away as though she had piddled on the floor. And she was angry at herself: she felt a fool and she felt the need to prove herself.

For the first time she appreciated the destruction of time during transit. To sleep for a month: convenient, impossible. She first must deal with her new existence, her new body; then she would deal with a new environment.

Perhaps she dozed. The deep sea admitted no time: the lights pierced the same indigo darkness day or night. Time was the least real of all dimensions to Laenea's people, and she was free of its dictates, isolated from its stabilities.

When she opened her eyes again she had no idea how long they had been closed, a second or an hour.

The time must have been a few minutes, at least, for the young man who had been sleeping was now sitting up, watching her. His eyes were dark blue, black-flecked, a color like the sea. For a moment he did not notice she was awake, then their gazes met and he glanced quickly away, blushing, embarrassed to be caught staring.

"I stared, too," Laenea said.

Startled, he turned slowly back, not quite sure Laenea was speaking to him. "What?"

"When I was a grounder, I stared at crew, and when I was crew I stared at pilots."

"I *am* crew," he said defensively.

"From—?"

"Twilight."

Laenea knew she had been there, a long while before; images of Twilight drifted to her. It was a new world, a dark and mysterious place of high mountains and black, brooding forests, a young world, its peaks just formed. It was heavily wreathed in clouds that filtered out much of the visible light but admitted the ultraviolet. Twilight: dusk, on that world. Never dawn. No one who had ever visited Twilight would think its dimness heralded anything but night. The people who lived there were strong and solemn, even confronting disaster. On Twilight she had seen grief, death, loss, but never panic or despair.

Laenea introduced herself and offered the young man a place nearer her own. He moved closer, reticent. "I am Radu Dracul," he said.

The name touched a faint note in her memory. She followed it until it grew loud enough to identify. She glanced over Radu Dracul's shoulder, as though looking for someone. "Then—where's Vlad?"

Radu laughed, changing his somber expression for the first time. He had good teeth, and deep smile lines that paralleled the drooping sides of his mustache. "Wherever he is, I hope he stays there."

They smiled together.

"This is your first tour?"

"Is it so obvious I'm a novice?"

"You're alone," she said. "And you were sleeping."

"I don't know anyone here. I was tired," he said, quite reasonably.

"After a while . . ." Laenea nodded toward a nearby group of people, hyper and shrill on sleep repressors, energizers. "You don't sleep when you're on the ground when there are people to talk to, when there are other things to do. You get sick of sleep, you're scared of it."

Radu stared toward the ribald group that stumbled its way toward the elevator. "Do all of us become like them?" He held his low voice emotionless.

"Most."

"The sleeping drugs are bad enough. They're necessary, everyone says. But that—" He shook his head slowly. His forehead was smooth except for two parallel vertical lines that appeared between his eyebrows when he frowned; it was below his cheekbones, to the square-angled corner of his jaw, that his skin was scarred.

"No one will force you," Laenea said. She was tempted to reach out and touch him; she would have liked to stroke his face from temple to chin, and smooth a lock of hair rumpled by sleep. But he was unlike other people she had met, whom she could touch and hug and go to bed with on short acquaintance and mutual whim. Radu had about him something withdrawn and protected, almost mysterious, an invisible wall that would only be strengthened by an attempt to broach it, however gentle. He carried himself, he spoke, defensively.

"But you think I'll choose it myself."

"It doesn't always happen," Laenea said, for she felt he needed reassurance; yet she also felt the need to defend herself and her former colleagues. "We sleep so much in transit, and it's such a dark time, it's so empty . . ."

"Empty? What about the dreams?"

"I never dreamt."

"I always do," he said. "Always."

"I wouldn't have minded transit time so much if I'd ever dreamed."

Understanding drew Radu from his reserve. "I can see how it might be."

Laenea thought of all the conversations she had had with all the other crew she had known. The silent emptiness of their sleep was the single constant of all their experiences. "I don't know anyone else like you. You're very lucky."

A tiny luminous fish nosed up against the sea wall. Laenea reached out and tapped the glass, leading the fish in a simple pattern drawn with her fingertip.

"I'm hungry," she said abruptly. "There's a good restaurant in the Point Stabilizer. Will you come?"

"A restaurant—where people . . . buy food?"

"Yes."

"I am not hungry."

He was a poor liar; he hesitated before the denial, and he did not meet Laenea's glance.

"What's the matter?"

"Nothing." He looked at her again, smiling slightly: that at least was true, that he was not worried.

"Are you going to stay here all night?"

"It isn't night, it's nearly morning."

"A room's more comfortable—you were asleep."

He shrugged; she could see she was making him uneasy. She realized he must not have any money. "Didn't your credit come through? That happens all the time. I think chimpanzees write the bookkeeping programs." She had gone through the red tape and annoyance of emergency credit several times when her transfers were misplaced or miscoded. "All you have to do—"

"The administration made no error in my case."

Laenea waited for him to explain or not, as he wished. Suddenly he grinned, amused at himself but not self-deprecating. He looked even younger than he must be, when he smiled like that. "I'm not used to using money for anything but . . . unnecessaries."

"Luxuries?"

"Yes, things we don't often use on Twilight, things I do not need. But food, a place to sleep—" He shrugged again. "They are always freely given on colonial worlds. When I got to Earth, I forgot to arrange a credit transfer." He was blushing faintly. "I won't forget again. I miss a meal and one night's sleep—I've missed more on Twilight, when I was doing real work. In a few hours I correct my error."

"There's no need to go hungry now," Laenea said. "You can—"

"I respect your customs," Radu said. "But my people never borrow and we never take what is unwillingly given."

Laenea stood up and held out her hand. "I never offer unwillingly. Come along."

His hand was warm and hard, like polished wood.

At the top of the elevator shaft, Laenea and Radu stepped out into the end of the night. It was foggy and luminous, sky and sea blending into uniform gray. No wind revealed the surface of the sea or the limits of the fog, but the air was cold. Laenea swung the cloak around them both. A light rain, almost invisible, drifted down, beading mistily in tiny brilliant drops on the black velvet and on Radu's hair. He was silver and gold in the artificial light.

"It's like Twilight now," he said. "It rains like this in the winter." He stretched out his arm, with the black velvet draping down like quiescent wings, opened his palm to the rain, and watched the minuscule droplets touch his fingertips. Laenea could tell from the yearning in his voice, the wistfulness, that he was painfully and desperately homesick. She said nothing, for she knew from experience that nothing could be said to help. The pain faded only with time and fondness for other places. Earth as yet had given Radu no cause for fondness. But now he stood gazing into the fog, as though he could see continents, or stars. She slipped her arm around his shoulders in a gesture of comfort.

"We'll walk to the Point." Laenea had been enclosed in testing and training rooms and hospitals as he had been confined in ships and quarantine: she, too, felt the need for fresh air and rain and the ocean's silent words.

The sidewalk edged the port's shore; only a rail separated it from a drop of ten meters to the sea. Incipient waves caressed the metal cliff obliquely, sliding into darkness. Laenea and Radu walked slowly along, matching strides. Every few paces their hips brushed together. Laenea glanced at Radu occasionally and wondered how she could have thought him anything but beautiful. Her heart circled slowly in her breast, low-pitched, relaxing, and her perceptions faded from fever clarity to misty dark and soothing. A veil seemed to surround and protect her. She became aware that Radu was gazing at her, more than she watched him. The cold touched them through the cloak, and they moved closer together; it seemed only sensible for Radu to put his arm around her too, and so they walked, clasped together.

"Real work," Laenea said, musing.

"Yes . . . hard work with hands or minds." He picked up the second possible branch of their previous conversation as though it had never gone in any other direction. "We do the work ourselves. Twilight is too new for machines—they evolved here, and they aren't as adaptable as people."

Laenea, who had endured unpleasant situations in which machines did not perform as intended, understood what he meant. Older methods than automation were more economical on new worlds where the machines had to be designed from the beginning but people only had to learn. Evolution was as good an analogy as any.

"Crewing's work. Maybe it doesn't strain your muscles, but it is work."

"One never gets tired. Physically or mentally. The job has no challenges."

"Aren't the risks enough for you?"

"Not random risks," he said. "It's like gambling."

His background made him a harsh judge, harshest with himself. Laenea felt a tinge of self-contempt in his words, a gray shadow across his independence.

"It isn't slave labor, you know. You could quit and go home."

"I wanted to come—" He cut off the protest. "I thought it would be different."

"I know," Laenea said. "You think it will be exciting, but after a while all that's left is a dull kind of danger."

"I did want to visit other places. To be like— In that I was selfish."

"Ahh, stop. Selfish? No one would do it otherwise."

"Perhaps not. But I had a different vision. I remembered—" Again, he stopped himself in mid-sentence.

"What?"

He shook his head. "Nothing." Laenea had thought his reserve was dissolving, but all his edges hardened again. "We spend most of our time carrying trivial cargoes for trivial reasons to trivial people."

"The trivial cargoes pay for the emergencies."

Radu shook his head. "That isn't right."

"That's the way it's always been."

"On Twilight . . ." He went no farther; the guarded tone had disappeared.

"You're drawn back," Laenea said. "More than anyone I've known before. It must be a comfort to love a place so much."

At first he tensed, as if he were afraid she would mock or chide him for weakness, or laugh at him. The tense muscles relaxed slowly. "I feel better, after flights when I dream about home."

The fortunate dreamer: if Laenea had still been crew, she would have envied him. "Is it your family you miss?"

"I have no family—I still miss them sometimes, but they're gone."

"I'm sorry."

"You couldn't know," he said quickly, almost too quickly, as though he might have hurt her rather than the other way around. "They were good people, my clan. The epidemic killed them."

Laenea gently tightened her arm around his shoulder in silent comfort.

"I don't know what it is about Twilight that binds us all," Radu said. "I suppose it must be the combination—the challenge and the result. Everything is new. We try to touch the world gently. So many things could go wrong."

He glanced at her, his eyes deep as a mountain lake, his face solemn in its strength, asking without words a question Laenea did not understand.

The air was cold. It entered her lungs and spread through her chest, her belly, arms, legs . . . she imagined that the machine was cold metal, sucking the heat from her as it circled in its silent patterns. Laenea was tired.

"What's that?"

She glanced up. They were near the midpoint of the port's edge, nearing lights shining vaguely through the fog. The amorphous pink glow resolved itself into separate globes and torches. Laenea noticed a high metallic hum. Within two paces the air cleared.

The tall frames of fog-catchers reared up, leading inward to the lights in concentric circles. The long wires, touched by the wind, vibrated musically. The fog, touched by the wires, condensed. Water dripped from wires' tips to the platform. The intermittent sound of heavy drops on metal, like rain, provided irregular rhythm for the faint music.

"Just a party," Laenea said. The singing, glistening wires formed a multilayered curtain, each layer transparent but in combination translucent and shimmering. Laenea moved between them, but Radu, hanging back, slowed her.

"What's the matter?"

"I don't wish to go where I haven't been invited."

"You are invited. We're all invited. Would you stay away from a party at your own house?"

Radu frowned, not understanding. Laenea remembered her own days as a novice of the crew; becoming used to one's new status took time.

"They come here for us," Laenea said. "They come hoping we'll stop and talk to them and eat their food and drink their liquor. Why else come here?" She gestured—it was meant to be a sweeping movement, but she stopped her hand before the apex of its arc, flinching at the strain on her cracked ribs—toward the party, lights and tables, a tasselled pavilion, the fog-catchers, the people in evening costume, servants and machines. "Why else bring all this here? They could be on a tropical island or under the Redwoods. They could be on a mountaintop or on a desert at dawn. But they're here, and I assure you they'll welcome us."

"You know the customs," Radu said, if a little doubtfully.

When they passed the last ring of fog-catchers the temperature began to rise. The warmth was a great relief. Laenea let the damp velvet cape fall away from her shoulders and Radu did the same. A very young man, almost still a boy, smooth-cheeked and wide-eyed, appeared to take the cloak for them. He stared at them both, curious, speechless; he saw the tip of the scar between Laenea's breasts and looked at her in astonishment and admiration. "Pilot . . ." he said. "Welcome, Pilot."

"Thank you. Whose gathering is this?"

The boy, now speechless, glanced over his shoulder and gestured.

Kathell Stafford glided toward them, holding out her hands to Laenea. The white tiger followed.

Gray streaked Kathell's hair, like the silver thread woven into her blue silk gown, but her eyes were as dark and young as ever. Laenea had not seen her in several years, many voyages. They clasped hands, Laenea amazed as always by the delicacy of Kathell's bones. Veins glowed blue beneath her light brown skin. Laenea had no idea how old she was. Except for the streaks of gray, she was just the same. They embraced.

"My dear, I heard you were in training. You must be very pleased."

"Relieved," Laenea said. "They never know for sure if it will work till afterward."

"Come join us, you and your friend."

"This is Radu Dracul of Twilight."

Kathell greeted him, and Laenea saw Radu relax and grow comfortable in the presence of the tiny self-possessed woman. Even a party on the sidewalk of the world's largest port could be her home, where she made guests welcome.

The others, quick to sense novelty, began to drift nearer, most seeming to have no particular direction in mind. Laenea had seen all the ways of approaching crew or pilots: the shyness or bravado or undisguised awe of children; the unctuous familiarity of some adults; the sophisticated nonchalance of the rich. Then there were the people Laenea seldom met, who looked at her, saw her, across a street or across a room, whose expressions said aloud: *She has walked on other worlds, she has traveled through a place I shall never even approach.* Those people looked, and looked reluctantly away, and returned to their business, allowing Laenea and her kind to proceed unmolested. Some crew members never knew they existed. The most interesting people, the sensitive and intelligent and nonintrusive ones, were those one seldom met.

Kathell was one of the people Laenea would never have met, except that she had young cousins in the crew. Otherwise she was unclassifiable. She was rich, and used her wealth lavishly to entertain her friends, as now, and for her own comfort. But she had more purpose than that. The money she used for play was nothing compared to the totality of her resources. She was a student as well as a patron, and the energy she could give to work provided her with endurance and concentration beyond that of anyone else Laenea had ever met. There was no sycophancy in either direction about their fondness for each other.

Laenea recognized few of the people clustering behind Kathell. She stood looking out at them, down a bit on most, and she almost wished she had led Radu around the fogcatchers instead of between them. She did not feel ready for the effusive greetings due a pilot; she did not feel she had earned them. The guests outshone her in every way, in beauty, in dress, in knowledge, yet they wanted her, they needed her, to touch what was denied them.

She could see the passage of time, one second after another, that quickly, in their faces. Quite suddenly she was overcome by pity.

Kathell introduced people to her. Laenea knew she would not remember one name in ten, but she nodded and smiled. Nearby Radu made polite and appropriate responses. Someone handed Laenea a glass of champagne. People clustered around her, waiting for her to talk. She found that she had no more to say to them than to those she left behind in the crew.

A man came closer, smiling, and shook her hand. "I've always wanted to meet an Aztec . . ."

His voice trailed off at Laenea's frown. She did not want to be churlish to a friend's guests, so she put aside her annoyance. "Just 'pilot,' please."

"But Aztecs—"

"The Aztecs sacrificed their captives' hearts," Laenea said. "We don't feel we've made a sacrifice."

She smiled and turned away, ending the conversation before he could press forward with a witty comment. The crowd was dense behind her, pressing in, all rich, free, trapped human beings. Laenea shivered and wished them away. She wanted quiet and solitude.

Suddenly Kathell was near, stretching out her hand. Laenea grasped it. For Kathell, Kathell and her tiger, the guests parted like water. But Kathell was in front. Laenea grinned and followed in her friend's wake. She saw Radu and called to him. He nodded; in a moment he was beside her, and they moved through regions of fragrances: mint, carnation, pine, musk, orange blossom. The boundaries were sharp between the odors.

Inside the pavilion, the three of them were alone. Laenea immediately felt warmer, though she knew the temperature was probably the same outside in the open party. But the tent walls, though busily patterned and self-luminous, made her feel enclosed and protected from the cold vast currents of the sea.

She sat gratefully in a soft chair. The white tiger laid his chin on Laenea's knee and she stroked his huge head.

"You look exhausted, my dear," Kathell said. She put a glass in her hand. Laenea sipped from it: warm milk punch. A hint that she should be in bed.

"I just got out of the hospital," she said. "I guess I over-did it a little. I'm not used to—" She gestured with her free hand, meaning: everything. My new body, being outside and free again . . . this man beside me. She closed her eyes against blurring vision.

"Stay awhile," Kathell said, as always understanding much more than was spoken. Laenea did not try to answer; she was too comfortable, too sleepy.

"Have you eaten?" Kathell's voice sounded far away. The words, directed elsewhere, existed alone and separate, meaningless. Laenea slowed her heart and relaxed the ar-terial constricting muscles. Blood flowing through the di-lated capillaries made her blush, and she felt warmer.

"She was going to take me to . . . a restaurant," Radu said.

"Have you never been to one?" Kathell's amusement was never hurtful. It emerged too obviously from good humor and the ability to accept rather than fear differences.

"There is no such thing on Twilight."

Laenea thought they said more, but the words drowned in the murmur of guests' voices and wind and sea. She felt only the softness of the cushions beneath her, the warm fragrant air, and the fur of the white tiger.

Time passed, how much or at what rate Laenea had no idea. She slept gratefully and unafraid, deeply, dreaming, and hardly roused when she was moved. She muttered something and was reassured, but never remembered the words, only the tone. Wind and cold touched her and were shut out; she felt a slight acceleration. Then she slept again.

Laenea half woke, warm, warm to her center. A recent dream swam into her consciousness and out again, leaving no trace but the memory of its passing. She closed her eyes and relaxed, to remember it if it would come, but she could recall only that it was a dream of piloting a ship in transit. The details she could not perceive. Not yet. She was left with a comfortless excitement that upset her drowsiness. The machine in her chest purred fast and seemed to give off heat, though that was as impossible as that it might chill her blood.

The room around her was dim; she did not know where she was except that it was not the hospital. The smells were wrong; her first perceptions were neither astringent antiseptics nor cloying drugs but faint perfume. The sensation against her skin was not coarse synthetic but silky cotton. Between her eyelashes reflections glinted from the ceiling. She realized she was in Kathell's apartment in the Point Stabilizer.

She pushed herself up on her elbows. Her ribs creaked like old parquet floors, and deep muscle aches spread from the center of her body to her shoulders, her arms, her legs. She made a sharp sound, more of surprise than of pain. She had driven herself too hard: she needed rest, not activity. She let herself sink slowly back into the big red bed, closing her eyes and drifting back toward sleep. She heard the rustling and sliding of two different fabrics rubbed one against the other, but did not react to the sound.

"Are you all right?"

The voice would have startled her if she had not been so nearly asleep again. She opened her eyes and found Radu standing near, his jacket unbuttoned, a faint sheen of sweat on his bare chest and forehead. The concern on his face matched the worry in his voice.

Laenea smiled. "You're still here." She had assumed without thinking that he had gone on his way, to see and do all the interesting things that attracted visitors on their first trip to Earth.

"Yes," he said. "Of course."

"You didn't need to stay . . ." But she did not want him to leave.

His hand on her forehead felt cool and soothing. "I think you have a fever. Is there someone I should call?"

Laenea thought for a moment, or rather felt, lying still and making herself receptive to her body's signals. Her heart was spinning much too fast; she calmed and slowed it, wondering again what adventure had occurred in her dream. Nothing else was amiss; her lungs were clear, her hearing sharp. She slid her hand between her breasts to touch the scar: smooth and body-temperature, no infection.

"I overtired myself," she said. "That's all. . . ." Sleep was overtaking her again, but curiosity disturbed her ease. "Why did you stay?"

"Because," he said slowly, sounding very far away, "I wanted to stay with you. I remember you . . ."

She wished she knew what he was talking about, but at

last the warmth and drowsiness were stronger lures than her curiosity.

When Laenea woke again, she woke completely. The aches and pains had faded in the night—or in the day, for she had no idea how long she had slept, or even how late at night or early in the morning she had visited Kathell's party.

She was in her favorite room in Kathell's apartment, one gaudier than the others. Though Laenea did not indulge in much personal adornment, she liked the scarlet and gold of the room, its intrusive energy, its Dionysian flavor. Even the aquaria set in the walls were inhabited by fish gilt with scales and jeweled with luminescence. Laenea felt the honest glee of compelling shapes and colors. She sat up and threw off the blankets, stretching and yawning in pure animal pleasure. Then, seeing Radu asleep, sprawled in the red velvet pillow chair, she fell silent, surprised, not wishing to wake him. She slipped quietly out of bed, pulled a robe from the closet, and padded into the bathroom.

Comfortable, bathed, and able to breathe properly for the first time since her operation, Laenea returned to the bedroom. She had removed the strapping in order to shower; as her cracked ribs hurt no more free than bandaged, she did not bother to replace the tape.

Radu was awake.

"Good morning."

"It's not quite midnight," he said, smiling.

"Of what day?"

"You slept what was left of last night and all today. The others left on the mainland zeppelin, but Kathell Stafford wished you well and said you were to use this place as long as you wanted."

Though Kathell was as fascinated with rare people as with rare animals, her curiosity was untainted by possessiveness. She had no need of pilots, or indeed of anyone, to enhance her status. She gave her patronage with affection and friendship, not as tacit purchase. Laenea reflected that she knew people who would have done almost anything for Kathell, yet she knew no one of whom Kathell had ever asked a favor.

"How in the world did you get me here? Did I walk?"

"We didn't want to wake you. One of the large serving

carts was empty so we lifted you onto it and pushed you here."

Laenea laughed. "You should have folded a flower in my hands and pretended you were at a wake."

"Someone did make that suggestion."

"I wish I hadn't been asleep—I would have liked to see the expressions of the grounders when we passed."

"Your being awake would have spoiled the illusion," Radu said.

Laenea laughed again, and this time he joined her.

As usual, clothes of all styles and sizes hung in the large closets. Laenea ran her hand across a row of garments, stopping when she touched a pleasurable texture. The first shirt she found near her size was deep green velvet with bloused sleeves. She slipped it on and buttoned it up to her breastbone, no farther.

"I still owe you a restaurant meal," she said to Radu.

"You owe me nothing at all," he said, much too seriously.

She buckled her belt with a jerk and shoved her feet into her boots, annoyed. "You don't even know me, but you stayed with me and took care of me for the whole first day of your first trip to Earth. Don't you think I should—don't you think it would be friendly for me to give you a meal?" She glared at him. "Willingly?"

He hesitated, startled by her anger. "I would find great pleasure," he said slowly, "in accepting that gift." He met Laenea's gaze, and when it softened he smiled again, tentatively. Laenea's exasperation melted and flowed away.

"Come along, then," she said to him for the second time. He rose from the pillow chair, quickly and awkwardly. None of Kathell's furniture was designed for a person his height or Laenea's. She reached to help him; they joined hands.

The Point Stabilizer was itself a complete city in two parts, one, a blatant tourist world, the second a discrete and interesting permanent supporting society. Laenea often experimented with restaurants here, but this time she went to one she knew well. Experiments in the Point were not always successful. Quality spanned as wide a spectrum as culture.

Marc's had been fashionable a few years before, and now

was not, but its proprietor seemed unperturbed by cycles of fashion. Pilots or princes, crew members or diplomats could come and go; Marc did not care. Laenea led Radu into the dim foyer of the restaurant and touched the signal button. In a few moments a screen before them brightened into a pattern like oil paint on water. "Hello, Marc," Laenea said. "I didn't have a chance to make a reservation, I'm afraid."

The responding voice was mechanical and harsh, initially unpleasant, difficult to understand without experience. Laenea no longer found it ugly or indecipherable. The screen brightened into yellow with the pleasure Marc could not express vocally. "I can't think of any punishment terrible enough for such a sin, so I'll have to pretend you called."

"Thank you, Marc."

"It's good to see you back after so long. And a Pilot, now."

"It's good to be back." She drew Radu forward a step, farther into the range of the small camera. "This is Radu Dracul, of Twilight, on his first Earth landing."

"Hello, Radu Dracul. I hope you find us neither too depraved nor too dull."

"Neither one at all," Radu said.

The headwaiter appeared to take them to their table.

"Welcome," Marc said, instead of goodbye, and from drifting blues and greens the screen faded to darkness.

Their table was lit by the blue reflected glow of light diffusing into the sea, and the fish watched them like curious urchins.

"Who is Marc?"

"I don't know," Laenea said. "He never comes out, no one ever goes in. Some say he was disfigured, some that he has an incurable disease and can never be with anyone again. There are always new rumors. But he never talks about himself and no one would invade his privacy by asking."

"People must have a higher regard for privacy on Earth than elsewhere," Radu said drily, as though he had had considerable experience with prying questions.

Laenea knew boorish people too, but had never thought about their possible effect on Marc. She realized that the least considerate of her acquaintances seldom came here, and that she had never met Marc until the third or fourth time she had come. "It's nothing about the people. He protects himself," she said, knowing it was true.

She handed him a menu and opened her own. "What would you like to eat?"

"I'm to choose from this list?"

"Yes."

"And then?"

"And then someone cooks it, then someone else brings it to you."

Radu glanced down at the menu, shaking his head slightly, but he made no comment.

"Do you wish to order, Pilot?" At Laenea's elbow, Andrew bowed slightly.

Laenea ordered for them both, for Radu was unfamiliar with the dishes offered.

Laenea tasted the wine. It was excellent; she put down her glass and allowed Andrew to fill it. Radu watched scarlet liquid rise in crystal, staring deep.

"I should have asked if you drink wine," Laenea said. "But do at least try it."

He looked up quickly, his eyes focusing; he had not, perhaps, been staring at the wine, but at nothing, absently. He picked up the glass, held it, sniffed it, sipped from it.

"I see now why we use wine so infrequently at home."

Laenea drank again, and again could find no fault. "Never mind, if you don't like it—"

But he was smiling. "It's what we have on Twilight that I never cared to drink. It's sea water compared to this."

Laenea was so hungry that half a glass of wine made her feel lightheaded; she was grateful when Andrew brought bowls of thick, spicy soup. Radu, too, was very hungry, or sensitive to alcohol, for his defenses began to ease. He relaxed; no longer did he seem ready to leap up, take Andrew by the arm, and ask the quiet old man why he stayed here, performing trivial services for trivial reasons and trivial people. And though he still glanced frequently at Laenea—watched her, almost—he no longer looked away when their gazes met.

She did not find his attention annoying; only inexplicable. She had been attracted to men and men to her many times, and often the attractions coincided. Radu was extremely attractive. But what he felt toward her was obviously something much stronger; whatever he wanted went far beyond sex. Laenea ate in silence for some time, finding nothing, no answers, in the depths of her own wine. The tension rose until she noticed it, peripherally at first, then clearly, sharply, almost as a discrete point separating her from Radu. He sat feigning ease, one arm resting on the table, but his soup was untouched and his hand was clenched into a fist.

"You—" she said finally.

"I—" he began simultaneously.

They both stopped. Radu looked relieved. After a moment Laenea continued.

"You came to see Earth. But you haven't even left the port. Surely you had more interesting plans than to watch someone sleep."

He glanced away, glanced back, slowly opened his fist, touched the edge of the glass with a fingertip.

"It's a prying question but I think I have the right to ask it of you."

"I wanted to stay with you," he said slowly, and Laenea remembered those words, in his voice, from her half-dream awakening.

" 'I remember you,' you said."

He blushed, spots of high color on his cheekbones. "I hoped you wouldn't remember that."

"Tell me what you meant."

"It all sounds foolish and childish and romantic."

She raised one eyebrow, questioning.

"For the last day I've felt I've been living in some kind of unbelievable dream. . . ."

"Dream rather than nightmare, I hope."

"You gave me a gift I wished for for years."

"A gift? What?"

"Your hand. Your smile. Your time . . ." His voice had grown very soft and hesitant again. He took a deep breath. "When the plagues came, on Twilight, all my clan died, eight adults and the four other children. I almost died, too . . ." His fingers brushed his scarred cheek. Laenea thought he was unaware of the habit. "But the serum came, and the vaccines. I recovered. The crew of the mercy mission—"

"We stayed several weeks," Laenea said. More details of her single visit to Twilight returned: the settlement in near collapse, the desperately ill trying to attend the dying.

"You were the first crew member I ever saw, the first offworlder. You saved my people, my life—"

"Radu, it wasn't only me."

"I know. I even knew then. It didn't matter. I was sick for so long, and when I came to and knew I would live it hardly mattered. I was frightened and full of grief and lost and alone. I needed . . . someone . . . to admire. And you were there. You were the only stability in our chaos, a hero . . ." his voice trailed off in uncertainty at Laenea's smile, though she was not laughing at him. "This isn't easy for me to say."

Reaching across the table, Laenea grasped his wrist. The beat of his pulse was as alien as flame. She could think of nothing to tell him that would not sound patronizing or parental, and she did not care to speak to him in either guise. He raised his head and looked at her, searching her face. "When I joined the crew I don't think I ever believed I would meet you. I joined because it was what I always wanted to do, after . . . I never considered that I might really meet you. But I saw you, and I realized I wanted . . . to be something in your life. A friend, at best, I hoped. A shipmate, if nothing else. But—you'd become a pilot, and everyone knows pilots and crew stay apart."

"The first ones take pride in their solitude," Laenea said, for Ramona-Teresa's rejection still stung. Then she relented, for she might never have met Radu Dracul if they had accepted her completely. "Maybe they needed it."

"I saw a few pilots, before I met you. You're the only one who ever spoke to me or even glanced at me. I think . . ." He looked at her hand on his, and touched his scarred cheek again, as if he could brush the marks away. "I think I've loved you since the day you came to Twilight." He stood abruptly, but withdrew his hand gently. "I should never—"

She rose too. "Why not?"

"I have no right to . . ."

"To what?"

"To ask anything of you. To expect—" Flinching, he cut off the word. "To burden you with my hopes."

"What about my hopes?"

He was silent with incomprehension. Laenea stroked his rough cheek, once when he winced like a nervous colt, and again; the lines of strain across his forehead eased almost imperceptibly. She brushed back the errant lock of dark blond hair. "I've had less time to think of you than you of me," she said, "but I think you're beautiful, and an admirable man."

Radu smiled with little humor. "I'm not thought beautiful on Twilight."

"Then Twilight has as many fools as any other human world."

"You . . . want me to stay?"

"Yes."

He sat down again like a man in a dream. Neither spoke. Andrew appeared, to remove the soup plates and serve the main course. He was diplomatically unruffled, but not quite oblivious to Laenea and Radu's near departure. "Is everything satisfactory?"

"Very much so, Andrew. Thank you."

He bowed and smiled and pushed away the serving cart.

"Have you contracted for transit again?"

"Not yet," Radu said.

"I have a month before my proving flights." She thought of places she could take him, sights she could show him. "I thought I'd just have to endure the time—" She fell silent, for Ramona-Teresa was standing in the entrance of the restaurant, scanning the room. She saw Laenea and came toward her. Laenea waited, frowning; Radu turned, froze, struck by Ramona's compelling presence: serenity, power, determination. Laenea wondered if the older pilot had relented, but she was no longer so eager to be presented with mysteries, rather than to discover them herself.

Ramona-Teresa stopped at their table, ignoring Radu, or, rather, glancing at him, dismissing him in the same instant, and speaking to Laenea. "They want you to go back."

Laenea had almost forgotten the doctors and administrators, who could hardly take her departure as calmly as did the other pilots. "Did you tell them where I was?" She knew immediately that she had asked an unworthy question. "I'm sorry."

"They always want to teach us that they're in control. Sometimes it's easiest to let them believe they are."

"Thanks," Laenea said, "but I've had enough tests and plastic tubes." She felt very free, for whatever she did she would not be grounded: she was worth too much. No one would even censure her for irresponsibility, for everyone knew pilots were quite perfectly mad.

"Don't use your credit key."

"All right . . ." She saw how easily she could be traced,

and wished she had not got out of the habit of carrying cash. "Ramona, lend me some money."

Now Ramona did look at Radu, critically. "It would be better if you came with the rest of us." Radu flushed. She was, all too obviously, not speaking to him.

"No, it wouldn't." Laenea's tone was chill. The dim blue light glinted silver from the gray in Ramona's hair as she turned back to Laenea and reached into an inner pocket. She handed her a folded sheaf of bills. "You young ones never plan." Laenea could not be sure what she meant, and she had no chance to ask. Ramona-Teresa turned away and left.

Laenea shoved the money into her pants pocket, annoyed not so much because she had had to ask for it as because Ramona-Teresa had been so sure she would need it.

"She may be right," Radu said slowly. "Pilots, and crew—"

She touched his hand again, rubbing its back, following the ridges of strong fine bones to his wrist. "She shouldn't have been so snobbish. We're none of her business."

"She was . . . I never met anyone like her before. I felt like I was in the presence of someone so different from me—so far beyond—that we couldn't speak together." He grinned, quick flash of strong white teeth behind his shaggy mustache, deep smile lines in his cheeks. "If she'd cared to." With his free hand he stroked her green velvet sleeve. She could feel the beat of his pulse, rapid and upset. As if he had closed an electrical circuit, a pleasurable chill spread up Laenea's arm.

"Radu, did you ever meet a pilot or a crew member who wasn't different from anyone you had ever met before? I haven't. We all start out that way. Transit didn't change Ramona."

He acquiesced with silence only, no more certain of the validity of her assurance than she was.

"For now it doesn't make any difference anyway," Laenea said.

The unhappiness slipped from Radu's expression, the joy came back, but uncertainty remained.

They finished their dinner quietly, in expectation, anticipation, paying insufficient attention to the excellent food. Though annoyed that she had to worry about the subject at all, Laenea considered available ways of preserving her freedom. She wished Kathell Stafford were still on the island, for she of all people could have helped. She had already helped, as usual, without even meaning to.

But the situation was hardly serious; evading the administrators as long as possible was a matter of pride and personal pleasure. "Fools . . ." she muttered.

"They may have a special reason for wanting you to go back," Radu said. Anticipation of the next month flowed through both their minds. "Some problem—some danger."

"They'd've said so."

"Then what do they want?"

"Ramona said it—they want to prove they control us." She drank the last few drops of her brandy; Radu followed suit. They rose and walked together toward the foyer. "They want to keep me packed in styrofoam padding like an expensive machine until I can take my ship."

Andrew awaited them, but as Laenea reached for Ramona-Teresa's money Marc's screen glowed into brilliance. "Your dinner's my gift," he said. "In celebration."

She wondered if Ramona had told him of her problem. He could as easily know from his own sources; or the free meal might be an example of his frequent generosity. "I wonder how you ever make a profit, my friend," she said. "But thank you."

"I overcharge tourists," he said, the mechanical voice so flat that it was impossible to know if he spoke cynically or sardonically or if he were simply joking.

"I don't know where I'm going next," Laenea told him, "but are you looking for anything?"

"Nothing in particular," he said. "Pretty things—" Silver swirled across the screen.

"I know."

The corridors were dazzling after the dim restaurant; Laenea wished for gentle evenings and moonlight. Between cold metal walls, she and Radu walked close together, warm, arms around each other. "Marc collects," Laenea said. "We all bring him things."

"Pretty things."

"Yes . . . I think he tries to bring the nicest bits of all the worlds inside with him. I think he creates his own reality."

"One that has nothing to do with ours."

"Exactly."

"That's what they'd do at the hospital." Radu said. "Isolate you from what you'll have to deal with, and you disagree that that would be valuable."

"Not for me. For Marc, perhaps."

He nodded. "And . . . now?"

"Back to Kathell's for a while at least." She reached up and rubbed the back of his neck. His hair tickled her hand. "The rule I disagreed with most while I was in training was the one that forbade me any sex at all."

The smile lines appeared again, bracketing his mouth parallel to his drooping mustache, crinkling the skin around his eyes. "I understand entirely," he said, "why you aren't anxious to go back."

Entering her room in Kathell's suite, Laenea turned on the lights. Mirrors reflected the glow, bright niches among red plush and gold trim. She and Radu stood together on the silver surfaces, hands clasped, for a moment as hesitant as children. Then Laenea turned to Radu, and he to her; they ignored the actions of the mirrored figures. Laenea's hands on the sides of Radu's face touched his scarred cheeks; she kissed him lightly, again, harder. His mustache was soft and bristly against her lips, against her tongue. His hands tightened over her shoulder blades, moved down. He held her gently. She slipped one hand between their bodies, beneath his jacket, stroking his bare skin, tracing the taut muscles of his back, his waist, his hip. His breathing quickened.

At the beginning nothing was different—but nothing was the same. The change was more important than motions, positions, endearments; Laenea had experienced those in all their combinations, content with involvement for a few moments' pleasure. That had always been satisfying and sufficient; she had never suspected the potential for evolution that depended on the partners. Leaning over Radu, with her hair curling down around their faces, looking into his smiling blue eyes, she felt close enough to him to absorb his thoughts and sense his soul. They caressed each other leisurely, concentrating on the sensations between them. Laenea's nipples hardened, but instead of throbbing they tingled. Radu moved against her and her excitement heightened suddenly, irrationally, grasping her, shaking her. She gasped but could not force the breath back out. Radu kissed her shoulder, the base of her throat, stroked her stomach, drew his hand up her side, cupped her breast.

"Radu—"

Her climax was sudden and violent, a clasping wave contracting all through her as her single thrust pushed Radu's hips down against the mattress. He was startled into a climax of his own as Laenea shuddered involuntarily, straining against him, clasping him to her, unable to catch his rhythm. But neither of them cared.

They lay together, panting and sweaty.

"Is that part of it?" His voice was unsteady.

"I guess so." Her voice, too, showed the effects of surprise. "No wonder they're so quiet about it."

"Does it—is your pleasure decreased?" He was ready to be angry for her.

"No, that's not it, it's—" She started to say that the pleasure was tenfold greater, but remembered the start of their loveplay, before she had been made aware of just how many of her rhythms were rearranged. The beginning had nothing to do with the fact that she was a pilot. "It was fine." A lame adjective. "Just unexpected. And you?"

He smiled. "As you say—unexpected. Surprising. A little . . . frightening."

"Frightening?"

"All new experiences are a little frightening. Even the very enjoyable ones. Or maybe those most of all."

Laenea laughed softly.

They lay wrapped in each other's arms. Laenea's hair curled around to touch the corner of Radu's jaw, and her heel was hooked over his calf. She was content for the moment with silence, stillness, touch. The plague had not scarred his body.

In the aquaria, the fish flitted back and forth before dim lights, spreading blue shadows across the bed. Laenea breathed deeply, counting to make the breaths even. Breathing is a response, not a rhythm, a reaction to levels of carbon dioxide in blood and brain; Laenea's breathing had to be altered only during transit itself. For now she used it as an artificial rhythm of concentration. Her heart raced with excitement and adrenalin, so she began to slow it, to relax. But something disturbed her control: the rate and blood pressure slid down slightly, then slowly slid back up. She could hear nothing but a dull ringing in her inner ears. Perspiration formed on her forehead, in her armpits, along her spine. Her heart had never before failed to respond to conscious control.

Angry, startled, she pushed herself up, flinging her hair back from her face. Radu raised his head, tightening his hand around the point of her shoulder. "What—?"

He might as well have been speaking underwater. Laenea lifted her hand to silence him.

One deep inhalation, hold; exhale, hold. She repeated the sequence, calming herself, relaxing voluntary muscles. Her hand fell to the bed. She lay back. Repeat the sequence, again. Again. In the hospital and since, her control over involuntary muscles had been quick and sure. She began to be afraid, and had to imagine the fear evaporating, dissipating. Finally the arterial muscles began to respond. They lengthened, loosened, expanded. Last the pump answered her commands as she recaptured and reproduced the indefinable states of self-control.

When she knew her blood pressure was no longer likely to crush her kidneys or mash her brain, she opened her eyes. Above, Radu watched, deep lines of worry across his forehead. "Are you—?" He was whispering.

She lifted her heavy hand and stroked his face, his eyebrows, his hair. "I don't know what happened, I couldn't get control for a minute. But I have it back now." She drew his hand across her body, pulling him down beside her, and they relaxed again and dozed.

Later, Laenea took time to consider her situation. Returning to the hospital would be easiest; it was also the least attractive alternative. Remaining free, adjusting without interference to the changes, meeting the other pilots, showing Radu what was to be seen: outwitting the administrators would be more fun. Kathell had done them a great favor, for without her apartment Laenea would have rented a hotel suite. The records would have been available, a polite messenger would have appeared to ask her respectfully to come along. Should she overpower an innocent hireling and disappear laughing? More likely she would have shrugged and gone. Fights had never given her either excitement or pleasure. She knew what things she would not do, ever, though she did not know what she would do now. She pondered.

"Damn them," she said.

His hair as damp as hers, after their shower, Radu sat down facing her. The couches, of course, were both too low. Radu and Laenea looked at each other across two sets of knees draped in caftans that clashed violently. Radu lay back on the cushions, chuckling. "You look much too un-dignified for anger."

She leaned toward him and tickled a sensitive place she had discovered. "I'll show you undignified—" He twisted away and batted at her hand but missed, laughing help-lessly. When Laenea relented, she was lying on top of him on the wide, soft couch. Radu unwound from a defensive curl, watching her warily, laugh lines deep around his eyes and mouth.

"Peace," she said, and held up her hands. He relaxed. Laenea picked up a fold of the material of her caftan with one of his. "Is anything more undignified than the two of us in colors no hallucination would have—and giggling as well?"

"Nothing at all." He touched her hair, her face. "But what made you so angry?"

"The administrators—their red tape. Their infernal tests." She laughed again, this time bitterly. " 'Undignified'—some of those tests would win on that."

"Are they necessary? For your health?"

She told him about the hypnotics, the sedatives, the sleep, the time she had spent being obedient. "Their redundancies have redundancies. If I weren't healthy I'd be back out on the street wearing my old heart. I'd be . . . nothing."

"Never that."

But she knew of people who had failed as pilots, who were reimplanted with their own saved hearts, and none of them had ever flown again, as pilots, as crew, as passengers. *"Nothing."*

He was shaken by her vehemence. "But you're all right. You're who you want to be and what you want to be."

"I'm angry at inconvenience," she admitted. "I want to be the one who shows you Earth. They want me to spend the next month shuttling between cinderblock cubicles. And I'll have to if they find me. My freedom's limited." She felt very strongly that she needed to spend the next month in the real world, neither hampered by experts who knew, truly, nothing, nor misdirected by controlled environments. She did not know how to explain the feeling; she thought it must be one of the things pilots tried to talk about during their hesitant, unsyncopated conversations with their insufficient vocabularies. "Yours isn't, though, you know."

"What do you mean?"

"Sometimes I come back to Earth and never leave the port. It's like my home. It has everything I want or need. I can easily stay a month and never see an administrator nor have to admit receiving a message I don't want." Her fingertips moved back and forth across the ridge of new tissue over her breastbone. Somehow it was a comfort, though the scar was the symbol of what had cut her off from her old friends. She needed new friends now, but she felt it would be stupid and unfair to ask Radu to spend his first trip to Earth on an artificial island. "I'm going to stay here. But you don't have to. Earth has a lot of sights worth seeing."

He did not answer. Laenea raised her head to look at him. He was intent and disturbed. "Would you be offended," he said, "if I told you I am not very interested in historical sights?"

"Is this what you really want? To stay with me?"

"Yes. Very much."

Laenea led Radu through the vast apartment to the swimming pool. Flagstones surrounded a pool with sides and bottom of intricate mosaic that shimmmered in the dim light. This was a grotto more than a place for athletic events or children's noisy beach ball games.

Radu sighed; Laenea brushed her hand across the top of his shoulder, questioning.

"Someone spent a great deal of time and care here," he said.

"That's true." Laenea had never thought of it as the work of someone's hands, individual and painstaking, though of course it was exactly that. But the economic structure of her world was based on service, not production, and she had always taken the results for granted.

They took off their caftans and waded down the steps into body-warm water. It rose smooth and soothing around the persistent soreness of Laenea's ribs.

"I'm going to soak for a while." She lay back and floated, her hair drifting out, a strand occasionally drifting back to brush her shoulder, the top of her spine. Radu's voice rumbled through the water, incomprehensible, but she glanced over and saw him waving toward the dim far end of the pool. He flopped down in the water and thrashed energetically away, retreating to a constant background noise. All sounds faded, gaining the same far-away quality, like audio slow-motion. Something was strange, wrong . . . Laenea began to tense up again. She turned her attention to the warmth and comfort of the water, to urging the tension out of her body through her shoulders, down her outstretched arms, out the tips of spread fingers. But when she paid attention again, something still was wrong. Tracing unease, slowly and deliberately, going back so far in memory that she was no longer a pilot (it seemed a long time), she realized that though she had become well and easily accustomed to the silence of her new heart, to the lack of a pulse, she had been listening unconsciously for the echo of the beat, the double or triple reverberation from throat and wrists, from femoral artery, all related by the same heartbeat, each perceived at a slightly different time during moments of silence.

She thought she might miss that, just a little, for a little while.

Radu finished his circumnavigation of the pool; he swam under her and the faint turbulence stroked her back. Laenea let her feet sink to the pool's bottom and stood up as Radu burst out of the water, a very amateur dolphin, hair dripping in his eyes, laughing. They waded toward each other through the retarding chest-deep water and embraced. Radu kissed Laenea's throat just at the corner of her jaw; she threw her head back like a cat stretching to prolong the pleasure, moving her hands up and down his sides.

"We're lucky to be here so early," he said softly, "alone before anyone else comes."

"I don't think anyone else is staying at Kathell's right now," Laenea said. "We have the pool to ourselves all the time."

"This is . . . this belongs to her?"

"The whole apartment does."

He said nothing, embarrassed by his error.

"Never mind," Laenea said. "It's a natural mistake to make." But it was not, of course, on Earth.

Laenea had visited enough new worlds to understand how Radu could be uncomfortable in the midst of the private possessions and personal services available on Earth.

What impressed him was expenditure of time, for time was the valuable commodity in his frame of reference. On Twilight everyone would have two or three necessary jobs, and none would consist of piecing together intricate mosaics. Everything was different on Earth.

They paddled in the shallow end of the pool, reclined on the steps, flicked shining spray at each other. Laenea wanted Radu again. She was completely free of pain for the first time since the operation. That fact began to overcome a certain reluctance she felt, an ambivalence toward her new reactions. The violent change in her sexual responses disturbed her more than she wanted to admit.

And she wondered if Radu felt the same way; she discovered she was afraid he might.

In the shallow water beside him, she moved closer and kissed him. As he put his arm around her she slipped her hand across his stomach and down to his genitals, somehow less afraid of a physical indication of reluctance than a verbal one. But he responded to her, hardening, drawing circles on her breast with his fingertips, caressing her lips with his tongue. Laenea stroked him from the back of his knee to his shoulder. His body had a thousand textures, muted and blended by the warm water and the steamy air. She pulled him closer, across the mosaic step, grasping him with her legs. They slid together easily. Radu entered her with little friction between them. This time Laenea anticipated a long, slow increase of excitement.

"What do you like?" Radu whispered.

"I—I like—I" Her words changed abruptly to a gasp. Imagination exaggerated nothing: the climax again came all at once in a powerful solitary wave. Radu's fingers dug into her shoulders, and though Laenea knew her short nails were cutting his back, she could not ease the wire-taut muscles of her hands. Radu must have expected the intensity and force of Laenea's orgasm, but the body is slower to learn than the mind. He followed her to climax almost instantly, in solitary rhythm that continued, slowed, finally ceased. Trembling against him, Laenea exhaled in a long shudder. She could feel Radu's stomach muscles quiver. The water around them, that had seemed warmer than their bodies, now seemed cool.

Laenea liked to take more time with sex, and she suspected that Radu did as well. Yet she felt exhilarated. Her thoughts about Radu were bright in her mind, but she could put no words to them. Instead of speaking she laid her hand on the side of his face, fingertips at the temple, the palm of her hand against deep scars. He no longer flinched when she touched him there, but covered her hand with his.

He had about him a quality of constancy, of dependability and calm, that Laenea had never before encountered. His admiration for her was of a different sort entirely than what she was used to: grounders' lusting after status and vicarious excitement. Radu had seen her and stayed with her when she was as helpless and ordinary and undignified as a human being can be; that had not changed his feelings. Laenea did not understand him yet.

They toweled each other dry. Radu's hip was scraped from the pool steps, and he had long scratches down his back.

"I wouldn't have thought I could do that," Laenea said. She glanced at her hands, nails shorter than fingertips, cut just above the quick. "I'm sorry."

Radu reached around to dry her back. "I did the same to you."

"Really?" She looked over her shoulder. The angle was wrong to see anything, but she could feel places stinging. "We're even, then." She grinned. "I never drew blood before."

"Nor I."

They dressed in clean clothes from Kathell's wardrobes and went walking through the multileveled city. It was, as Radu had said, very early. Above on the sea it would be nearing dawn. Below only street cleaners and the drivers of delivery carts moved here and there across a mall. Laenea was more accustomed to the twenty-four-hour crew city in the second stabilizer.

She was getting hungry enough to suggest a shuttle trip across to #2, where everything would be open, when ahead they saw waiters arranging the chairs of a sidewalk café, preparing for business.

"Seven o'clock," Radu said. "That's early to open around here, it seems."

"How do you know what time it is?"

He shrugged. "I don't know how, but I always know."

"Twilight's day isn't even standard."

"I had to convert for a while, but now I have both times."

A waiter bowed and ushered them to a table. They

breakfasted and talked, telling each other about their home worlds and about places they had visited. Radu had been to three other planets before Earth. Laenea knew two of them, from several years before. They were colonial worlds, which had grown and changed since her visits.

Laenea and Radu compared impressions of crewing, she still fascinated by the fact that he dreamed.

She found herself reaching out to touch his hand, to emphasize a point or for the sheer simple pleasure of contact. And he did the same, but they were both right-handed and a floral centerpiece occupied the center of their table. Finally Laenea picked up the vase and moved it to one side, and she and Radu held left hands across the table.

"Where do you want to go next?"

"I don't know. I haven't thought about it. I still have to go where they tell me to, when there's a need."

"I just . . ." Laenea's voice trailed off. Radu glanced at her quizzically, and she shook her head. "It sounds ridiculous to talk about tomorrow or next week or next month . . . but it feels so right."

"I feel . . . the same."

They sat in silence, drinking coffee. Radu's hand tightened on hers. "What are we going to do?" For a moment he looked young and lost. "I haven't earned the right to make my own schedules."

"I have," Laenea said. "Except for the emergencies. That will help."

He was no more satisfied than she.

"We have a month," Laenea said. "A month not to worry."

Laenea yawned as they entered the front room of Kathell's apartment. "I don't know why I'm so sleepy." She yawned again, trying to stifle it, failing. "I slept the clock around, and now I want to sleep again—after what? Half a day?" She kicked off her boots.

"Eight and a half hours," Radu said. "Somewhat busy hours, though."

She smiled. "True." She yawned a third time, jaw-hinges cracking. "I've got to take a nap."

Radu followed as she padded through the hallways, down the stairs to her room. The bed was made, turned down on both sides. The clothes Laenea and Radu had arrived in were clean and pressed. They hung in the dressing room along with the cloak, which no longer smelled musty. Laenea brushed her fingers across the velvet. Radu looked around. "Who did this?"

"What? The room? The people Kathell hires. They look after whoever stays here."

"Do they hide?"

Laenea laughed. "No—they'll come if we call. Do you need something?"

"No," he said sharply. "No," more gently. "Nothing."

Still yawning, Laenea undressed. "What about you, are you wide awake?"

He was staring into a mirror; he started when she spoke, and looked not at her but at her reflection. "I can't usually sleep during the day," he said. "But I am rather tired."

His reflection turned its back; he, smiling, turned toward her.

They were both too sleepy to make love a third time. The amount of energy Laenea had expended astonished her; she thought perhaps she still needed time to recover from the hospital. She and Radu curled together in darkness and scarlet sheets.

"I do feel very depraved now," Radu said.

"Depraved? Why?"

"Sleeping at nine o'clock in the morning? That's unheard of on Twilight." He shook his head; his mustache brushed her shoulder. Laenea drew his arm closer around her, holding his hand in both of hers.

"I'll have to think of some other awful depraved Earth customs to tempt you with," she said sleepily, chuckling, but thought of none just then.

Later (with no way of knowing how much later) something startled her awake. She was a sound sleeper and could not think what noise or movement would awaken her when she still felt so tired. Lying very still she listened, reaching out for stimuli with all her senses. The lights in the aquaria were out, the room was dark except for the heating coils' bright orange spirals. Bubbles from the aerator, highlighted by the amber glow, rose like tiny half moons through the water.

The beat of a heart pounded through her.

In sleep, Radu still lay with his arm around her. His hand, fingers half curled in relaxation, brushed her left breast. She stroked the back of his hand but moved quietly away from him, away from the sound of his pulse, for it formed the links of a chain she had worked hard and wished long to break.

The second time she woke she was frightened out of sleep, confused, displaced. For a moment she thought she was escaping a nightmare. Her head ached violently from the ringing in her ears, but through the clash and clang she heard Radu gasp for breath, struggling as if to free himself from restraints. Laenea reached for him, ignoring her racing heart. Her fingers slipped on his sweat. Thrashing, he flung her back. Each breath was agony just to hear. Laenea grabbed his arm when he twisted again, held one wrist down, seized his flailing hand, partially immobilized him, straddled his hips, held him.

"Radu!"

He did not respond. Laenea called his name again. She could feel his pulse through both wrists, feel his heart as it pounded, too fast, too hard, irregular and violent.

"Radu!"

He cried out, a piercing and wordless scream.

She whispered his name, no longer even hoping for a response, in helplessness, hopelessness. He shuddered beneath her hands.

He opened his eyes.

"What . . . ?"

Laenea remained where she was, leaning over him. He tried to lift his hand and she realized she was still forcing his arms to the bed. She released him and sat back on her heels beside him. She, too, was short of breath, and hypertensive to a dangerous degree.

Someone knocked softly on the bedroom door.

"Come in!"

One of the aides entered hesitantly. "Pilot? I thought— Pardon me." She bowed and backed out.

"Wait—you did right. Call a doctor immediately."

Radu pushed himself up on his elbows. "No, don't, there's nothing wrong."

The young aide glanced from Laenea to Radu and back to the pilot.

"Are you sure?" Laenea asked.

"Yes." He sat up. Sweat ran in heavy drops down his

temples to the edge of his jaw. Laenea shivered from the coolness of her own evaporating sweat.

"Never mind, then," Laenea said. "But thank you."

The aide departed.

"Gods, I thought you were having a heart attack." Her own heart was beginning to slow in rhythmically varying rotation. She could feel the blood slow and quicken at her temples, in her throat. She clenched her fists reflexively and felt her nails against her palms.

Radu shook his head. "It was a nightmare." His somber expression suddenly changed to a quick but shaky grin. "Not illness. As you said—we're never allowed this job if we're not healthy." He lay back, hands behind his head, eyes closed. "I was climbing, I don't remember, a cliff or a tree. It collapsed or broke and I fell—a long way. I knew I was dreaming and I thought I'd wake up before I hit, but I fell into a river." She heard him and remembered what he said, but knew she would have to make sense of the words later. She remained kneeling and slowly unclenched her hands. Blood rushed through her like a funnelled tide, high, then low, and back again.

"It had a very strong current that swept me along and pulled me under. I couldn't see banks on either side—not even where I fell from. Logs and trash rushed along beside me and past me, but every time I tried to hold onto something I'd almost be crushed. I got tireder and tireder and the water pulled me under—I needed a breath but I couldn't take one . . . have you felt the way the body tries to breathe when you can't let it?"

She did not answer but her lungs burned, her muscles contracted convulsively, trying to clear a way for the air to push its way in.

"Laenea—" She felt him grasp her shoulders: she wanted to pull him closer, she wanted to push him away. Then the change broke the compulsion of his words and she drew deep, searing breath.

"What—?"

"A . . . moment . . ." She managed, finally, to damp the sine-curve velocity of the pump within her. She was shivering. Radu pulled a blanket around her. Laenea's control returned slowly, more slowly than any other time she had lost it. She pulled the blanket closer, seeking stability more than warmth. She should not slip like that: her biocontrol, to now, had always been as close to perfect as anything associated with a biological system could be. But now she felt dizzy and high, hyperventilated, from the needless rush of blood through her brain. She wondered how many millions of nerve cells had been destroyed.

She and Radu looked at each other in silence.

"Laenea . . ." He still spoke her name as if he were not sure he had the right to use it. "What's happening to us?"

"Excitement—" she said, and stopped. "An ordinary nightmare—" She had never tried to deceive herself before, and found she could not start now.

"It wasn't an ordinary nightmare. You always know you're going to be all right, no matter how frightened you are. This time—until I heard you calling me and felt you pulling me to the surface, I knew I was going to die."

Tension grew: he was as afraid to reach toward her as she was to him. She threw off the blanket and grasped his hand. He was startled, but he returned the pressure. They sat crosslegged, facing each other, hands entwined.

"It's possible . . ." Laenea said, searching for a way to say this that was gentle for them both, "it's possible . . . that there is a reason, a real reason, pilots and crew don't mix."

By Radu's expression Laenea knew he had thought of that explanation too, and only hoped she could think of a different one.

"It could be temporary—we may only need acclimatization."

"Do you really think so?"

She rubbed the ball of her thumb across his knuckles. His pulse throbbed through her fingers. "No," she said, almost whispering. Her system and that of any normal human being would no longer mesh. The change in her was too disturbing, on psychological and subliminal levels, while normal biorhythms were so compelling that they interfered with and would eventually destroy her new biological integrity. She would not have believed those facts before now. "I don't. Dammit, I don't."

Exhausted, they could no longer sleep. They rose in miserable silence and dressed, navigating around each other like sailboats in a high wind. Laenea wanted to touch Radu, to hug him, slide her hand up his arm, kiss him and be tickled by his mustache. Denied any of those, not quite by fear but by reluctance, unwilling either to risk her own stability or to put Radu through another nightmare, she understood for the first time the importance of simple, incidental touch, directed at nothing more important than momentary contact, momentary reassurance.

"Are you hungry?" Isolation, with silence as well, was too much to bear.

"Yes . . . I guess so."

But over breakfast (it was, Radu said, midafternoon), the silence fell again. Laenea could not make small talk; if small talk existed for this situation she could not imagine what it might consist of. Radu pushed his food around on his plate and did not look at her: his gaze jerked from the sea wall to the table, to some detail of carving on the furniture, and back again.

Laenea ate fruit sections with her fingers. All the previous worries, how to arrange schedules for time together, how to defuse the disapproval of their acquaintances, seemed trivial and frivolous. The only solution now was a drastic one, which she did not feel she could suggest herself. Radu must have thought of it; that he had said nothing might mean that volunteering to become a pilot was as much an impossibility for him as returning to normal was for Laenea. Piloting was a lifetime decision, not a job one took for a few years' travel and adventure. The way Radu talked about his home world, Laenea believed he wanted to return to a permanent home, not a rest stop.

Radu stood up. His chair scraped against the floor and fell over. Laenea looked up, startled. Flushing, Radu turned, picked up the chair, and set it quietly on its legs again. "I can't think down here," he said. "It never changes." He glanced at the sea wall, perpetual blue fading to blackness. "I'm going on deck. I need to be outside." He turned toward her. "Would you— ?"

"I think . . ." Wind, salt spray on her face: tempting. "I think we'd each better be alone for a while."

"Yes," he said, with gratitude. "I suppose . . ." His voice grew heavy with disappointment. "You're right." His footsteps were soundless on the thick carpet.

"Radu—"

He turned again, without speaking, as though his barriers were forming around him again, still so fragile that a word would shatter them.

"Never mind . . . just . . . oh—take my cape if you want, it's cold on deck in the afternoons."

He nodded once, still silent, and went away.

In the pool Laenea swam hard, even when her ribs began to hurt. She felt trapped and angry, with nowhere to run, knowing no one deserved her anger. Certainly not Radu; not the other pilots, who had warned her. Not even the administrators, who in their own misguided way had tried to make her transition as protected as possible. The anger could go toward herself, toward her strongwilled stubborn character. But that, too, was pointless. All her life she had made her own mistakes and her own successes, both usually by trying what others said she could not do.

She climbed out of the pool without having tired herself in the least. The warmth had soothed away whatever aches and pains were left, and her energy was returning, leaving her restless and snappish. She put on her clothes and left the apartment to walk off her tension until she could consider the problem calmly. But she could not see even an approach to a solution; at least, not to a solution that would be a happy one.

Hours later, when the grounder city had quieted to night again, Laenea let herself into Kathell's apartment. Inside, too, was dark and silent. She could hardly wonder where Radu was: she remembered little enough of what she herself had done since afternoon. She remembered being vaguely civil to people who stopped her, greeted her, invited her to parties, asked for her autograph. She remembered being less than civil to someone who asked how it felt to be an Aztec. But she did not remember which incident preceded the other or when either had occurred or what she had actually said. She was no closer to an answer than before. Hands jammed in her pockets, she went into the main room, just to sit and stare into the ocean and try to think. She was halfway to the sea wall before she saw Radu, standing silhouetted against the window, dark and mysterious in her cloak, the blue light glinting ghostly off his hair.

"Radu—"

He did not turn. Her eyes more accustomed to the dimness, Laenea saw his breath clouding the glass.

"I applied to pilot training," he said softly, his tone utterly neutral.

Laenea felt a quick flash of joy, then uncertainty, then fear for him. She had been ecstatic when the administrators accepted her for training. Radu did not even smile. Making a mistake in this choice would hurt him more, much more, than even parting forever could hurt both of them. "What about Twilight?"

"It doesn't matter," he said, his voice unsteady. "They refused—" He choked on the words and forced them out. "They refused me."

Laenea went to him, put her arms around him, turned him toward her. The fine lines around his blue eyes were deeper, etched by distress and failure. She touched his cheek. Embracing her, he rested his forehead on her shoulder. "They said . . . I'm bound to our own four dimensions. I'm too dependent . . . on night, day, time . . . my circadian rhythms are too strong. They said . . ." His muffled words became more and more unsure, balanced on a shaky edge. Laenea stroked his hair, the back of his neck, over and over. That was the only thing left to do. There was nothing at all left to say. "If I survived the operation . . . I'd die in transit."

Laenea's vision blurred, and the warm tears slipped down her face. She could not remember the last time she had cried. A convulsive sob shook Radu and his tears fell cool on her shoulder, soaking through her shirt. "I love you," Radu whispered. "Laenea, I love you."

"Dear Radu, I love you too." She could not, would not, say what she thought: *That won't be enough for us. Even that won't help us.*

She guided him to a wide low cushion that faced the ocean; she drew him down beside her, neither of them really paying attention to what they were doing, to the cushions too low for them, to anything but each other. Laenea held Radu close. He said something she could not hear.

"What?"

He pulled back and looked at her, his gaze passing rapidly back and forth over her face. "How can you love me? We could only stay together one way, but I failed—" He broke the last word off, unwilling and almost unable to say it.

Laenea slid her hands from his shoulders down his arms and grasped his hands. "You can't fail at this, Radu. The word doesn't mean anything. You can tolerate what they do to you, or you can't. But there's no dishonor."

He shook his head and looked away: he had never, Laenea thought, failed at anything important in his life, at

anything real that he desperately wanted. He was so young
. . . too young to have learned not to blame himself for
what was out of his control. Laenea drew him toward her
again and kissed the outer curve of his eyebrow, his high
cheekbone. Salt stung her lips.

"We can't—" He pulled back, but she held him.

"I'll risk it if you will." She slipped her hand inside the
collar of his shirt, rubbing the tension-knotted muscles at
the back of his neck, her thumb on the pulse-point in his
throat, feeling it beat through her. He spoke her name so
softly it was hardly a sound.

Knowing what to expect, and what to fear, they made
love a third, final, desperate time, exhausting themselves
against each other beside the cold blue sea.

Radu was nearly asleep when Laenea kissed him and left
him, forcibly feigning calm. In her scarlet and gold room
she lay on the bed and pushed away every concern but
fighting her spinning heart, slowing her breathing. She had
not wanted to frighten Radu again, and he could not help
her. Her struggle required peace and concentration. What
little of either remained in her kept escaping before she
could grasp and fix them. They flowed away on the channels of pain, shallow and quick in her head, deep and slow
in the small of her back, above the kidneys, spreading all
through her lungs. Near panic, she pressed the heels of her
hands against her eyes until blood-red lights flashed; she
stimulated adrenalin until excitement pushed her beyond
pain, above it.

Instantly she forced an artificial, fragile calmness that
glimmered through her like sparks.

Her heart slowed, sped up, slowed, sped (not quite so
much this time), slowed, slowed, slowed.

Afraid to sleep, unable to stay awake, she let her hands
fall from her eyes, and drifted away from the world.

In the morning she staggered out of bed, aching as if she
had been in a brawl against a better fighter. In the bathroom she splashed ice water on her face; it did not help.
Her urine was tinged but not thick with blood; she ignored
it.

Radu was gone. He had told the aide he could not sleep,
but he had left no message for Laenea. Nor had he left
anything behind, as if wiping out the traces of himself could

wipe out the loss and pain of their parting. Laenea knew nothing could do that. She wanted to talk to him, touch him—just one more time—and try to show him, insist he understand, that he could not label himself with the title failure. He could not demand of himself what he could break himself—break his heart—attempting.

She called the crew lounge, but he did not answer the page. He had left no message. The operator cross-checked, and told Laenea that Radu Dracul was in the crew hold of A-28493, already prepared for transit.

An automated ship, on a dull run, the first assignment Radu could get: nothing he could have said or done would have told Laenea more clearly that he did not want to see or touch or talk to her again.

She could not stay in Kathell's apartment any longer. She threw on the clothes she had come in; she left the vest open, defiantly, to well below her breastbone, not caring if she were recognized, returned to the hospital, anything.

At the top of the elevator shaft the wind whipped through her hair and snapped the cape behind her. Laenea pulled the black velvet close and waited. When the shuttle came she boarded it, to return to her own city and her own people, the pilots, to live apart with them and never tell their secrets.

Peter Dillingham

The Spirit of Asilomar—will it save us? The 1975 Asilomar conference codified the decisions of a group of molecular biologists who, in 1974, determined that certain lines of genetic research should either be terminated or else placed under stringent safety precautions. The threat is that artificially combined genetic materials from unrelated organisms, whether viral, bacterial or animal, could result in deadly strains resistant or immune to existing medical treatment. As I write this in May 1976, I read in my morning paper of the concern of National Cancer Institute researchers about a successful experiment at the Southwest Institute in San Antonio. The Texas experimenters have produced a new "pseudotype" virus by combining separately harmless (to humans) mouse cancer and baboon viruses. The product is capable of crossing broad species lines to produce tumors. Another chapter in the Biological Revolution begins . . .

Peter Dillingham is a transplanted easterner now living in the west. *Salome Among the Stars and Other SF Poems,* his first volume of poetry, will soon be published.

Oh my America, my new found land.
                    —John Donne

He has broken loose
Our recombinant man
Heir of X-1776
Self-regenerating like a newt
Hyper immunoresponsive
A prototypal homo futurus
Commemorating Asilomar
When creation passed
From God to man

Bound by that prime directive
Containment
We made him purposely flawed
Genetically sabotaged
With extreme sensitivity to UV radiation
To hydro-carbon pollutants
Where else could he possibly survive
Or want to
But in that pristine artificial ecosystem
Of our laboratory
And Adam gifted with a new Eden
A microcosmic recreation
Of that fresh green breast
Of our lost new world

Delivered from his glass cocoon
A stranger vexed and tormented
By the nightmarish incoherence
The failure of this strange land
Of forgotten promise

197

A pustulating
Always healing Frankenstein
Gasping
Cough wracked parody
Of once and future man
Slouching down the dark alleys
Of our ashen cities
Until he is caught
I fear the incorruptibility
Of the vision we programmed him with
The impossible dreams
He may resurrect
The futile hope . . .

THE BIOLOGICAL REVOLUTION

Robert E. Vardeman and Jeff Slaten

This is the first of two collaborative short stories in 2076. Bob Vardeman is a native Texan now living in Albuquerque. Having degrees in physics and nuclear engineering, he worked for four years in the solid state physics department of Sandia Laboratories. These days he's turned to writing full-time, producing novels both under his own name and as part of a popular pseudonymous adventure series. Jeff Slaten is another Albuquerque resident. Under his alter-ego identity of Sir Bien, he is a practicing member of the Society for Creative Anachronism. That means he recreates the medieval past without recourse to a time machine.

THE BIOLOGICAL REVOLUTION

*July 4, 2076, Speech given by Bren Edwards, MCP, Ph.D.,
at the launch site of the First Interstellar Colonisation
Fleet, White Sands, New Mexico, USA:* Thank you, Madam
President, for the kind introduction. And thank you, people of the United States, for your interest in the words of
an aged historian.

I am doubly honored to be speaking to you on this great
occasion, the three hundredth anniversary of our nation's
founding. First, because I know that every American, including myself, is thrilled at the prospect of our Tricentennial. And second, because I, more than anyone, have a
unique appreciation of what this day commemorates—for I
was there when it happened!

I have stood in awe watching the battles of Concord
and Lexington. I have personally witnessed Washington
struggling against overwhelming odds and adversity such
as we, in the twenty-first century, can only vaguely comprehend. I have seen fifty-six men sign the Declaration of
Independence from England!

January 6, 2047, Excerpts from the Journal of Bren Edwards: I'm so excited that words fail me. Today, my application to the Department of Science was approved! I, of
all my colleagues, will be granted the privilege of traveling
back through time and witnessing firsthand the events of
the American Revolution!

Oh, how I envied Bartleson when he was granted Fourteenth Century France, and McPherson when he was given
Seventeenth Century Britain. But my years of diligent
work have not gone unnoticed, it seems. The panel was
unanimous in its decision—Eighteenth Century North
America is all mine!

I can hardly believe it! Me, a relatively obscure professor

with nothing to my credit but thirty years of research into American history being chosen to walk with the great men of our past.

Who would have believed such a wonderful thing could happen, even a mere two decades ago? History was considered a dead subject, a field for scholars to amuse themselves with among dusty tomes of muddled lore! But with the advent of Proctor's time displacement equipment, it's finally being given the attention it so richly deserves. Now, perhaps for the first time in history, man can learn from his mistakes because he will be able to see them firsthand.

July 4, 2076, White Sands: It is nothing short of fantastic that the spirit of America has not died since those perilous days in the 1770's and '80's. If anything, it has grown stronger, for in those days we were divided, though not in courage—Americans have never lacked that. We were divided in loyalty.

The Tories were not the evil men so often portrayed. Benedict Arnold, with whom I have talked, was a traitor by the strict definition of the word, but he acted from an inner sense of duty. He did what he thought best for the country. In his own way, he typifies the best of our American characteristics for he acted selflessly. He did not benefit from his acts; he did what his conscience told him was the best for our country.

His mistake, however, made little impact on our early forces. The revolutionaries were firm enough of will to overcome any adversity. And they triumphed just as surely as this country suffered and triumphed over two civil wars. Slavery split the country asunder in the 1860's. Religion brought son to father's throat in 2010. But we survived both, and grew stronger, more unified.

This is America, the land of the free and the home of the brave! It was built on the shoulders of great men like Washington, John and Samuel Adams, and Thomas Jefferson, on the quiet bravery of Crispus Attucks, the firm resolve of Abe Lincoln, and the justice of Watson. The list is long, my fellow Americans.

June 10, 2051, the Journal of Bren Edwards: I never realised that preparing for temporal displacement took so long. The scientists at Cal Tech have been hammering in lessons that seem strange to me, an historian. The NEBULA II computer has been lecturing to me about the language difference probabilities until I find myself slipping into colonial English without even meaning to. 'Tis marvelous!

I still know nothing of the mechanics of Proctor's time machine. But then, I'm not sure I'd even want to know what makes the eye-crossing wheels spin and seem to vanish into eternity.

But the scientists know what they're talking about. I've seen the NEBULA II computer projections on time dislocations, or so they call them. I call them time botches. Creating a time botch is a frightening prospect. If I alter the fabric of history, the computer says I might start what's called a positive temporal energy feedback loop and destroy the world as I know it!

Small botches seem acceptable, though. Temporal inertia assures that such changes will soon vanish as if they'd never existed. But Dr. Taragon and his crew have spent over four years teaching me how to avoid meddling.

With luck, I will be allowed to make a preliminary excursion back to the eighteenth century in a few more months. It's odd, though. I cannot escape the feeling, somehow, that it will escape if I don't get back there soon. But of course, that's nonsense. Too, I have the *exclusive* privilege of traveling there. The NEBULA and Taragon both say that two people in the same century and place form a synergistic combination that could bring about a dozen botches of monumental proportions. Imagine Latvia conquering the world or blowing up the moon!

July 4, 2076, White Sands: Who could have imagined that, from our humble beginnings as a country in 1776, we would grow to be the most powerful country in the history of the world? Our impetuosity has been tempered, our curiosity and bravery have been honed to a fine edge. We have colonised the moon, and managed to reach Mars and establish a permanent outpost even in the middle of the Third World War. And now, showing that the pioneer spirit still lives, the Starmaster and fourteen companion interstellar ships orbit 37,500 kilometers above us, preparing to leave for the very stars!

August 3, 2051, the Journal of Bren Edwards: It was a hard decision for me to make. Where did I want to go on my first jaunt into the past? It seemed such an easy question when I was given the grant four and a half years ago. But of late, I'm uncertain. I want to see it all! I finally decided to start on a relatively quiet event, but one that would shape this entire country's destiny: the birth of Benjamin Franklin. I told Dr. Taragon to set the machine for January 17, 1706, the Boston, Massachusetts colony.

The instant of transition left me dazed, confused, and stumbling like a drunk. The first thing I noticed was a change in odor from the oily smell of the time machine to that of eighteenth century Boston, which did not have the benefits of modern sewers. No one seemed to notice when I appeared on the street less than two blocks from the Commons. I oriented myself and hurried to the tallow chandler shop of the Franklins. It seemed fitting that a crowd gathered in the store, muttering softly in the way of all crowds, no matter what the century or place.

Such an auspicious birth required guns firing in salute, fireworks flaring! But none of the people could possibly know that young Ben would mature into the most astute statesman of the century, a true Renaissance Man.

Just then, a plump woman burst out the front door, wailing and crying incoherently. It took several minutes to calm her down enough to speak. My heart almost ceased when I heard what she said.

The baby had been stillborn.

July 4, 2076, White Sands: Yes, America is the greatest country on earth. Our citizens have comforts undreamed of in the past. And we've been generous with our bounty. We've helped the other countries of the world to create the closest thing to a lasting peace that has ever existed on the face of the earth.

This is not to say there aren't problems. Even in our wonderful land there are problems. We do not have the smog and pollution rampant in the nineteenth and twentieth centuries; fusion power has freed us from those bonds. There is no starvation, but some of our citizens live at only subsistence level. But we have created a two-edged sword of Damocles.

At the birth of our nation, the infant mortality rate was approximately nine per cent. At our hundredth anniversary it had dropped to 2.2 per cent. Our vast medical technology has reduced this to a mere 1.2 per cent. But in this saving of lives is the hidden danger which now plagues us. Population growth is the challenge of the century. We continue to expand, now, to the stars, but not quickly enough.

August 3, 2051, the Journal of Bren Edwards (continued): I was shocked. I spent three hours wandering the streets of Boston soaking in the "feel" of the city. But the horror gripping me increased. Benjamin Franklin had died at birth. My entire reputation was based on this great man's exploits, his scientific discoveries, his political life, even the conflicts he felt when his son decided to remain loyal to the King of England. What had happened? Franklin dead!?

I covered my shock upon returning by telling Taragon that the temporal displacement had been more of a jolt than I had anticipated. But my mind seethed. What had happened? What *would* happen? The history books all told of Franklin's birth, his life, his death. *My* books among them.

The realisation of what must be done slowly dawned on me.

July 4, 2076, White Sands: As I look out over the assembled crowd in front of me, the last of the shuttle craft for the majestic Starfleet standing proud behind, I am humbled. I am also proud. Proud to be a part of this great country, this country with a history of overcoming even the mightiest of obstacles. Like no other nation in the world, the United States of America is famous for *doing* while others merely dreamed.

October 12, 2051, the Journal of Bren Edwards: The decision wasn't easy to reach. I've spent many sleepless nights wondering if I should tell Taragon of my shocking discovery, or program my findings into the NEBULA II. But somehow, I think neither he nor the computer would understand. This is a human decision. And all mine. If this journal ever finds its way into another's hand, may God prove me right in my actions. If not, then let me be forever damned.

November 18, 2051, the Journal of Bren Edwards: I finally started the wheels turning today. It has taken considerable preparation and research, and much soul searching, but I finally did it. I went to one of the most illegal of all twenty-first century businesses—black market cloning.

The concept of cloning has always somewhat disturbed

me. The very thought that someone could take the merest fragment of living tissue from a person and "grow" a complete genetic duplicate of him in a matter of weeks feels almost blasphemous. Certainly frightening.

And it makes some sense that cloning has been outlawed. We are overpopulated. The proposed starships, if and when they ever come to completion, will bleed off thousands, perhaps even millions, but that will not be enough.

Like all things illegal, there is always somewhere to go. In this case, the 32-Flavours Ice Cream Parlor. I entered and went through the underworld ritual of passwords, told them what I wanted (but not why), paid an outrageous sum, let them nick my arm for the necessary cells, and then left. The clone will be the size of a newborn baby by this New Year's. I can only trust to God Almighty that the creature grown from my very own flesh will never be torn by any dilemma such as that which now prevents me from peaceful sleep.

July 4, 2076, White Sands: Davy Crockett had a motto that I would like to pass on to you; he said, "Make sure you're right, then go ahead." Simple words? Perhaps. And yet, those words describe our entire history. Sometimes, we would become impetuous and get slapped in the face for it; but then we would remember, and benefit. When other countries stormed and fought, we stopped, and made sure, and then we stepped in to end the nuclear conflict of World War Three. Who but America could fashion its political practice on the simple but wise words of a humble trapper?

January 23, 2052, the Journal of Bren Edwards: The cosmetic pre-programming took longer than expected with the clone. Even at my ripe old age I have a full head of hair. Also, I am a fraction over two meters in height, which few people were then. Ben Franklin was balding by age thirty, and certainly under a hundred and eighty centimeters tall. Having the eyes altered to make him a bit nearsighted puzzled the clone makers, but I clearly specified that no questions were to be asked, and they complied. For a price, but they complied.

The time machine crew never gave a second thought to the small black bag I carried. In it was the clone child in a drug-induced state of suspended animation. I gave Dr.

Taragon the total mass for myself and the package, and he went about his work setting the controls.

I had been watching them for years, and I knew what to do. The second I had the opportunity, I reset their time controls from my specified April 10, 1774 to January 17, 1706. It went totally unnoticed, because I was dropped back to the rear of the Franklins' chandlery at the very same instant my younger self was appearing out on the Commons.

This time, I rushed up the back stairs to the woman in labor. Benjamin had just been born, and the midwife had begun her bawling at seeing the blue face. I don't remember exactly what I said. I shouted her out of the room, took the baby, and put my clone in its place. A hot compress on its forehead and a swift slap to its bottom for verisimilitude completed my mission. Benjamin Franklin was squalling and alive. My clone.

When I returned to my own time line, I immediately started railing at poor Dr. Taragon for missetting the controls and sending me back to the same time as before. I painted a picture of myself running to hide just as my other, earlier self walked by on his/my way to the Franklins'. I said that in the process, I had lost my satchel, and feigned fear that a time botch might occur if anyone found a twenty-first century product, even one crafted for the period.

Taragon apologised, though I think he was suspicious. I had to testify before the Time Committee that I was probably in the way during preparation, and therefore distracting. Fortunately, he was given no reprimand and was allowed to return to his regular post at the time machine. For that, I am glad. Taragon's a good man.

July 4, 2076, White Sands: Our history is laced with the noble deeds of individuals. Yet even more, it is the record of an entire nation's nobility. The old saying, "A chain is as strong as its weakest link" shows just how vital the man on the street, the common citizen is, to America. His courage has kept us free. Indeed, it is a slander to even say "common citizen." Our citizens have shown throughout history just how very uncommon they are.

February 29, 2052, the Journal of Bren Edwards: It's taken me a month to realise that Franklin's stillbirth might not be unique. Under the guise of taking a couple of months off to recover from the shock of existing simultaneously with myself, I've had plenty of time to consider this. It worries me more and more.

I've learned the hard way how intricate it is preventing major time botches. I need not worry about the clones carrying over any of my memories somatically. There is nothing but a vague, misty remembrance of a former life, or so I'm told. At the very worst, my clones might become known as visionaries. Something the clone maker said does bother me, however.

I had never known before that I carried XYY chromosomes. All my clones will carry this stigma, this social unreliability. And yet I wonder. Might this not be the very quality needed to insure a rebellious nature and guarantee the outcome I so desperately seek? And might not the presence of several clones, all with XYY chromosomes, make the revolution absolutely inevitable!?

I don't dare check beforehand to see if any of the others in history were stillborn, or even not born at all. By checking, I would determine history. And I dare not bind history to the non-existence of any of its great men.

The decision wasn't easy, but I finally made it. I've gone back to the ice cream store many times. And, in direct violation of the rules, I've smuggled a small Utility-Medkit with me on my trips. Using it, I've anesthetized fifty-five women, surgically implanted my fetus clones in fifty-five wombs, and guaranteed that fifty-five healthy pregnancies occurred to my specifications. Learning to use the Medkit was no problem. I grew so proficient with it after a time, that it took me mere minutes to perform each operation and be gone before I was discovered in the act.

But as easy as it is to be a doctor with computer-controlled equipment, I find that I'm simply not emotionally suited to being a gynecologist. And as if that were not enough, I had to live with the knowledge that each one of the women would in essence be mother to another version of me. A version genetically tampered with to resemble none of the other versions, true, but basically each one still me. I would have to rely solely on environment for differences in character.

I was very glad when I had finished.

Only after all this could I journey farther into the eighteenth century; only then could I hope it would follow the course the history books said that it did.

I was heartened to find the arrow of time flying swiftly to the target I knew. I had succeeded.

July 4, 2076, White Sands: They were the propertied class, but they represented the opinions of freedom-loving men everywhere. Fifty-six patriots, including such prominent men as Benjamin Franklin, Thomas Jefferson, Richard Henry Lee, John Hancock, Samuel and John Adams, made the decision with the backing of the Continental Congress and thirteen colonies—states!—to declare independence and form the New World's first democracy. Their words ring down through the corridors of time, and will live forever as long as there are men; "We hold these truths to be self-evident, that all men are created equal . . . !"

ONE ROAD TO DAMASCUS

James Sallis and David Lunde

There is no nuclear disaster in this story, no worldwide famine, no pollution doom, no giant spiders or purple Spican menaces; none of the traditional bogeycreatures of dystopian writing. Yet I find this a chiller vision than most I've lately read. It is the second collaborative effort in this book. David Lunde is an often-published American poet and editor of the Basilisk Press. He is currently Associate Professor of English at the State University College, Fredonia, New York. James Sallis, once editor of *New Worlds*, has written the story collection *A Few Last Words*.

For those readers lax in their Sunday school lessons, Damascus was the scene of St. Paul's conversion.

ONE ROAD TO DAMASCUS

We can't appraise the time in which we act.
　　　　　　　　　　　　　—Robert Frost,
　　　　　　　　　　　　　　"Lesson for Today"

Dr. Samuel Cutler sat in an outer office somewhere in the leviathan belly of Sowhat Enterprises, counting his change from pocket to pocket and watching the huge gilt-and-enamel clock boom through the minutes towards three. Submissive, subsumed.

Periodically Miss Berth (the desk placard read), Alexander Sowhat's confidential secretary (that was the rest of the placard), rose from behind the organ-like banks of recording and processing machines to enter the (he supposed, smaller) inner office. Moments later she would come prowling silently back, smile and shake her small head apologetically, take her seat at the scooped-out console, then, fingers poised on the upbeat, fall of a sudden to her steeplechase scherzo.

Dr. Cutler had been here since ten. At ten-thirty a voice had spoken somewhere inside his skull (subaudial? newave?): "Time for coffee, time for tea. Time for talk and amity." The building's music had phased subtly out of its sprightly tempos into a new smoothness, a murmur of soothing, glissando melodies (the manufacture of which occupied some small part of Composoflex's time in the basement complex): pianissimo, inviting talk. Doors opened like floodgates and workers gushed into the outer office, an Autoservit scurrying behind them. Mistaking him for one of the staff perhaps, the machine pushed into Cutler's hand a coffee. He hated coffee but drank it, gulping, from a peculiar respect for gratuitous events, then dropped the cup into one of the many chutes. Sundered from all but the waiting, wholly adrift, his mind idly traced

213

the cup's route through subterranean veins, the Undercity capillaries like cylindrical spiderwebs. Down through them, ever and ever deeper into the vast maze of intersecting flush-tubing and finally into the Sequoia-size bowels—to the vats, where it would join the pulp of a million suits of clothing, millions of cups and containers and scraps of paper slowly soaking apart in the mild acid, slowly becoming re-formed for others to wear, others to feed again into the 'plexes, others to drink or eat from yet again. And again. And again. *Waste, the great immorality* . . . In his doctoral thesis Cutler had adopted this process—and that slogan—as the final symbol of his society's, his time's, converging forces . . . *Nothing* must be wasted!

At eleven the workers went away, back to their work, vanishing (again like water) into the labyrinthine, plexiglass corridors. Two young men came and waited for a while with him, sitting together across the room and talking quietly, finally leaving their cards and fumbling away down the halls in search of a Guide. He watched them for several minutes as they wandered among the plexiglass panels, growing ever more distorted with the accretion of layer upon layer until, at last, they vanished.

At noon he was served spiced chicken and oatbread from a cart which came rolling down the halls and into the room, halting before him. He ate slowly, relishing every nuance of taste, holding each bite of food in his mouth till it was fully drained of flavor. A card laid alongside the warm ceramic plate begged him to have patience, Mr. Sowhat would be with him shortly. Close inspection revealed it to be a form; the typeface in which his name had been printed across the top was minutely different from that in the body of the message. When he finished and pushed the cart slightly away from him it clicked to life, swiveled about and moved towards the door, which swung open just as the cart reached it.

In the space since noon Dr. Cutler had: changed seats eleven times; drunk four cups of coffee from the lobby servits; been after at least two dozen drinks of water; tied his arms and legs in a variety of unmanageable knots; and narrowly avoided a second break, slipping out of the office against a tide of workers, waiting in the hall and looking away, down the corridors, until (swarming out of the bowl) they left. He had a dim memory of a face pressed close to the glass, looking out at him.

Three now. Not a nibble at the line.

Miss Berth got up for the fourteenth time and went into the inner office (for the twelfth time: the other two were breaks, and she had skipped lunch). Cutler pulled the copyscript from his pocket and read it again. Precise, economical. Employment Central had sent it to him three days ago; he had made the appointment immediately. He wondered now if this was because he'd been *afraid* to hesitate, to act from other than reflex.

> Wanted. Tutor, companion for
> children agd 12, 7. Require
> Ph.D., equivalent. Prefrnce
> gvn to multiple degree, M pre-
> frd, sngle. Apply A. Sowhat,
> Sowhat Enterprises.

"Dr. Cutler. Mr. Sowhat will see you now. This way please."

He stared blankly at her and she had to repeat herself before he shambled to his feet, portfolio under one arm, and allowed himself to be led to the door. As he entered, she was relapsing into her console. He imagined that her hummingbird fingers were about to start some comic overture, all staccato chords and leaping soprano.

It was definitely not smaller. That was the first thing he noticed, his first impression of the inner office.

A gaping highway of a room, bare, flat, stretching away from the door: gray. Colored rugs scattered about at random with chairs and small tables on them, making islands. In one far corner a child's swing depended from the twelve-foot ceiling. The room was trimmed in silver, gleaming against the flat gray walls. The swing was composed of silver chains and something which looked very much like wood. Virtually the entire half of one wall was given over to a window which, judging from its distortion and the smeared surface, could only be glass. Real glass.

Cutler walked down the room towards the desk looming like a tollgate on its horizon. As he neared it, Alexander Sowhat rose from his chair, a bell buoy rolling to a slow wave—and the room suddenly seemed not so large after all. It was not just the size of the man, though that *was* in itself substantial enough, but the air of *presence* about him, which made the room at once subordinate, *his*. Here was a man who gathered everything—image, gesture, object, form —close about him.

Seesaw greeting: Sowhat up, Cutler down. Sowhat stayed on his feet, maintaining what he would likely call "a proper distance". Cutler slid forward in his chair and offered the portfolio.

"That won't be necessary, Dr. Cutler. I'm a blunt man, make a point of it. Don't waste words. *Or* my time—so I'll tell you right off, I've had you investigated—you realize, I hope, the necessity. Less than an hour after your call, I had on my desk all the pertinent facts and information concerning your . . . qualifications. Not prying into your affairs, I hope you understand. Just protecting myself. The organization. Standard procedure."

"Certainly, Mr. Sowhat."

"Sorry to have to keep you waiting so long. Business, you know." He made a vague, expansive gesture about the room then looked, almost sadly, down at the desk, as though he'd forgotten what, under all the papers, forms, and folders, its surface looked like. "Never lets you stop." He looked back up. "Never."

"Yes sir. I understand."

"End of the year, absolute hell on the schedule. But then, I suppose you know something of what that's like. I guess what we do's finally not that different." He waved his hand again, dismissing the matter, which flew away into the corner of the room. "Still, sorry you had to wait.

"EC sent your file over, of course. Seems to be in order and our, ah, checking would appear to corroborate it. Principal degree in history. Auxiliaries in sociology and comparative anthropology. Separate ones—Pragmatic—in Fine Arts, physics . . . In fact, Doctor, I'd call you a modest man. No mention in the dossier of your *honorary* degrees. Perhaps EC overlooked them?"

"No, sir." Leaning forward nervously. An organizational mind such as Sowhat's might read more into the gesture than was intended. Omission to him could well be confusing, enigmatic; indicating inefficiency or (in this case, more likely) some attempt at deception. "It's just that they don't really mean much. I didn't bother putting them in the file, didn't think they could matter."

"No, I suppose not . . ." Sowhat reached down to his desk and riffled the edge of a stack of papers there. "Might even prejudice some people. Still, I'm surprised at EC. For missing them. Not like EC at all."

Cutler paused. "I have a friend there . . ."

"A former student of yours?"

He nodded. Resigned. "For a few months." He raised his head, started to say something, then looked down again.

"Don't worry. He's safe. We covered for him." Cutler looked back up just in time to catch Sowhat's smile before he went on: "I must say, though, it's quite surprising to find a man of such manifest drive and, ah, efficiency, outside the business world. Shame you never joined us. Our loss; you could have gone a long way." He touched the papers again. Corners clicked together and Cutler could tell from the sound that they were neither plastifilm nor synthesized pulp, but actually wood-derived. "The most we'd hoped for was, say, an M.A., something like that. Afraid we'd have a hell of a time finding *that*, after we found out Harvard had closed down finally."

"There aren't many of us left." Cutler hooked one angular knee over the other and hugged the portfolio into his lap. His eyes strayed to the thin silver chains supporting the swing.

"No, I guess not. And they're all pretty old by now. Or dead. A young man like you . . ." For a moment Sowhat stood behind the desk like a Gorgon, regarding Cutler. Then he smiled. "I guess the hypnotechs and comp-plexes pretty much did away with your kind. Man can learn something he needs for a job, really learn it just the way he'll be doing it, and it takes just a night, maybe two, while he's sleeping—or dial through the 'plexes for information, get just what he needs—he doesn't have much use for the old ways. Teachers and so on, they're not much good far as he's concerned."

Sowhat remained silent for several moments, staring down at the papers on his desk.

" 'Subtler dangers', Doctor? I think we all realize that; the same way people used to realize what cigarette smoking meant to them, personally—but they didn't stop smoking because of it. The hypnotechs break down a few of the old channels in his mind, I guess a man's willing to take the chance, for what he gets from it. And it's the same for the specialists. If prolonged exposure to threshold consciousness makes for schizoid tendencies, or modifies motor control, or all the rest that the Learners claim—he's willing to accept that, he figures it all balances out. And besides, it's necessary. Our society just got too complex to work any other way; it had to randomize and organize at the same time, and the 'plexes showed the way. They saved us, Dr. Cutler; saved our society. More than that: they made it possible to go on. To progress. And if it's a mixed blessing it's still a blessing, and the mix is a good one. The 'plexes, 'techs, they were inevitable. They're also the best thing that ever happened to us."

He spread his hand flat on top of the papers. Cutler waited.

"Credit where it's due, though; I believe in that. And it's scholars, people like you that made it all possible. Did all the groundwork, organization, so the Comps could be programmed."

Again, he paused, looking down at Cutler and smiling, as though in a kind of sympathy. How many hearts, how many kidneys had this man used up, Cutler wondered; how many times had that face been shaped back around the bones? For a man to rise to his position would take more than intelligence, will, character: it would also take many decades of perseverance, of struggling upwards millimeter by millimeter, of waiting—and it had been "Sowhat Enterprises" for as long as he remembered. This man would have to be well over one hundred . . . Cutler looked back at the chains on the swing.

"Pretty hard on you, I guess. You spend all that time, put all that work into getting something, then there's nothing to do with it; all the reasons jerked out from under you. Progress, though: we've all got to make a few adjustments. Our own decisions. But a man who works that hard for something, he could do a lot for the business world. And a lot for himself at the same time."

"Yes, sir. But I knew fairly well what I was doing. What was happening." Cutler's hands burrowed beneath his coat, into crumpling paper pockets. "What it meant."

"Yes, I suppose you did. Thirty-four, aren't you . . . Yes, I think you did." He motioned to the papers on his desk and for the first time Cutler noticed among them a slim bound volume of plastifilm. The reference index on the spine was familiar enough: it was his initial dissertation. "And that makes it a bit strange, doesn't it?"

Sowhat strode meters to the window, looked out as if

checking the progress of his world, then came back to the desk, considering.

"You go for all that Learner propaganda, Dr. Cutler? I mean, if we had The War and all the 'plexes were destroyed? Side effects? Image accretion and under-stimulation? All that?"

Cutler shook his head. "No sir, I've never allied myself with them. You must know that from my files. A bit too much emotion, too little reason. But I do believe much of what they have to say. The ones who began the movement, they were concerned, rational; they had the right questions and they asked them. But the same thing happened that always happens with such 'idealistic' movements. The cranks, the fanatics, neurotics and people who just plain panicked, they all came huddling around it. And since there are always so many more of them—"

"Visionaries, Mr. Sowhat. The kind of people any reactionary movement will inevitably attract. Unbalanced, looking for 'meaning' or 'fulfillment,' always thinking the problem's out there, with the world, and not theirs, not inside them. Look at all the religious movements, surrogate beliefs—or the sixties. The odd thing is, they're quite often brilliant—"

"But, as you say, neurotic."

Cutler nodded. "And when they take over, and they always do, it's the neurosis that shows most strongly. Their personal confusions, the inability to act, to direct their intentions towards a single goal. That's what we see happening now." He paused. "And of course there are some others, a few, like the people in that old Cavafy poem, *Waiting for the Barbarians:* 'And now what are we going to do without the barbarians? Those people were a kind of solution.' They—"

"Yes. I know the poem, Dr. Cutler. And I see what you mean." Sowhat picked up a pen and began to swivel it between his thumb and forefinger, pushing it against the desk so that his fingers ran from one end to the other, again and again. Cutler noticed that he was left-handed, which meant an incredibly strong will or human teaching—probably both, considering his age. That was one extremely minor danger of the 'techs; they were programmed statistically, and too often (even more often than before, with human instruction) left-handed people were forced to make basically artificial motor connections to the opposite lobe. A slight aphasia was the general result.

"Well, at least we aren't going to have that war," Sowhat said. "Can't." He shuffled through a stack of papers, made a note on one, set it aside. The pen remained poised, like a thought, above the paper. "Look at it from the business angle. Balance of interest. No waste. We've got our two major economies running together like a couple of worn gears. Our production, their consumption; we've got organizational complexes like nothing they could ever work up to, efficiency that developed out of our way of life—and they've got a hard core of technology, resources, a damned near endless labor source. And what's left, it sheds off onto the others. No one wants to interfere with a smoothly running machine, political bickering to the contrary." Sowhat took up the paper, scratched out the note he'd made a moment before, scribbled a new one. Then he signed it and returned it to the stack. And smiled. "That's what *I* think."

"Yes sir. But you had the correct word a moment ago: propaganda. Rather crude hyperbole, all the Learners are saying. But sometimes a shout will make people stand still, make them listen to what comes *after* the shout, to the real reasons, the quiet ones. Maybe we *are* becoming too dependent upon the Comps; there's a difference between information and knowledge; having the tool doesn't mean the job's done. If China hadn't—"

"But it was. That was necessary."

Cutler paused. "Yes. I know." He shifted his weight in the chair and it began to throb, massaging his spine back to relaxation.

Sowhat grinned.

"I hate those damned chairs. Secretary put them in here; fun at board meetings, though. Just twist around a bit when you want to stop it."

Cutler squirmed. Mercifully, it stopped.

"You know, I'm not one to hold what a man believes against him," Sowhat said, "and I think we might have more in common than you'd expect. Sometime I'd like to hear more about what you think, your reasons. Always good to get a perspective on the problem: that's why I don't hire yes-men . . . someday when I have a little more time, then?"

"Of course, Mr. Sowhat, any time you'd like. I look forward to it."

"Soon, then."

"Soon, Mr. Sowhat."

The big man looked down at him for a moment, then subsided into his own chair.

"Nice, isn't it?" he said, noticing Cutler's look of interest. "Wife gave it to me. Anniversary. Real leather, imported of course. Took a bit of getting used to: no buttons to push, one position; keeps its own shape, doesn't contour to your body and all that—but surprisingly comfortable. Now. If there are any questions you'd like to ask while we're waiting . . ."

"Waiting?"

"For the children. After all, they're the ones who are really hiring you. Don't mind telling you, you pass with me. It's them you'll have to satisfy now. So I'm afraid the final choice has to be theirs. Now: questions?"

"The obvious one. Why? Why a human teacher?"

Elbows on the desk, Sowhat steepled his fingers and peered through them. "More than a teacher, Dr. Cutler. Your educational duties would be but a small part of the job; you'd be expected to look after the children's amusement as well. A companion. *Au pair*, so to speak: I thought that was understood."

"I see. Yes . . . yes, of course."

Sowhat settled deeper in the chair and laid his arms along the padding.

"My wife is a career woman, Dr. Cutler, and a very successful one at that. We need someone to oversee the children fulltime. 'The human touch,' Dr. Cutler. Yet we obviously can't place our children in a crèche—*quite* out of the question. As for the rest . . . well, we deal in anachronisms here at Sowhat Enterprises: books, wood and leather goods, antiques, direct lighting, vegetable and animal fiber, things like that. Snob value—or in the trade, 'specialist appeal'—that's what we depend on and why our profits are so high. Of course, Objects-of-Art is only one of our departments, and a small one—but it's close to our most profitable. I don't mind telling you that. My wife heads it, and she's developed a decided taste for the things she deals in. It happens."

Sowhat waved a hand the size of a book.

"You'll enjoy our home, Dr. Cutler. Most of the furniture is wood, the mirrors are glass, we even have glass tables. Natural products. It's all rather striking. Quaint, you might say. Seemed odd at first, of course; wrong somehow, too. Things that break or wear out—and of course we had to have specially programmed cleaners made to handle them. But my wife loves it and I have to admit I'm beginning to see why. Pride myself on keeping an open mind. And what she says, goes, as far as our home is concerned. Still, when she suggested an, ah—educator?—for the children, I thought for a while maybe she was going too far. Automatics could do it better."

"But not as cheaply."

He nodded. "Plus the problem of companionship. And, as I said, she runs the house and I go along."

Sowhat leaned back in his chair. "Now, if you don't have any more questions, there's one I'd like to ask you."

"Yes, sir?" Cutler leaned forward, trying to reach an upright position in the shifting chair, that remolded itself with every movement he made.

"Your last job."

"You must know about that, Mr. Sowhat. The investigators surely obtained that information for you."

Sowhat rocked his own chair from side to side, then leaned towards him.

"Don't need them, there," he said. "Personnel sheets tell me all that. But I'd like to hear it from you. Your side of it." He waited.

"I doubt the story's much different from the reports you got. I won a position as a trend-stat technician in one of the Pro-Products contests, and took the job on a provisional status-credit wage."

"Where did you get the training?" Sowhat interrupted.

"I taught myself."

Sowhat paused a moment. "Admirable." He lit a syntho-cigar the size of his thumb and puffed at it wetly. "Most admirable indeed." He held the cigar out in profile. One end glowed pink, the other glistened. It gave off no odor, no smoke. "Better than real ones," he said. "Have one with me?"

"No thank you. I've never cared for them, myself."

"Records say you left within a month. What was the problem?"

"I'm not sure, sir. It's difficult to explain. I just couldn't get used to it, couldn't seem to get the work done. I wanted to, and I tried, but—" He slumped in his chair. It collapsed around him; conformed to every hollow, every part of his body. It was warm, like a hand. "I couldn't."

"I see . . ." Sowhat rolled the cigar between his thumb and fingers, back and forth, back and forth, staring at the wet end as though life were about to begin there. "A shame. But I guess every man's got his place and he feels *out* of place anywhere else. Takes some a while to find it. Some never do."

Suddenly he looked up at Cutler.

"You'll get a room, meals served by the automatics, and I can manage to let a small part of the company's SC quota leak your way. Just a little—but it all helps, you know. And it would have to be confidential, that part of it, of course. And a lifetime contract, you understand."

"Certainly, sir. I understand."

"Your time with the children would be monitored, of course. No propaganda, unorthodoxy, nothing like that."

"Of course." Cutler felt a sudden urge to try out the ridiculous swing in the corner, see how near he could get to the ceiling.

"Then—"

Miss Berth was at the door, apologizing for the intrusion.

"Yes?"

"The children are here, Mr. Sowhat."

They came in, beaming at their father, wearing vinyl-and-silk. Evidently, they enjoyed being here. The boy was tall, asthenic, with watery eyes and a long face which made him look like a dreaming horse; his clothes had a permanently rumpled appearance. His younger sister was like the father, larger and sure of herself; sure of the way she walked, the way she held her head; certain of success on anybody's terms. Attractive children, both of them.

"Susan, David, this is Dr. Cutler. Dr. Cutler: our children."

Susan came boldly down the floor to shake his hand, while her brother loped along behind, nodding shyly at him, grinning.

"You'll find them both to be well-behaved children," Sowhat told him. "Intelligent, understanding, undemanding. They know how to care and cope for themselves." He went over and put an arm around the girl's shoulders. She grinned. "Susan likes music, friends over, the usual sort of thing. Gets a bit overexcited, enthusiastic, occasionally;

nothing more than that. David tends to be quieter, likes to be alone, has a little trouble making friends."

He returned to his desk, stood there leaning out over it.

"They're affectionate, bright children, and we try to respect their being individuals. All they need is a little nudge now and then. A word or two of advice, someone to talk things over with."

Sowhat smiled broadly and looked at the children.

"You've both read through Dr. Cutler's file, and now you've met him. What do you think?"

"The board votes yes, Father. He's nice. I like him." That was Susan.

David nodded serenely, distantly. "Yes, sir."

Sowhat smiled and looked back at Cutler. "Our arrangements will be satisfactory, Doctor?"

"Yes, sir. Very much so."

"Then you may consider yourself hired."

"Thank you, Mr. Sowhat."

"And, Doctor . . ."

"Yes?"

"*Do* remember what I've said this afternoon, won't you?"

"Yes, sir."

"I think that will be all, then." Sowhat shoved his hand across the desk. "Good luck, Cutler. I'm sure it will work out for both of us. I'll have the papers sent over tonight. You're still at the 'Plex?"

Cutler nodded, stood and took the hand, shook it limply. The portfolio slipped out from under his arm just then, and he had to take his hand away to rescue it.

Sowhat smiled. "Sorry again about keeping you waiting."

"Perfectly all right, sir. Thank you, Mr. Sowhat, thank you very much."

Cutler turned and trudged down the gray floor. Dimly, he could hear them talking behind him: three voices, one keen, one gentle, one steady and strong.

He stepped into the outer office and Miss Berth, in full concert, smiled and nodded as he went past her. There were two men waiting to see Mr. Sowhat, both in paper clothes, both huddled in their chairs with portfolios across their laps.

Cutler wondered if he was smiling.

He went out into the white-lit corridor and walked in what he thought the correct direction. Within moments he was hopelessly lost in the plexiglass. He had passed corridor after corridor; each had seemed equally familiar, equally anonymous. Behind the maze of clear panes all the offices appeared the same, coagulating into one massive optical, and spatial, illusion; he felt as though he were being passed through the intestines of some vast plastic beast. Deeper in, several of the panes were lightly tinted—rose, lime, lemon, pearl—but even this, from overlapping, failed to be any useful aid.

Some time later, a Guide found him wandering somewhere among the halls and conducted him safely to one of the basement stations. He took the submaze across the city, got off, inserted his nose filters and ascended the ramps into the flaming heat.

It was his first time Up for years. He looked with surprise at the purple sky. Sunset already: he hadn't thought it that late, hadn't known it was that bad—even though there was still an hour, possibly two, till true dark. As the smog grew heavier, swaddling the earth in layers of refuse that fell and drifted within one another, the day grew shorter, the heat mounted ever higher; for all their vaunted efficiency, they'd still not solved *that* problem.

The buildings rose like jagged teeth, black against the sky. He became suddenly aware of the film of sweat which slid over the skin; his clothes logged with the salty water and threatening any moment to come apart. Quickly he turned and reentered the gorge of the station, down again among the vats, and was shuttled two kilometers over and two kilometers up to his room in Complex E-27-43.

He remembered from his studies, rooms long ago which had seemed welcoming, familiar: had stared for hours at photographs of the study in which Darwin worked, brown like a Rembrandt—the piled books and papers, the globes, artifacts, brown padded leather chairs and the large French window, skulls and bones and stuffed animals containing the residue of things once warm and alive; he knew the tiny shack where Dylan Thomas had sat through afternoons over his poems—the small oil stove, the rumpled papers, bottles, empty cigarette cartons on the floor, portraits of Whitman and Auden looking down at him; he could recall every detail of the room in which Keats had lived and worked—the dainty curved legs of furniture, the order and disarray. And it seemed to him that a room long lived in should take on the personality of its occupant, that this should be in the nature of a natural process—yet nothing he did to this one could make the faintest impression on its polymeric austerity. He always entered it as though it were a stranger's, as he might enter another body. Neither his arrival nor residence had changed it, had in the least way modified it. Nor, he knew, would his departure.

It was well lighted, but with things cast off and about so as to invest the corners with shadow: his sole influence. The lights, in fact, were never off, but rose and sank on the rhythms of the 'day' shut inside its walls. Soft blue walls, one of them a bed. Chair in one corner. The table he used as a desk, with a viewer, and a single book beside it. Standard plastic packing cases in the center of the room, four of them, containing his few possessions; they, and the small antique filing cabinet as yet unmoved from against the wall. Rounded corners on every side, for the automatics. (Once, he had secured the cabinet in place with epoxy. Coming against it the next day, the cleaner had attempted to move it the same as every morning, butting softly against the gray side, then stopped dead still, buzzing loudly, then humming and apparently emitting some signal which registered as distress, at least confusion—for within half an hour another machine, a Servicer, arrived and began to dissemble various components of the cleaner, swallowing them for inspection. This had continued for several minutes, after which the Servicer itself sat quietly humming. Further machines came and began to disembowel *both* the cleaner and the Servicer . . . then finally, over two hours later, three men in white arrived, with identical frowns on their faces. The cabinet had been gently pried away and the crusted epoxy removed from floor and cabinet bottom by the grateful cleaner. The men departed without a word. Cutler sat on the bed watching all this; later, he had been reprimanded, his few remaining SC's rescinded.)

He put the portfolio on the desk and lay on the bed. He looked at the dull green packing cases: yesterday he'd been assigned to the Communals; now the job saved him from that at least.

He turned his head and looked up at the painting he liked to imagine was a window: a Picabia, the landscape of a monstrous mechanical organism sweeping down, grinding, devouring . . .

A society may be studied as a highly organized rite of cannibalism or sacrifice, as a sublimation of these two

primary urges: it is here that we find our most proper
analogy. A man gives his time and function, and receives in
turn only a grant to subsist off others. The more complex a
society, the greater the consumption of men, or of a single
man; he must give up more of himself and he must take
more that belongs to others. This absorption, this consump-
tion is ever increasing . . .

That was from his first doctoral thesis. Fifteen years now
—no, close to twenty—since he'd got up in the night to
scribble those words for the first time, the first of many
times; sitting at his desk in the dim light, printing them
boldly, hurriedly, in red pen across the top of a stack of
false starts.

He rose and drew a cup of tea from the tap, took it back
to bed, lay against the wall sipping. The lights were beginning, subtly, to sink.

Why. Why can't I accept it. It should be so easy, so
simple. The decision. A gesture.

He looked at the portfolio and thought: there. There I
am. And there, in the boxes, the cabinet, the file cards. In
this room. And here on the bed, scattered.

Inasmuch as there is an answer, the answer is mediation.
The problem cannot be avoided; its replications amplify
with the rise of our buildings; it is rooted in our every
conviction, every initial assumption of our society. A man
cannot decline this invitation to his own absorption, cannot
refuse to witness the consumption of others. It is inevitable,
and necessary. *He must learn to juggle . . .*

He got up again, stripped, and shoved the sogged clothing into the chute, where it would be flushed down into the
vats, soaked apart, reformed. In an hour, two, others would
be wearing these clothes: a hundred people would be wearing them, combined now with the fibers of a hundred, a
thousand identical suits. Behind him, the bed was slightly
damp. He looked back at the painting, at the mirror.
Pigeons, he thought. *There used to be a pigeon problem in*
New York.

He lay down again. Threw the empty cup towards the
chute. It missed and rolled with a ticking sound back towards him, spilling tiny beads of tea across the floor.

The Pagliacci routine. Have to try on my suit, two colors
meeting down the middle, the pointed shoes, the jingling
cap; make sure it fits; rehearse my tricks.

Laughing, he rose and deposited the cup in the chute, then stood there with his hand still out, laughing at himself. He pulled another cup out of the feeder and walked around the room, again and again, laughing madly, holding the cup out in front of him like a torch, an offering, like something sacred—balancing it on top of his head, putting it on the floor and dancing about it—throwing his heels high and flailing his arms wildly . . . finally crushing his heel down hard and smashing it into the floor. He went over to the chair, dragged it across the room to face the painting and put the mirror in it, then returned to the feeder and began to pull out cup after cup, throwing them into the air, more and more, trying to catch them and throw them back up, pulling out others, others, others. They fell all around him and rolled and struck together silently on the floor.

He must learn to juggle . . .

The small red eye on the feeder began to blink violently, indicating that he was expending more than his quota. He continued to pull the cups out and throw them against the ceiling—the eye blinking ever more frantically: a week's, two weeks', a month's quota—until the feeder refused to provide any more. The last cups arced slowly through the air and began to fall. Still, he walked through the room, through the cups, laughing, laughing, till he was out of breath. Then he went over to the chair and slammed his fist into the plastic mirror again and again and again. It wouldn't break. Silently, it regarded the painting, oblivious to his blows. He stood there by it for several minutes.

And after that he sat down on the bed, looking from cup to cup, waiting for the papers to come.

WELCOME TO THE TRICENTENNIAL

Patrick Henry Prentice

Patrick Henry Prentice describes himself as a 32-year-old househusband living in Alexandria, Virginia. And no, he is not a lineal descendant of his namesake, though the byline makes a fine note on which to end this volume. Of all the people in the pieces in this book, I think I enjoy the character of 106-year-old Jacob Pacheco the best. Without cryogenics, without time machines, he has seen the *Bicentennial*, endured, and now he views the Tricentennial. Human connective tissue for society, he binds our era with that dim future a century removed. Jacob's eyes are ours.

WELCOME TO THE TRICENTENNIAL

The old man remembered the day perfectly.

The earliest part of it, as in all his days then, had been spent moving in and out of dreams. On that particular morning he had been dreaming of fireworks; and what six-year-old boy was not, on the morning of the Bicentennial.

His father, looking for ways to snare his son's attention, had begun with the fireworks: had described the Monument, and the Reflecting Pool with the Lincoln Memorial hunched in the background ("See, that's this one, here, on a five-dollar bill.") and how it would get dark shortly before nine P.M. ("That's just about your bedtime, but tonight you get to stay up, get to take in the whole thing.") and how the whole thing would be just like the fireworks in the square back home, only more of them, many more, and of beautiful colors, going higher and exploding larger, spurting out in huge bright circles against the night sky, and louder! Louder by far than anything you could hear in South Carolina, with the ones to especially watch and listen for being tiny white blasts that would shatter your eardrum within the three seconds that it took for the sound to travel to where they would be sitting; and the whole thing, the whole great flaming display would last—for one whole hour! Imagine! ("One hour, son, that's how long it takes us to drive to your Aunt Kitty's in Spartanburg.")

Just six years old, he had fallen for the whole idea of the Bicentennial, hook, line, and sinker, so proud that he was now old enough to begin learning about such things as history, heritage, traditions.

His dream had been of fireworks then, when his father shook him awake, and he blinked open to the unfamiliar room in the Sheraton-Arlington, and followed his father wordlessly to the bathroom which had white towels wrapped in paper sheafs and tiny bars of soap.

He brushed his teeth while Jake Senior ran the shaver over his face, and then both of them stepped into the shower—the first shower he ever remembered. And felt (he had thought about this a good deal) not small and insignificant next to that great hairy body, but bigger and older than ever, as if he sensed for the first time in his life that one day he too would be tall and hairy and thirty-two years old with a son of his own to take showers with and explain things to. While it hadn't happened precisely that way (he'd never had a son, and his only daughter had died along with her mom from the Galveston A-strain back in '99), that first dim intuition served as a durable base for the perceptions he developed later in life about how the world worked and what it meant ("All things have their seasons, son, plants, people, even countries . . . it's like the old cycle of the perpetual phoenix, spring over and over again from the ashes . . .").

First stop was the International House of Pancakes (OPEN 24 HOURS A DAY TO SERVE YOU!); then, bloated with corn meal and sausage and syrup, they drove over the river to the Maryland side, down Indian Head Highway to Fort Washington. It was completely deserted at that hour.

There was a serenity to the place he'd never gotten over. They stood next to the cannons on the highest parapet, totally alone, while his father waited for dawn and instructed him in the importance of omens, concluding: "We'll see how the day breaks now. It might tell us what the country is in for these next hundred years."

It hadn't broken all that great, to tell the truth. Overcast, as the weatherman said, with a chance of rain. His father chewed on his lower lip, making the mental adjustments which are characteristic of all omen-haunted men: "Oh well . . . Rain is a many-sided symbol. If we were still neolithic farmers, we'd be ecstatic."

Then riding into the city, he had dozed and dreamed of being a cannoneer in the War of 1812, of lofting heavy iron balls over 300 yards of air and water to go ker-plop, right in the captain's cabin. Deadeye Pacheco, the kid who saved America.

The old man chuckled. Was it from such childish dreams of glory that his present determination to outwit Val was born? Probably not, he concluded. He hadn't much use for glory any more, and besides, if he succeeded no one would know; only if he failed might his name be whispered around. No, he was going to stop Val because he, Jacob Pacheco, was one of the last down-home American boys, brought to near-manhood by a father who took his Constitution seriously; and because he'd been waiting for this day, America's 300th birthday, for precisely one hundred years, a wait that had taken him through two wars and eighty years of a battered civilization climbing its way out of the mud and ash. He wasn't about to let some young kid with prehistoric ideas about the use and aim of government mess it up at the last moment.

Since he was in no hurry, the old man's mind clicked to the past again, effortlessly hurtling that one hundred years, and he was back holding hands with his dad, wandering through the throngs of celebrants gathered around the Reflecting Pool towards the end of that afternoon long ago, July 4, 1976. They had already visited the monuments honoring the early Presidents: Washington, Jefferson, Lincoln; they'd stood in line at the Archives to see the yellow parchments with their faded brown calligraphy ("It's called the Constitution, and it's the rules we all live under," his father explained. "They change a bit here and there, but basically it's the same as it was two hundred years ago, back in the beginning.").

They finally claimed a tiny patch of grass where they could spread a blanket, dig into their cooler full of fried chicken and lemonade, and wait for the fireworks. His body tingled with excitement, being with so many people, all in one place, celebrating the same event.

He could see sparklers being lit, and an occasional Roman candle gushing fountains of pure white light. From all directions came the chatter of firecracker chains, punctuated now and again by the heavier bass of cherry bombs. He shivered, his excitement mingled with fear. Were the cherry bombs being thrown at people, little people like himself?

His father shook his head. He hoped not, anyway. Then inexplicably he'd launched into an explanation that lasted the better part of an hour: how even in the best of nations in the best of times there would always be people who didn't like the way things were, people who didn't follow the rules, or didn't care, or held a grudge. Such people were capable of incalculable harm, capable in some extreme instances of bringing whole nations to their knees with the strategies of terror—assassinations, bombings, sniper attacks.

"Desperate men are almost as inevitable as death and taxes, so a country has to be able to absorb their onslaughts without coming apart at the seams," he had concluded, quietly, and that was it. No mention of the dark unsettling images which must have been making the rounds of his mind about that time, must have been at the root of that sudden lecture: that it took only one mad act to light the powder keg, fuse the old hatreds, unleash the old doubts; that never is a nation more vulnerable than in the process of healing ancient wounds, or when it is trying hard to celebrate itself; so that a single spooked man, climbing the statue of Lincoln with a rifle, crouched in that marble lap, timing his shots to the rocketfire, could with a dozen random volleys spook an entire nation. And that, more or less, was Val's intention, but Jacob Pacheco aimed to stop him—even if he had to act like a goddamn fool.

The young man with the red hair had come to Washington from Eau Claire, in late June. The eleven-hundred-mile trip over the shimmering asphalt of the Interstates had taken Val fourteen days, much of it spent in Pennsylvania suffering from leg cramps, alternately cursing the forces which had made such mountains in the first place, and the forces which had combined to outlaw the automobile 55 years before his birth. Never having ridden in a "car" he could only imagine what it must have been like; you sat in it as if in a chair, and pushed a lever with your foot, and it moved, taking you with it. The madness which had compelled society to turn its back on such a spectacular invention was beyond him completely.

Bicycles, on the other hand, he knew and he hated. They were, at best, antidemocratic, favoring those who were slim and in shape, those who had legs of steel, who didn't mind huffing and puffing unprotected through the elements, heat or cold, rain or snow, at a miserly speed. At worst, they were an instrument of torture, pure and simple, especially if you were on the pudgy side to begin with, especially if you were fair skinned and slightly asthmatic, and most especially if you were carrying a long, awkward package and a suitcase that weighed a ton. Every labored, down-thrust of his feet, as he rode eastward through the corn and bean fields, served to remind Val of the essential justness of his mission, of the need to cry halt to a society bent on erasing the best from its past.

The trip itself had been largely uneventful. Since the thought of sleeping outside with the gnats and mosquitos was repugnant to him, he'd stayed with clanfolk along the way. It had surprised him to find how easy it was for a total stranger like himself to pedal into a small town at sundown, check the phonebook for the address of the nearest *Kway* who was head-of-household, and present himself for dinner, and more often than not, his very own bed. He even got laid, once, in Indiana.

As he rolled out of the Blue Ridge mountains, past Leesburg, and caught his first view of Washington, the success of his mission seemed assured. He felt anonymous and at ease: just another huffing pilgrim on another yellow bicycle on the way to the Tricentennial to have a few laughs and see a few national shrines before he did his thing and the revolution came and swept everything away in its path.

"Yes?"

The pretty blond girl bearing the insignia of the *Teh-Khiu* clan on her dress looked up at Val expectantly. He lowered his suitcase to the floor, and propped the long, thin package gently against the counter. The large hall of the Clan Assignment Offices was nearly empty.

"I'm a visitor," he said, though that must have been obvious. "Is there a *Kway* around here who can help me find a room?"

The girl nodded and pointed to a hallway on the opposite side of the room. "Just follow that corridor and you'll find all the clan assignment services. *Kway's* will be halfway down, on your left."

Val grunted his thanks, picked up the package and the suitcase and moved across the great tiled floor toward the corridor. He was already sweating fiercely. Hearing tales of Washington summers was one thing, he decided, experiencing them in person was another. The trickle of perspiration down his sides irritated him profoundly, and as he moved down the dimly lighted hallway he recalled yet another example of society's present idiocy. Back in the old days, they'd had something called air-conditioning—a way of pumping cool dry air into buildings to make them habitable during the hottest summer months. If there was any rational objection to a device that ingenious he'd yet to hear it. As he trudged down the corridor his sense of righteous indignation mounted; his mind toyed absently with the example, as if with an old wound.

He came to the door marked with the number 43. Beneath that was the *Kway* insignia, painted black: six concentric circles, the outermost of which had a gap at either side. He walked in, without bothering to knock.

Another young woman, seated at a desk, glanced up from the book she was reading.

"Hello. May I help you?"

"Hi." Val nodded politely and laid his gear near the door, wishing there were some way he could disguise the two large spreading circles of wetness under his arms. He felt soiled and vulnerable, and it took some effort to smooth the brusqueness from his voice.

"I'm looking for a room?"

The woman nodded and indicated that he should sit down in the chair facing the desk. "You've come to the right place. Now, let's see. First I'll need your clan-card, and then we'll see if we can fix you up."

Val fumbled in his wallet, wet and sour-smelling, extracted the small plastic card with the raised letters and numbers, and slid it across the desk. He tried, with only partial success, to assume a joking tone. "What is this? Some kind of security check?"

The woman smiled briefly and shook her head.

"Actually, it just saves me a whole lot of paperwork." She inserted the card in a small desk terminal, punched up three buttons, and waited. Within seconds a single sheet of paper slid down into the wire basket. She examined it cheerfully.

"Eau Claire, hunh? That must be awfully pretty country up there."

"It is."

"Not as hot as here I'll bet."

"Jeez. You can say that again."

Val waited stiffly in the chair while the woman punched up some more numbers on the console. "As you know," she said, "we're awfully tight on space here this week, what with the Tricentennial and all, so I'm afraid you'll have to double up with someone. The main clanhouse was filled weeks ago, and it's really been kind of a madhouse around here."

Val stared at the woman blankly.

For the first time it dawned on him that he'd made a

serious miscalculation. It had never crossed his mind that he might have difficulty finding a single room in the nation's largest metropolitan area—one of the few cities in the country which hadn't suffered a direct hit during the Forty-Eight Bomb War. And a place of his own, where he could go about his business unmolested, was a virtual necessity. Not only was he carrying illegal weapons—he could get life if he were caught—but he was fearful of any kind of socializing at all. As if even polite chitchat over dinner might soften his resolve, wake him up from his angry dream, and force him to cancel his mission altogether.

It was not the first time that possibility had occurred to him.

"No single rooms you say?"

"Afraid not. But don't worry, we'll figure something out."

She reached into a drawer and pulled out a small microfilm cassette. "This is a complete list of all the *Kways* in the D.C. area. You can take it to that machine over there and check through it. If you find somebody you'd like to stay with, just give me the number and I'll see if it's still vacant."

Wordlessly Val took the cassette and trudged over to the readout console. His mood was black. The seriousness of his error was beginning to sink in. In all likelihood he would be forced to find a secluded spot outdoors, among the dreaded gnats and mosquitos and the terrible heat, causing him to wonder for the hundredth time if the whole thing were worth it. Still, with the girl watching him, he had to at least go through the motions, pretend to check the list, in order not to arouse suspicions.

He plunged the tape home and flicked on the monitor.

Names and addresses, birthdates and occupations, swam before his eyes. He read them through, mechanically, swiftly, until halfway through the list one entry caught his eye.

NAME: PACHECO, JACOB H.

BIRTHDATE: MAY 31, 1970.

Val turned, and called over his shoulder to the girl. "Hey, I think you've got an error here. It says this guy was born in 1970. Pacheco. Jacob H. Pacheco."

"That's no mistake," the girl said, looking up from her book. "He really was born in 1970."

"No fooling." He felt his mind at work, slowly digesting this bit of news. "You know him?"

The girl smiled wryly. "Every *Kway* around here knows Mr. Pacheco. In fact, I believe he's the oldest living *Kway* in America."

"Well, I'll be damned." His thoughts were picking up speed. It occurred to him that rooming with an old man, a *very* old man, might be almost the same thing as being alone. He whistled softly. "One hundred and six. That's amazing. What's he like, anyway?"

The girl shrugged. "Oh, you know, he has his good days and his bad. I mean, after all, he's over a century old. What can you expect?"

Val paused, framing his words carefully. "But is he, you know . . . senile? Does he take part in clan business, that sort of thing?"

"He comes to most of the monthlies," she said.

"Yeah, sure." Val forced his voice to be casual. "But what I mean is, just out of curiosity . . . Do his opinions carry much weight in the meetings? Do people listen to him . . . *believe* him? Like if he came to you with some wild story about something he'd seen . . . ?"

The girl laughed. "Mr. Pacheco has more wild stories than you could shake a stick at. I mean, he was actually here, in Washington, at the . . . whaddycallit . . . the Bicentennial, can you imagine? God knows what kind of weird things he remembers from way back then, before the wars and all. We're just hoping he doesn't have a stroke or something before the Fourth."

Val nodded, absently. "I guess if he's that old, though, he probably spends most of his time in his room?"

"Actually," she smiled, "he's really quite fit, considering. I think he spends a lot of his time out in the garden, watching the sparrows hop up and down or something. Do you think you might like to try him?"

"I was thinking of it, yes."

"Well, I'm sure the room is available. There's not too many people want to stay with someone that old. You know . . ." And her voice trailed off while she waited for Val to decide.

At last he nodded. Rooming with a very old man seemed infinitely preferable to bedding down with the bugs; and if the old geezer somehow happened to stumble onto the truth . . .

He experienced a curious plummeting sensation, and

forced the thought from his mind. He'd just have to cross that bridge when he came to it.

The oldest living *Kway* in America was in the garden, dozing under a peach tree, dreaming of fireworks, when he felt a shadow pass before him. He opened his eyes. Against the glare of the sun he could make out a short, stocky figure thatched with hair of the brightest orange imaginable, watching him.

Jacob Pacheco closed his eyes again, feigning sleep—a trick old age had taught him, which he used whenever he didn't want to be bothered, or when he felt like stalling for time. He flapped his mouth once or twice for good measure, and jerked his shoulders slightly, whimpering softly, as if in the grip of some gentle, ancient nightmare.

Meanwhile, he was thinking. Even with his eyes clamped tightly shut he could feel the presence of the shadow, observing him. He tried to imagine what the stranger might want.

He decided he needed more information. To this end, he blinked his eyes open, wide open, as if surfacing from a dream which still mesmerized him. For two seconds he stared straight ahead, then clamped his eyes shut; he flapped his mouth, twitched, and pretended once again to be asleep. The boy was obviously a *Kway* sent over from the billeting center for a room. That much could be deduced from the clan's insignia embroidered on his shirt, and the suitcase resting by his leg. It was only a little less obvious that the young man was standing silently out of respect for an old man's afternoon nap.

"Mr. Pacheco?"

The old man flapped his lips and pretended to brush away an imaginary fly. He was curiously pleased. He realized he hadn't had a young person—a *really* young person—around for a long time, and he was feeling vaguely out of touch with what the latest crop of grownups were thinking. His usual source of news and gossip was Mrs. Slattery, his landlady, and though he thought of her as a youngster, she was damn near seventy; and she believed the country was going to hell in a handcart, which limited her usefulness as an information-gathering device. And now he had the real McCoy.

"Mr. Pacheco?" The voice was louder and more insistent

this time, accompanied by the barest hint of pressure on his shoulder.

He decided it was time to wake up.

"What—! Hanh!" Flapping and blinking and snorting.

"Mr. Pacheco, I'm sorry to bother you, but I'm here about a room. The clan billeting office sent me? My name is Val Gardener?"

Jacob Pacheco nodded brightly.

"Val Gardener," the boy repeated, framing the words distinctly. "I'm here about a room. A *room*."

"Glad to meet you, Mr. Gardener," said Jacob Pacheco, extending a steady right hand.

"Oh, gee, don't bother moving. I can—"

The old man cackled merrily. "If I didn't bother moving now and then, people might get to thinking I was dead. Shake!"

Solemnly the two shook hands, studying each other.

"Say, if it wouldn't be too much trouble, I'd like to see the room."

"No trouble at all," said the old man, steadying his hands on the arm of the chair. Concentrating fiercely, he prepared himself for his next move—the transition from a sitting to a standing position with no sign of infirmity, or clumsiness. There was that within him which enjoyed showing off, demonstrating that nimbleness was not merely a function of age. When he was confident that he had the young man's undivided attention he made his move, springing to his feet in a single and largely fluid motion; one of his best embarkations ever.

Flushed with success, wobbling only slightly, he felt a mischievous need to augment the astounding impression he must have made, and grasped the handle of the large black suitcase resting near Val's chunky leg. He pulled.

He had never actually intended to carry it up the stairs, or even all the way across the yard to the porch. Surely Mr. Gardener would intercede and relieve him quickly of his burden with an appropriate venting of amazement. But he *had* been reasonably sure of budging the thing. Instead, he almost fell over.

"My God Almighty!" he cried. "What've you got in there, a howitzer? Must weigh a quarter ton!"

The young man stared at him blankly.

"Never mind, you wouldn't know what a howitzer is. Afraid you'll have to manage by yourself," he muttered, crestfallen, and walked across the lawn to the porch, hoping he hadn't given himself a hernia. The boy trailed silently behind him, without so much as a smile on his show of grit. Oh well, he thought philosophically. Americans never did spend much time eulogizing failure.

Then, holding the door wide open, he let Val precede him up the stairs.

It was shortly after swallowing the last bite of Mrs. Slattery's magnificent vegetable curry that Jacob Pacheco concluded that something was troubling the young man from Wisconsin. He had barely touched his dinner. His manner seemed distracted, as if he were unable or unwilling to follow the thread of conversation. When pressed for details of his life in the nation's buttery, he had responded with grunts or monosyllables. When the old man had attempted to steer the discussion into his favorite topic—the state of the Union—Val had clammed up entirely. No amount of wheedling seemed to shake Val from his resolve not to offer an opinion, and Mr. Pacheco found this exceedingly strange. He believed himself to be a shrewd judge of character, and he would have given odds that Val Gardener had as many opinions as the next man, and quite possibly more.

The young man was hiding something, of that he was reasonably sure. As he mounted the steps to his bedroom, the old man wondered what that something was.

He entered the bedroom and found Val stretched out on the couch, his eyes wide open and apparently focused on the ceiling. A solitary fly could be heard buzzing angrily around the room. The air was still and hot, without any trace of breeze.

The old man walked to his bed, arranged the pillows against the backboard and carefully lowered himself to a nearly horizontal position. The two of them stayed like that for nearly half an hour, until the old man said, "Air conditioning."

Val turned his head slightly. "What?"

"Air conditioning," the old man repeated. "You might not know what that is. Back in the old days you could put this machine in your window, and the whole room would feel cool."

"Yeah," Val said. "I know."

Encouraged that his overture had not met with complete

silence, the old man continued. "Can't have them nowadays, on account the government says they use up too much electricity. But there's a bill in Congress to change all that, so maybe next year we'll all be able to cool down a bit."

Val's response was uttered so softly that Mr. Pacheco wasn't positive he'd heard it correctly. He thought the young man said, *don't hold your breath.*

"You know, Mrs. Slattery downstairs makes an awfully good pitcher of root beer. I'd say a glass of root beer would be mighty refreshing along about now. How about you?" The bed creaked as he raised himself slowly into a sitting position. "You know root beer?"

Val grunted in the affirmative.

"Well, what do you say I go get us each a nice long glass of root beer. With ice cubes," he added.

He had intended to make a great display of having difficulty getting out of bed, but to his surprise it was Val who swung slowly to his feet. "Don't bother. I'll go get it."

"With plenty of ice," the old man called after him. "At least we still have refrigerators, right?"

The moment he heard Val's heavy steps on the stairs, the old man jerked himself to his feet and went to the closet. Heart pounding, he fumbled with the latches on the boy's suitcase. Locked. That left the tall, thin package, secured by a single strand of cord, looped into a cross. Quickly he worked the string off one corner, his ears focused tightly on the stairs.

He opened the flap and stared. He wasn't sure what he had expected, but as he examined the machine of gleaming black metal and polished walnut he couldn't say he was surprised. He closed things up and went to sit in his rocker by the window. Clearly he would have to do something . . . but what? The simplest procedure would be a telephone call to the clan deputy. Val would be taken before the Council, and inevitably disciplined—perhaps a tour of duty in the clan's canning factory, possibly a period of actual confinement. Going through the regular channels was undoubtedly the proper thing to do, yet he hesitated. Deep inside him something stirred, an infantile memory, a childhood dream of heroism. He thought about his own father, still living in the son; about his wife and daughter, so long dead, and the son he'd never had.

He could always go to the deputy.

He rocked himself slowly, his hands folded neatly in an attitude of prayer. Already a plan was beginning to form.

When Val returned with the root beer, he found the old man sound asleep in his chair. He surprised himself by experiencing a small twinge of disappointment. All things considered, Jacob Pacheco was a right interesting old fellow. Val had actually enjoyed listening to some of his recollections about the days before the war, had wanted to question him further. That he had managed to control his impulses, had walked away from the dinner table without having revealed his own radical attitudes was, he believed, a tribute to his determination.

The old man stirred and whimpered in his sleep. It was strange, Val thought, the way he slipped in and out of sleep so effortlessly, as if his mind and body were attuned to an entirely different cycle. Val had never known his own grandparents, and the habits of old age had always been a mystery to him—usually a fearful one. He had always told himself that old age was a condition he would never permit; better to kill oneself than enter a state of decrepitude. Now he wasn't so sure. There was a calmness and an alertness to the old man which he found appealing. The absence of bedpans, wheelchairs, and dentures sitting in a glass of water on the bureau was a profound relief.

He was wondering whether he should drink the second glass of root beer when Mr. Pacheco's eyes blinked open.

"I got that drink for you," Val said, carrying it over.

"Fine, fine." His hand closed around the glass, but at the same moment his eyes closed again. Val hovered over him, ready to catch the drink if it fell. Then the old man said, "There's a wooden box in the top drawer of my dresser. Could you get it for me?"

Inside the box there was a mound of tiny, green flakes; a flat rectangular object made of red plastic, and some thin papers the size of a business card. Val watched curiously while the old man sprinkled the green flakes into the machine, licked a paper on one edge and inserted it, and suddenly squeezed the whole thing together. As if by magic a small white cylinder popped out into his gnarled fingers.

"I used to roll them by hand," the old man said sadly, "but then my fingers got stubborn, and I had to resort to this."

"What is it?" Val asked, frowning.

Mr. Pacheco pulled a pack of matches from under the mound of flakes. "Dope," he said, casually.

Val's eyes widened as he watched the lighted match flare against the tip of the white cylinder. The old man inhaled deeply, then blew out a long column of smoke.

"Dope?" Val stammered. "You mean . . ."

"I mean reefer," the old man smiled. "Marijuana. Hemp. You ever heard of it?"

"Of course I—" Val couldn't believe what he was seeing. "Of course I've *heard* of it."

"But of course you've never smoked it." The old man snorted mirthlessly. "Jesus."

"Well, no, I never actually . . . I mean, *nobody* smokes it any more."

"Except old folks," Pacheco whispered. "Relics of a gayer age, like me. I know, I know . . . even if it's not out-right illegal, it's considered a reactionary habit by all you youngsters. But if you were practically weaned on it . . ." He sighed and shook his head. "The truth is, I don't give a damn what you all think." And he took another puff.

"It doesn't bother me," Val said quickly.

The old man nodded dreamily. "You want some? Mighty nice stuff if I do say so myself." He clucked appreciatively. "My own strain, the result of years of patient breeding. Colombian, Jamaican, Nepalese, Thai . . ." His voice trailed off. "'Course being cured in opium doesn't hurt."

Val stared at the cigarette in the outstretched hand. Finally he took it between thumb and index finger, holding it daintily as he examined it. "I'd better not," he said, "on account of my asthma."

"Asthma," the old man repeated. "Seems to me I recall that opium is good for asthma." He reached out his hand, and grinned. "Better give it back before it bites you."

"I'm not saying I'm afraid," Val muttered defensively. "Just so it doesn't mess up my lungs."

With an air of studied nonchalance he took a puff, then coughed. The smoke had a strange sweet taste.

"Take just a little smoke, and a whole lot of air," the old man advised. "Then hold it for as long as you can, say fifteen seconds . . ."

Val inhaled again, and managed to hold it this time. *Five, ten, fifteen . . .*

He heard a voice, distantly. "You've got to let it out *some*time."

Val blew out a clean column of air.

"Have another toke," the old man said.

Val repeated the procedure. *Toke*, he thought. What a strange word. Five, ten, fifteen . . . A wave of euphoria passed over him. There was nothing to it. He didn't know just what he had expected dope to do to him, but something on the scary side anyway—nightmare images dragged up from his subconscious, weird stuff like ghouls, ghosts, and voluptuous women with blood on their teeth . . .

He started to giggle. This was fine, really fine. The giggle turned into a laugh which seemed to come from the pit of his stomach. His mind began to dance.

"You have had enough," he heard the old man say.

Grinning like an idiot, he watched the old man suck the last bit of life from the joint. He felt so good that he didn't even notice when the old man rose and went to the closet; and by the time Val's mind registered the fact that Pacheco had returned with the long, slender package it was already too late. So he merely looked on, an interested bystander, as the binding string was looped away, and the gleaming machine he'd carried so far was removed.

In some dim recess of his mind he heard Pacheco's satisfied murmur. "Winchester. Thirty-ought-six. A fine rifle. Haven't seen one of these in fifty years." And he was not even particularly dumbfounded when he heard the old man say, softly, "Now let's figure out how to use this baby without getting caught."

When Val awoke the next morning, shortly before noon, there was no sign of the old man. Experiencing a moment of confusion, even panic, he bolted to the closet, half expecting to find the weapons removed; but everything was in its place.

Sitting numbly on the edge of the bed, he tried to recall what had occurred the previous evening. It was all beginning to come back.

Under the influence of the drug, he had spilled his innermost feelings, his pent-up anger at the blindness of the nation's leaders. His harangue had touched virtually every aspect of modern American life—from the persistent reluctance to reintroduce the airplane and the automobile into the society that had invented them, to the alien nature of the clan system itself, which was based, after all, on the *I Ching*—a Chinese document.

"Why do we fool ourselves into thinking we live under the same rules as our ancestors," Val had cried with genuine anguish. "Why can't we admit that if the founding fathers were alive today, they'd throw up their hands in despair and give the country back to old King Henry!"

"George," the old man had corrected, absently.

"George," Val muttered disgustedly. "Whoever."

Now, sitting on the edge of the bed, contemplating the events of the previous night, Val felt a sense of relief that he had finally said his piece, and that the man he had exposed his secret to was himself a radical, and understood these things. His only regret was that this fleeting sense of well-being could not last long.

A wave of melancholy engulfed him. He tried to obliterate the fact that it was the morning of July Third, 2076, and that, for better or worse, the act which would ignite the Second American Revolution was less than thirty hours away.

Five miles away, across the Potomac, the oldest living *Kway* in America had just concluded a productive interview with a round-faced man of Oriental extraction, a Mr. Yukio Takamura, fellow *Kway* and novelty shop owner on temporary assignment to the Tricentennial Planning Commission, Division of Fireworks and Display.

The meeting had been hastily scheduled in the middle of a very hectic day, and Mr. Takamura was sweating profusely. Yet, Pacheco reflected, the man had listened to his story carefully, respectfully. Therein lay the genius of the clan system; the entire structure was based on the rule that no clanner could refuse a "reasonable request" when it came from the mouth of a fellow member.

After some deliberation, Mr. Takamura had evidently concluded that this particular request, though eccentric, was reasonable. He spoke softly into his desk intercom. Within minutes came word that the parcel had been placed in Mr. Pacheco's golf cart.

"The best time would be at the height of the finale," Mr. Takamura advised him. Pacheco nodded and shook his hand. Somehow, he doubted that he would ever have to use it. But it paid to be careful.

He made the trip back to Alexandria in less than twenty minutes, tooling across the 14th Street Bridge at a brisk 20 k.p.h. Along the way he passed scores of pedestrians, cyclists, and skaters, but only one other golf cart; mechanized wheels were a luxury reserved either for the very old or the very infirm.

Coming around the corner on North Patrick Street he spied Val's heavy figure standing on the front porch of the house, peering in his direction. Pacheco applied a final, exhilarating burst of speed and jammed to a stop directly in front of the house, raising, he noted with satisfaction, a little dust. Perched on his seat under the billowing canopy, swaying precariously, he affected languor and nonchalance while he waited for Val to approach.

"Get the stuff and hop in," he whispered conspiratorially. "We're going for a little ride."

Ten minutes later they were on the Jefferson Davis Highway, heading south. The old man could not help noticing that Val's knuckles were white as he gripped the cart's aluminum frame, his smile slightly forced. The cart negotiated the corners with singular abandon, then fishtailed crazily into the straightaways.

"Nothing like a little speed, eh?" Pacheco chirruped happily. "Nothing like a little risk."

At the southern limits of Alexandria they were forced into a slow crawl, weaving carefully in and out of a long procession of people, each one dressed in the distinctive clan costumes which were worn only on that most ceremonial of occasions—the initiation of a new member. Toward the end of the parade they spotted the object of all this attention—a small girl dressed entirely in white, holding flowers, surrounded by her relatives. Behind her walked a man carrying the placard of the *Shih-ho* clan, which told the passers-by that the child had already completed the initiation ritual, the throwing of the yarrow stalks which bound her to the *Shih-ho* clan for life.

Pacheco pulled the cart over to the curb and applauded politely when he caught the child's eye. Watching the procession recede he felt a throb of nostalgia for the initiation of his own daughter into the *Zhaou-kwo's*. He recalled as if it were yesterday the excitement she had felt on becoming a full-fledged member of her own clan—a second family that she could turn to for help and guidance throughout her life, a resource bank that numbered nearly two million persons throughout the land.

The old man shook his head sadly. That was eighty years ago. It didn't seem possible.

After crossing the river into Maryland over the Woodrow Wilson Bridge they proceeded south down Indian Head Highway at a steady clip. The heat shimmered off the asphalt in waves.

They rode for the most part in utter silence. Twice Val had asked where they might be heading, receiving only a mysterious smile in answer. He finally decided it was entirely too hot to think. His head was beginning to throb. He experienced flashes of dizziness. Somehow, riding under an electric motor's power was less entrancing than he had imagined, and his stubby hands gripped the rail with renewed vigor as the old man gunned the tiny cart through each successive curve in the road. They drove for a long time without seeing a soul.

After what seemed an interminable time they crested a hill to a full view of the river, then swerved sharply onto a road that was little more than a pathway covered with gravel and rocks. The cart slowed, bouncing up a substantial incline. The hard rubber tires transmitted every jolt to Val's throbbing skull. He closed his eyes and prayed that he wouldn't be sick. When they finally drew to a complete stop he was almost too weary to notice or care.

"Rough ride," Pacheco muttered sympathetically.

Val opened his eyes.

Before them stood an enormous ramshackle house, its wooden sides cracked and fading, painted an ancient white. Shards of cracked glass clung to the window sills like transparent teeth. Weeds and bushes curled up everywhere, gripping the structure in a patient green embrace.

The old man hopped onto the ground and gestured for Val to follow. Pushing aside a thick snarl of honeysuckle they entered the house.

It seemed to Val at first glance that there was almost as much vegetation inside as there was outside. Green creepers of ivy and kudzu clung to the walls, feeding on the shattered sunlight which seeped through the windows and chinks in the ceiling. There were cobwebs everywhere, and frantic scurrying noises could be heard coming from the other rooms. The old man held up his hand until these sounds had passed.

"I never was much of a hand at tidying up," he cackled happily. "But what the hell. It's only for a night."

Val was unable to conceal his horror. "We're going to *stay* here?" he croaked.

"It's not the Hilton," Pacheco admitted, "but desperate men can't be choosy, right?" He walked gingerly to the doorway of another room and nodded, satisfied. "I mean, when you're on the lam, you have to expect some minor inconveniences. Of course, I realize it'll be harder for you in the years to come than it will be for me," he added sympathetically, "because I'll be dead. But there's lots of places just like this one around the country, and if you're real careful you could probably hole up one way or another for decades."

Val put the back of his hand to his forehead, wondering if perhaps he weren't just a bit feverish. Everything was happening so fast—too fast. In a scant twenty-four hours the moment he had been pointing toward for a whole year would be upon him, and nothing was going the way he had expected.

"You look a little wobbly," the old man noted from the doorway. He pointed at a rotting sofa covered with moss and a scattering of dead leaves. "You'd better sit down while I get the show on the road. Mind there's no snakes . . ." And he was gone.

Val sat with his buttocks barely resting on the arm of the sofa, his head in his hands. The awfulness of his situation was just beginning to sink in. To think that he was going to spend one single night in such loathsome surroundings was unbearable; imagining a whole lifetime of similar accommodations was a horror beyond comprehension.

What in the name of God was he doing there?

He shook his head, shuddering. It had all seemed so simple back in Eau Claire. One loud, screaming gesture of defiance. He'd been prepared for violence ever since he came across the mortar in the abandoned half-track submerged in the lake behind the farm, ever since he'd actually fired it that one time, at dawn, down by the cliffs. He could still recall his sense of awe as the bomb left the mortar, the long moments of silence as it described its perfect arc over the water to the shelf of land five hundred meters away. In that five seconds of perfect silence the whole world had seemed poised on the brink of something inevitable, something he would be part of—*must* be part of. Then in the distance a soundless flowering of orange and red light burst against the muted early morning colors, thrilling him to the bone with its beauty, followed by the flat report, a sudden, muffled thud which flew across the water like an afterthought.

But violence was one thing, he thought. Living like a rat forever afterwards was something he hadn't counted on. Perhaps, he thought absently, without much hope, the old man could be persuaded to follow an alternate course. Might it not be wiser simply to throw themselves on the mercy of the clan?

He was wondering how he could present this alternative diplomatically when the old man popped his head through a door and motioned Val to follow. Through the ghastly remains of a kitchen, across a battered breezeway and down a short flight of steps they descended, into a tiny house adjoining the main one.

Val pulled up short, and stared.

"Well, what do you think?"

Val moved forward, slowly. His hand reached out as if hypnotized, touching the sleek blue metal.

"She's a beauty," Pacheco said with undisguised pride. "A Chrysler Imperial, one of the last ones built, and practically in mint condition. I've been coming out here every so often to keep her in shape."

Val trailed his hand over the smooth metal, unable to speak. His heart was pounding furiously. A car, he told himself over and over. A genuine goddamn car. He peered through the window at the plush leather and velvet interior, the dials and the buttons. Breathtaking.

"I found it here like this, oh, forty years ago. So far as I know, I'm the only human who knows it's here. Folks don't come out this way as a rule," he explained, "on account of a plutonium waste scare a while back."

Val shook his head in disbelief. "It doesn't actually work?" he stammered finally.

"Of course it works!" Pacheco snorted. "If I wanted to see one that didn't work, I'd go to a museum. This here is our getaway car!" He smiled craftily. "Now let's load your stuff in the trunk, and take it for a spin."

Two minutes later Val was sitting in the plush bucket seat, watching the old man's every movement with open-mouthed awe. He put a key in a slot on the steering column and turned it. There was a brief cranking noise before the engine roared into life with a din which seemed to rattle the entire garage.

"What's wrong with it?" Val cried with alarm. He had to scream to make himself heard.

The old man fixed him with a maniac's smile. *"Nothing!"* he shouted happily. "That's the way it's *supposed* to sound."

Then without warning the car leaped out of the garage onto the rough gravel driveway, slamming Val sharply against the seat. A low guttural cry of fear escaped his lips.

"Hold tight!" Pacheco yelled. "I haven't actually driven it in years!"

He took the curve out onto the side road without visibly slowing down and at the first straightaway he accelerated to a dazzling 120 k.p.h.

"Drives like a champ, eh?" He pretended not to notice Val's stricken expression. "Unfortunately there's nowhere around here to really give her the gun, but this'll give you the general idea."

He barreled out of a curve and pressed the accelerator to the floor, scaring even himself.

"Christ Almighty," Val whispered. "Jesus Christ Almighty."

"You can say that again," the old man smiled.

Moments later, without warning, the huge vehicle screeched to a halt, leaving a hundred feet of rubber smoking on the road. Val took his hands away from his ears and gave the old man a shaky smile.

"So *that's* how she stops," Val said wonderingly. Over his shoulder he gazed at the twin black scars against the shimmering asphalt. He tried not to think about what might have happened had there been a physical obstruction in that path.

"Well, it's time to push the baby bird out of the nest."

Val turned to face the old man.

"I beg your pardon?" Blinking.

"You know what I'm talking about." Pacheco gave him a mischievous wink. "When we're on the lam, you're going to have to do most of the driving, not me. Hell, I'm likely to have a stroke at the wheel and kill us both . . ." and before Val had a chance to answer the old man had opened his door and come around to Val's side. He pounded on the window impatiently. "Scoot on over before I get dehydrated and blow away!"

Obediently Val opened the door; and slipped, wide eyed and trembling, into the driver's seat.

If only the folks back in Eau Claire could have seen him

now! He tried to imagine their incredulous expressions should he happen to breeze into town during his fugitive years, to pick up supplies or say hello to his folks. The women, he thought, would be thunderstruck; the men openly envious. And no one would quite believe it was actually him.

In fact, he wasn't sure he believed it himself.

Gradually he became aware of the old man's voice feeding him the necessary instructions.

"Now this is your accelerator. And this one here's your brake. You push the first one when you want to go, the second one when you want to stop. Any questions?"

Val shook his head.

"And, seeing as how this is your first time," Pacheco observed judiciously, "what say we play it safe and buckle up."

He showed Val how to attach the belts that whirred out from the backs of the seats at the touch of a button.

"Ready when you are."

Val nodded and took a deep breath. He was conscious of a strange, rubbery sensation in the pit of his stomach. His stubby fingers gripped the steering wheel until the knuckles went white. Tentatively he pressed down on the accelerator. The car inched forward.

As if from a great distance he heard Pacheco's dry chuckle. "You've got to push harder than that," he said, "or those trees will beat us home."

As the car picked up speed Val kept his attention tightly focused on the narrow ribbon of asphalt stretched out before him, running nearly a half-mile before it curved away into the trees. One touch of a foot, he told himself, over and over. One touch of a foot and we'll be there. Effortlessly. A wave of heavy euphoria swept over him, a strange admixture of exhilaration and dread.

At the approach of the first curve his hands tensed on the steering wheel and he removed his foot from the accelerator.

"Easy does it," he heard Pacheco say. Then: "You may want to apply a little bit of brake."

But they were already well into the curve before Val realized that they were going too fast, before the panic set in. He was dimly conscious that his foot was groping, blindly, in the space between the accelerator and the brake, and he was forced to take his eyes off the road for the brief instant it took his foot to find the larger pedal. When he brought his eyes back to the road he felt completely disoriented. Trees seemed to be looming up on every side; he had the odd sensation that he was driving down the side of a cliff, that at any moment the back of the car would topple over, crushing both of them.

He closed his eyes while his right foot pushed the brake to the floor. He had no clear sense of what happened next. There was a terrifying shriek from the tires, a burning sensation in his nose. The actual moment of impact had a soft, dreamlike quality, as if he had been pitched forward into a giant marshmallow. For a split second it occurred to him that he might be dead.

Then he opened his eyes in time to see a great, shapeless bag of air deflating in front of him. He watched the soft, vinyl-like material crumple to the floor, and turned to Pacheco, uncomprehending.

"What—?" he began. And then stopped.

The old man's head was hanging limply to one side. His mouth and eyes were partly open, as if he'd been arrested in mid-speech.

Val let out a long involuntary moan. Then he fainted.

When he came to he was lying across the front seat. There was a flutter of green at his face which he traced to a branch poking through the open window. He was thinking how oddly serene it all was when he realized that his head was resting on someone's bony lap, and that a bony hand was making soothing motions at his forehead.

"Mr. Pacheco!" he cried, remembering. When he tried to sit up, a firm hand forced him down. He looked up into a pair of ancient eyes.

"Maybe you aren't cut out to be a revolutionary after all," the old familiar voice was saying. "Seeing as how I won't always be around to pick up the pieces." There was a dry, cackling wheeze. "Maybe you ought to try accounting."

That was when Val broke down openly and wept.

Amid the general bustle of midafternoon, three hundred years to the day after the signing of the Declaration of Independence, an ancient golf cart carrying a very old man and a very young one purred over Memorial Bridge and came to a stop on one of the roads leading away from the Lincoln Memorial. Just beyond them was a sign, lettered in blue and red against a white background; WELCOME TO THE TRICENTENNIAL!

The two men smiled, and walked without haste to the huge swath of grass which surrounded the reflecting pool. They carried with them a large cooler and an even larger package wrapped in plain brown paper. For the remainder of the afternoon they sat there, sipping lemonade and talking, apparently mindless of the great crowd gathering everywhere about them. The mood was festive, if slightly apprehensive. Most of the celebrants had never seen a fireworks display before.

Shortly after sundown a single white flare twisted up through the sky, glowed briefly, and was gone. A hush spread over the crowd. Heads craned upward. Then suddenly the sky exploded.

"Oh my Lord," the young man whispered. "I never imagined."

The old man couldn't hear him. His attention was fixed on the awesome tumult overhead, his face tilted upward in an attitude of rapture, or ecstatic prayer. For one full hour three hundred years of history were celebrated in smoke and color and cascading flame; the night sky blazed with likenesses of the early Presidents, with names and dates and flags, while under the canopy of fire the crowd shrieked and cheered. This time it was the old man who wept, unabashedly proud, astonished at his own longevity, overwhelmed at having shared one-third of a thriving nation's life. During the finale—those final eye-popping ear-shattering minutes—his mood shifted and he found himself convulsed with joy, standing on his feet and shaking his arms at the heavens, exhorting the sky to blaze without end.

It was only then that he remembered Mr. Takamura's package, and turned in time to see Val pointing the cluster of tubes skyward, waiting for the signal. The old man raised his arm, hesitated, like a conductor alerting the tympanist that his moment has finally come, then brought it down, hard.

"Now!" he howled, as Val plunged the lever home.

The six tubes puffed simultaneously, and moments later, hundreds of feet above them, six concentric circles—the outermost one with a gap at either side—flared out against the universe like rings.

Around them, the crowd applauded. Jacob Pacheco

bowed, elaborately, then turned to the younger man, leading a second wave of cheers. Val found himself blushing, and held up a modest hand. Later he joined in the general applause, but not without noting (proudly, to himself) that it had been, all in all, quite a coup for the *Kways.*

One minute past midnight,
it is July 5th . . .
America's fourth century begins.